About the Author

The author was born in London in October 1944. She enjoyed school, adored Elvis and loved to dance. She ruined her feet in winklepicker shoes in her teens and swung in the Swinging Sixties. She worked as a personal assistant, married Dave, had three sons and then worked in their garden centre in Essex.

She moved to Cornwall in 1980. She worked as an administrative assistant for a government quango. She retired and bought and rented out villas in Tenerife. She lost Dave after nearly fifty-two years of marriage, and is currently surrounded by three sons with gorgeous wives and twelve grandchildren.

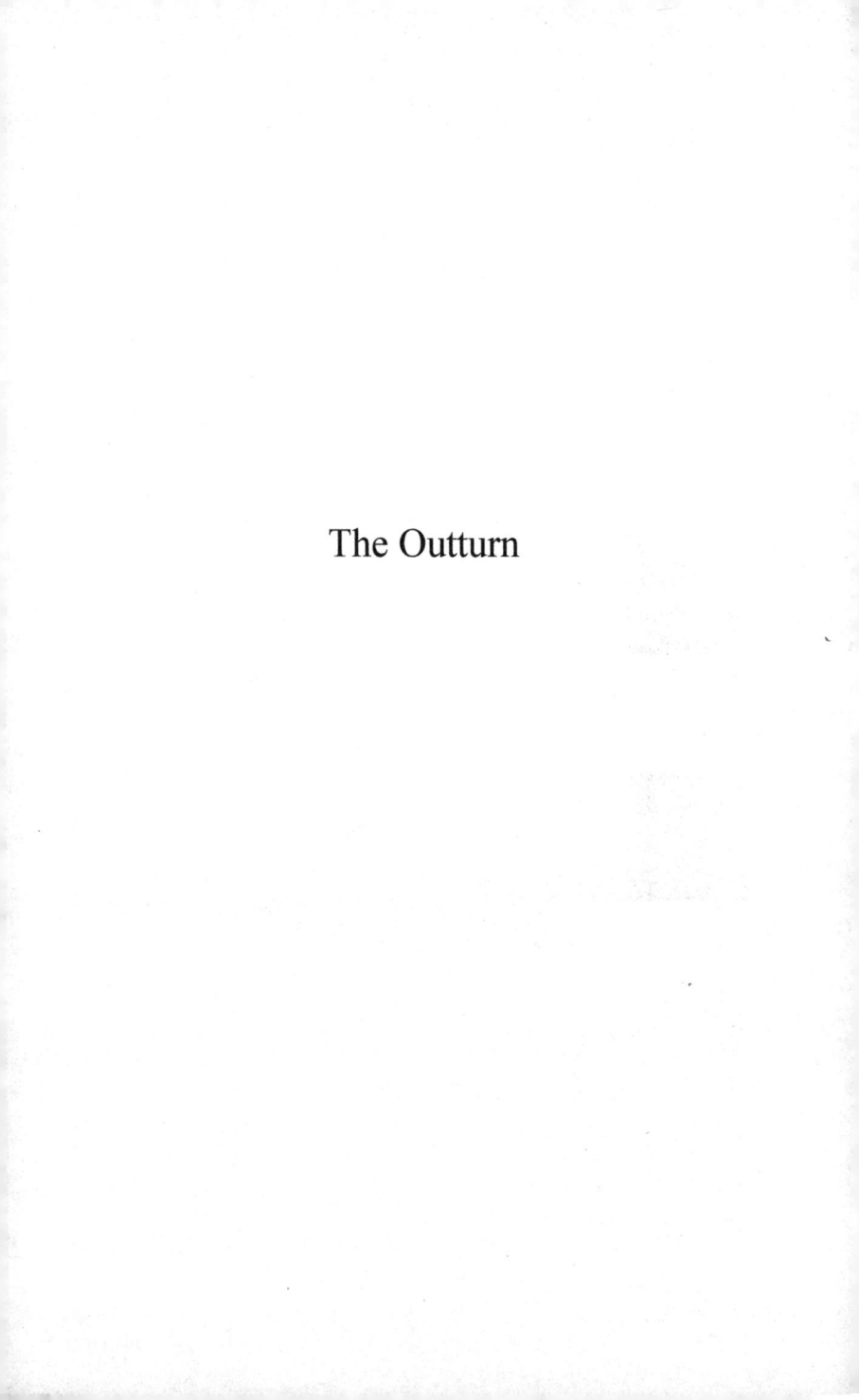

The Outturn

J. A. Ellery

The Outturn

Vanguard Press

VANGUARD PAPERBACK

© Copyright 2023
J. A. Ellery

The right of J. A. Ellery to be identified as author of
this work has been asserted by her in accordance with the
Copyright, Designs and Patents Act 1988.

All Rights Reserved

No reproduction, copy or transmission of this publication
may be made without written permission.
No paragraph of this publication may be reproduced,
copied or transmitted save with the written permission of the
publisher, or in accordance with the provisions
of the Copyright Act 1956 (as amended).

Any person who commits any unauthorised act in relation to
this publication may be liable to criminal
prosecution and civil claims for damages.

A CIP catalogue record for this title is
available from the British Library.

ISBN 978 1 80016 688 2

This is a work of fiction. Names, characters, businesses, places,
events and incidents are either the product of the author's
imagination or used in a fictitious manner. Any resemblance to
actual persons, living or dead, or actual events is purely
coincidental.

Vanguard Press is an imprint of
Pegasus Elliot Mackenzie Publishers Ltd.
www.pegasuspublishers.com
First Published in 2023

Vanguard Press
Sheraton House Castle Park
Cambridge England
Printed & Bound in Great Britain

For my amazingly loving and supportive family, thank you so much.

Dear Chris

Thank you for all your help

Lots of love

Jan xx

1

The divorce was amicable. Clive had not challenged or begged or expected. It is what it is. He had another woman. The extraordinary fact was that he loved his wife more than the other woman. It is only when you are about to lose the most precious thing in your life, you realize how devastated you are.

The family was in complete disbelief. There was no judgment on their part. Their parents were adults. It was just that they had no idea there was anything amiss. They loved their father and their mother. Equally. No contest. Maybe they were just numb.

Sarah Cook was in a kind of bubble. She had had so much time to come to terms with events that she seemed surprised that everyone else was in shock. Clive was. He had seen a remarkable recovery in his wife. From being in Intensive Care, the possibility of an induced coma, to finally regaining consciousness, was a miracle in itself. His sheer joy turned to despair, utter torment, when she told him she knew about Kiri.

She told him when she was at home, away from hospital tubes, physiotherapists, and medication. She was whole again. She really felt this. She felt she had come out of a huge vacuum. Strange noises no longer there, no more pain. Finally, no more pain. Even the pain she first felt at his betrayal had evaporated.

When she found the voicemail on his phone he had forgotten to take with him on an emergency call to New York, she was not really surprised. She had suspected for a long time that he had another life in New York that did not include her. She threw herself into her career and never mentioned the discovery to him. Maybe, if she had, there could have been at least a discussion. Maybe, deep down, she didn't want to have that discussion. Her life was progressing so well. She had enjoyed an amazing role as John Bartlett's personal assistant. She had created a secure cocoon around herself, confident and self-assured in her work and the children were independent and doing well.

For a marriage to survive such as theirs it would have had to be extraordinary. To be fair, not many marriages would cope with separation that became their routine. She thought that if they were truly together it could have worked. They were not, not any more. Once, early on, they were so determined that each could have a career, children and success.

Clive had achieved his ambition, success in America and in the UK. He worked meticulously hard to ensure his work was faultless. He brought in the business and he felt he was at the top of his game. He was confident that Sarah was also doing what she did best, happy in her work, and he thought, in their marriage. He felt a twinge. He had not really considered the marriage. It was a fact, he was more in New York than London and although his boss had asked him to seriously consider moving to New York permanently he had explained Sarah had her own career and that was her fulfillment.

He felt that he had it all. Kiri of course was always there for him, always playing her part, and he had thought that maybe one day he would settle for good in New York. He had not thought it through. He had his family, his children, in London, so maybe for now, keep it that way. Two separate lives in two capital cities.

He was completely and utterly shattered when Sarah had told him she knew about Kiri. That it had been going on for a long time, virtually since he set up the apartment in New York. She was incredibly sad at his betrayal. At the time it had seemed that it was possible to be with two women and treat them both as his partner. That said it was almost callous.

Sarah had come through the physiotherapy, the self-doubt, the pain and her mind was finally healing. The trauma of the accident paled into insignificance when divorce came into the equation. There was no conversation regarding can we at least have one more try? It wasn't an option. She had gone over and over it in her mind and she was sure this would be the only solution.

She was surprised, not shocked, that Clive seemed to think his actions were normal. To have Kiri in New

York and her, his wife, for better or for worse, in London. Well, no more.

John Bartlett was horrified when Sarah told him about the situation. He was a regular visitor to her home, wanting to be there for his 'right hand man', particularly when Clive had to return to New York. Sarah did not elaborate. It was she asking Clive for the divorce citing Kiri. John just asked, are you sure, but did not judge or offer an opinion. Privately, he was sad, then angry, then resigned. It was Sarah and Clive's lives that were involved here. He was on the sidelines with his support. He offered Sarah the use of the company solicitor but she had thought it best to keep it strictly personal and she sourced a lawyer. Really it was just a formality. Fifty-fifty split of all assets. The children were adult. Clive had his apartment in New York and Sarah kept the house. Clive used the company flat in London when needed.

Sarah knew John Bartlett wanted her to return to her old position but the accident had changed her. She believed she would make a full recovery, but the job demanded her complete confidence and flair. She was unsure she still had it within herself. Financially, she was sound, no money worries whatsoever. Emotionally, however, her confidence was not quite up to speed. To take on her old role would be demanding and she was not sure she could muster the energy, the courage, to get back to what she once excelled at.

It was with a heavy heart she met John for lunch and told him of her decision. He was both sad, yet happy for her. She was able to come to that decision after weighing everything up. They would always be friends, just not business colleagues any more. He had realized during her absence how much she brought to the table. She was second to none in presenting herself and representing the Corporation. He knew he would never be able to replace her, but he would need to consider how to go about filling the position.

For now, the most important thing was for Sarah to get completely well. She had come a long way and he knew she would succeed in turning the final corner. He held her so tight as they parted. It was all he could do not to break down. He held it together as did she and when he closed the taxi door and directed the driver, he felt as though part of him would never be the same again.

2

Kiri looked at herself in the mirror. She never expected things to turn out in the way they had. On the other hand, one day something would have to give. Clive had always said one day they would be together. Now that was on the cards. The divorce would be finalized, he would be free, and they could marry. She tried very hard to convince herself that this was how it would be.

Truth to be told, Clive was not the same man any more. He nearly lost his best client group, a lack of concentration allowing another company to infiltrate and pay off a few loose tongues. Had it not been for Kiri realizing what was happening, he would have lost the company millions. She didn't care about that, she wanted the old Clive back. The man that could make her laugh, escort her to dinner, make love to her, letting her know she was the only woman for him.

Clive, for his part, felt he was shutting down. He found it very hard to function at all. He realized what a prize idiot he had been. What was he thinking? Hindsight is a wonderful thing. Trouble is no one has it when you make decisions. It is only when those decisions were so wrong you realize you have carved a route that is untenable. You lose the most precious person, really the only one you needed.

The children had been so good. They made it clear that wherever he was, New York or London, he could count on them. They said the same to Sarah. They were just sad it had had to happen. They were loyal to them both, and Clive would be forever grateful to them for that.

His boss was understanding but dismissive. He had a business to run and Clive would need to step up to keep his position. Just like that. No sentiment involved. You are there to do a job and if you can't stand the heat get out of the kitchen.

Kiri was another dilemma. He realized, when he saw Sarah in the hospital, desperately ill and so vulnerable, his heart belonged to her and her's to him. He didn't think how this would impact on Kiri. He just wanted Sarah to be whole again and he would change his life, rearrange his work, to be there for her.

It sounded so simple. It would be if you didn't count emotion, commitment, future plans let alone other people's feelings. He had not considered Kiri to be a part of his future. He did not realize just how unbelievably selfish he was. Not a good trait.

He was in the apartment in New York, trying to avoid having a drink, not a practical solution. He poured his second Scotch and soda and waited for Kiri to come home from work. He just couldn't live a lie any more even though the actual lie had been lived for three years.

The lie was within him. He could no longer have a life with Kiri. It was all self-inflicted.

Kiri sat next to him on the sofa. He looked at her. She was as she always had been. Wide-eyed, attractive, but the happiness was gone from her. "Kiri, I can only say how sorry I am about everything."

"Of course, I understand, divorce is horrible, but at least Sarah is doing so well."

"No Kiri, I am sorry about us. I cannot be with you any more." At least he didn't continue with — I only want to be with Sarah.

Kiri didn't move. She stared at her hands. She realized a tear was running down her face. She honestly had not expected this. She thought he would be guilt ridden — it's a man thing— but now they had their future, just the two of them in their life in New York. A future together; she had dreamed of this.

"Of course you are upset, baby. It has been a dreadful time for you, but you are here now, we can plan, we can dream."

"Oh, my poor Kiri, can you ever forgive me? I cannot stay. I am just about holding on to my sanity, let alone my job. You deserve so much more."

"We made plans, we have a future together. You are reeling from the trauma of Sarah's accident and the divorce. I can make you strong again. Together we can grow stronger." Her voice was gradually lacking conviction. She was now realizing he actually didn't want to be with her. How could this be? He adored her. Their life was here in New York.

Clive stood, a little uncertainly as the Scotch kicked in. "Kiri, I have to leave now. I honestly do not know what I will do. If I stay here in New York I don't think I can cut it. In London I can see the children."

She jumped up, stood squaring up to him, "and who else will you want to see — your precious Sarah?"

Those words were actually the push he needed to get to the door. Yes, she was his precious Sarah — or at least she had been. He opened the door. He did not look back. If he had he would have seen a person crumpled on the floor, motionless. It looked as if Kiri was dead, and to all the world, she was.

3

Elaine Radley was ironing Harriet's school uniform. It had been two years since Charlie effectively left home to go to the Kevin Brownlow School and he had blossomed in every way. Funny to use the word blossomed, normally that is what you say about a girl, but he had found his niche. He was in his element, nothing fazed him and he absorbed the information he was taught like a sponge.

Harriet was not academic like Charlie. She had other skills. She excelled at IT. She also liked engineering and art, two very different skills but her mind was quick to grasp new things and although she decided on art as a distraction from facts and figures, she was actually rather good.

Elaine folded the last shirt and poured herself a coffee. She smiled to herself. Oh my goodness, thinking of the other parents at Charlie's school, she was hardly a lady that lunched. She was far too busy earning money in a very different way to the average mother. She had come to enjoy her evening work. Her mum still came round to be there for Harriet, although Harriet spent a lot of time in her room, chatting with friends on the internet, but grateful Nan was there. Miranda as she was known at the Pandora, a private club in Reading, was doing very well. She had a spark, a kind of electricity, which attracted her clients. She had an intelligence that they appreciated, good conversation to them was as important as amazing sex, and this did not go unnoticed by the management. She had been there four years and she grew in the role. It was apparent she enjoyed it. Her elegance, the way she moved and circulated around the room, made her one of the most desirable and requested women in the club.

Financially, she really did not need to work. It was just escapism, a life completely away from monotony. It was totally separate from her suburban existence. She had no reason to believe it would change.

One Friday evening she arrived home and her mum was waiting for her. Normally she would have her coat and bag by the door but she was sitting bolt upright in the chair in the kitchen. "Elaine, something dreadful has happened." Elaine stopped dead. "Charlie, is it Charlie? Harriet is okay, isn't she?"

"Oh no, it's not the kids, Elaine. My friend Sarah, it's her daughter Carol. Her husband has had a heart attack. He has died, Elaine."

"Oh mum, I am so sorry, I really am. When, when did this happen?"

"Last night. You won't believe it Elaine. He died on the train coming home from Reading. Carol is in total shock. He had been working late at the office and was not on his normal train. Sarah is looking after her but something isn't right. His office said he left at the normal time. Two hours unaccounted for Sarah said, and Carol is distraught."

"Have you met the husband, mum?"

"Many times, a lovely family-man, loved his kids to bits. It's dreadful. It's a shock because he was a fit man. I liked Fred, he was a normal happy man."

Elaine sat down. Not the Fred she knew, surely not. Oh, my God! Fred McIntosh. Could it be him? He was her six o'clock. How could it be him? But she knew nothing of his personal life. He was so much fun. He loved to tease her, loved talking to her about anything and everything, and was very generous in every way. He always made sure she enjoyed their time together. Not a normal occurrence. She was there to make sure the client had the very best time.

"They are trying to trace his movements. As far as everyone knew he always went straight home from work. He was taken to hospital and poor Carol had to identify the body. The police were called because at first no one knew it was a heart attack but the post mortem has confirmed it was."

"Elaine, are you all right, you have gone as white as a sheet?"

"Oh, yes, I think I was just reeling from the shock. I feel guilty. I immediately thought of the kids but I am so sorry for your friend's family. The loss is dreadful. What will happen now? Are the police still involved?"

"I don't know. They were at first because they did not know it was natural causes. Anyway Elaine, you look done in. I will let you know if I hear anything. I don't really like to keep bothering Sarah, but I will call her in the morning in case I can help with the grandchildren. Get to bed Elaine, we have all had an awful shock."

Elaine hugged her mum. "Take care, mum, let me know if you have any more news." Elaine phoned the Pandora. Over the years there was a mutual respect between Mark, the owner and Elaine. He had been more than happy to have her work for him and she felt appreciated and respected working there. "Mark, it's Elaine. Sorry to call you so late but I feel I must let you know what I have just learned from my mother. I believe Fred McIntosh, my six o'clock from last night, could be the same man who died last night on the train from Reading."

"Hold on Elaine, how can you possibly know it's the same man? Was it his real name? I will get the register checked. So often clients choose a different name for obvious reasons."

"My mum's best friend Sarah is his wife's mother. She told me tonight that he had told his wife he was working late. When they contacted his office they said he left at the normal time. The police are involved because it could be that the death was suspicious."

Mark listened and the register was put in front of him. "Fred McIntosh signed in at 5.45 last night. He must be the same person Elaine. I do not think that the police will pursue this. Their job was to get the cause of death established. The reason he left early and did not go straight home will not concern them. Don't worry about that. He could have met a friend, gone for a drink. There is nothing to tie him to the Pandora. I will erase the entry, correct the register." Elaine was trembling. She could not grasp that this was happening. Mark seemed so dismissive. Not at all concerned that a fit family man had died, a regular client of his. She felt it was beyond callous. "I just thought you should know, Mark. I am tired, I am going to bed and if I hear anything further I will call you. Goodnight."

"Elaine, don't worry, you are not to blame. No one is. It is just one of those things. He must have had a weak heart and it gave out. Try to get some sleep. I will speak to you tomorrow. Goodnight."

Elaine poured a glass of wine. She did not feel in the least bit tired. On the contrary, her head was buzzing. His last hug. His last words. See you next time Miranda Moo. She realized how happy she was when she knew he would be her client. He was fast becoming more than that, and she looked forward to their time together.

She had not really thought it through. She had always enjoyed their time together. It all seemed so natural. No questions, just a very enjoyable time. It was almost an affair, although just within the confines of the Pandora. Her other clients were literally just that, quite often professionals who needed to relax and unwind, and it had not become personal. With Fred it had. She felt instant chemistry when he first walked in to the Pandora, buying the champagne, then the natural progression. It was almost as if this is something he did every day, quite a normal turn of events.

She refilled her glass and thought of his family, his wife who was so suddenly alone, her husband never coming home. With her "Elaine" head on she realized this was really very serious. What if he had told someone he was going to the Pandora for a drink? What if that someone who worked with him and his wife tried to trace his movements? He obviously wasn't working late. Elaine realized his visits had become more frequent. His wife would be determined to find out as much as she could about where he was, where had he gone. Mark had said he would clear the register, but that would go back a few months and what if the police became involved? No, it wasn't a suspicious death, it was a heart attack and it was on the train. Nothing except the register would link him to the Pandora, other than for a drink, but Mark would erase all history of him being there.

Suddenly she felt very tired. She realized she would have just three hours' sleep before the alarm went off and Harriet's school day would begin. Harriet was her usual bubbly self, one of her favourite lessons today and she was going after school to a friend's for tea so tell Nan not to worry, she would be fine coming home and sorting herself out.

Elaine felt an enormous pang of guilt. Her mum had been quite a lifesaver when it came to Harriet. They both loved each other and were happy together, but wasn't that her place? Shouldn't she have been there for her daughter? If she hadn't had to find the money for the school she could have been there and although she was normally home when Harriet got in from school, she wasn't there when she went to bed.

Another thing, it irked her that Mark had been so offhand about it all. A man had died, and for the tenth time she thanked God he wasn't in her bed, yet it was business as usual. Strike him from the register, from life itself. She looked through her accounts. At the back of her mind she was wondering if she could survive on less wages. Maybe she could find another way of earning money. How much did she need? The account in the Cayman Islands was very healthy. She did the sums. She could pay the bills for another five years and have some left over. Somehow this dreadful incident had brought her to her senses. It wasn't senseless to have done what she had to do. It was necessary. If she could financially achieve paying all the bills, taking into account new books, uniforms, etc., it could save her sanity. She could find another job, albeit an unknown quantity, but she would be a mother to Harriet, and not in name only.

She arrived at the Pandora and went to her room to change. She needed to see Mark. She needed to tell him she was leaving the Pandora. She didn't want to give a reason, although he would guess anyway, she just wanted to sever the tie. She dressed in a beautiful black dress, figure hugging, flattering her legs in the highest of heels. She knocked on his door. "Come." She entered and Mark came from around the desk to hug her. "Miranda, I must introduce you to Mrs McIntosh. Miranda, this is Mrs McIntosh. Sadly she lost her husband a little while ago." "Three days ago," Mrs McIntosh said in an extremely calm voice. Summoning all her strength, Miranda turned to her and said, "How dreadful, I am so sorry Mrs McIntosh." Mark said that she was trying to trace where he had been before boarding the train, sadly he had died on the train. Miranda felt for the chair behind her and sat down. "How can we help? Do we know of him? Has he been here?" She hoped she wasn't speaking too fast. She felt sick and faint. "I am not sure. I am not sure what goes on here. My friend said she thought she saw him going up the steps to the front door, but she was on top of a bus and she just couldn't be sure. Any sighting of him is very important to me. I have a photograph, do you recognize him Mark?" Mark studied the photograph and said he was rarely by the bar. His job was administration and the basic running of the club. Miranda took the photograph and managed to look carefully, frowning as if trying to recall. "Do you know Mrs McIntosh, I honestly do not think I have seen this man. I am a hostess and my hours do vary. What time did your friend say she thought she saw him?"

"She cannot be sure, probably around six p.m. last Friday."

"I will check more thoroughly as to where I would have been in the lounge at that time. It could be that I wasn't in the lounge when he was."

"Just how thoroughly will you be able to check, Miranda?"

Miranda gathered her strength. "Friday is a busy day, I would think I would have been at one of the tables towards the back of the lounge and I honestly cannot recollect seeing your husband. I am so sorry. What about the station, do they have CCTV?"

"It is totally beyond my comprehension that the reel of film had not been changed and the police could not determine how he arrived at the station, or when he boarded the train. British Rail is investigating but there is only so much the police can do in this situation. Well, I can see I am getting nowhere here. Thank you for your time. In my heart I do not believe that Fred would come to a place such as this. He was a pint and pie man. That would hardly be found here, would it? Thank you for your time. I just have to cover every angle." Mark went to her and shook her hand. "Mrs McIntosh, if we can be of any further help to you?"

"No, thank you anyway but I do believe I just have to wonder how and why. He was a fit man, why would he have a heart attack? I am in despair. I am at a total loss as to how my beloved Fred could leave me in such a way. That's not for you to worry about however. He wasn't here. I must accept that and hope that may be there may be some footage that British Rail can uncover. Goodbye to you both." Mark escorted her down the stairs and opened the front door. She stepped out into the evening hustle and bustle and was gone.

Mark sprinted up the stairs. Elaine was sitting bolt upright in the chair. Tears were spilling down her cheeks. She was as pale as a ghost. Mark put his arms around her and handed her a brandy. "You can add acting to your list of talents, Elaine. You were outstanding. Thank you so much, I do believe we are home and dry."

"Mark, I have never felt such sadness for someone I have never met. I am so sorry for the whole episode, and that is how I must look at it. I can no longer do this, Mark. I cannot take a man to my bed. I cannot even begin to imagine how his poor wife must be thinking, feeling, wondering, maybe hoping that he was happy, on his way home to her. I will not be able to work my notice, you must do what you have to regarding my wages."

"Dear Elaine, you have come so far. Please reconsider, you are one of our very best young ladies. Your attitude towards the club, to your clients is as professional as it is outstanding. I really hope, if you take some time away, you will be able to put things into perspective."

"I am sorry, Mark, I am exhausted. The fear I felt when you introduced me to her was compounded by the grief I felt for her. I will never be able to do this again. There was a spontaneity that I enjoyed. I really could relate to the clients. The fact that Fred was with me, not her, before he died will cause me great pain for a very long time. I hope you will understand, I hope you will appreciate I really cannot do this any more."

"My dear Elaine. It is because you are such a kind and caring person that you are so good in this business. However, I do understand your feelings. In all honesty I do not think, even with time away from the club, you will change your mind. Reluctantly, I will let you go, and please believe me there will be a generous thank you in your wages. You have been a loyal and successful member of the Pandora. Take care of yourself and your lovely family. We will miss you, and we wish you all the best for your future."

He hugged her and held her until she stopped trembling. He took her down the stairs and waited until she had changed. He called a cab and she got in. As he closed the door he said, "The Pandora has lost one of its greatest assets. Thank you for your bravery, your honesty and your integrity. We will all miss you so much Elaine." She tried to smile but the tears wouldn't stop.

She called her mum when she got in. She said she felt it was about time she put Harriet before her work. She had resigned but felt it was for the best. She had done all of this for Charlie. It was about time she put Harriet first.

Her mum felt a huge surge of relief. She had been worried about Elaine for a long time. She knew how hard she worked but she also knew where she worked. She wasn't a fool. She realized there was more to her job than serving champagne and making small talk. It was none of her business. Elaine brought in the money. She had ensured Charlie's future and now it was the turn of Harriet. She finally felt so much calmer. She told her how very proud she was of all that she had achieved and was happy that she would be able to help Harriet in a similar way to Charlie. After all, what's sauce for the goose is sauce for the gander, and the smile that crossed her face was one of great happiness. All would be well.

4

Dawn and Ken Campbell were gradually gathering their thoughts. They were emotionally drained. The family had gathered for Dawn's mother's funeral and the reading of the will had proved to be a fortune beyond all expectations. Estelle Campbell had amassed a huge fortune from her work as P D Sycamore, a best-selling murder mystery writer, and had been more than generous in distributing her estate. This also included a castle in Scotland as well as the proceeds from the sale of her bungalow. This was enough to try to absorb.

Edward had been involved in a dreadful motorway accident on the M4. Anne was pronounced dead at the scene and Edward had been taken into intensive care. He was finally beginning to make good progress but would be in a wheelchair for the foreseeable future. Dawn and Edward took him to Anne's funeral and insisted he stay with them, at least until things calmed down. It was all too much for Dawn. The loss of her mother affected her in so many ways and to have her dear brother so badly injured and trying to cope with his wife's death was a body blow.

Gradually Dawn and Ken managed to settle back into some kind of routine. Ken returned to his job, one in which he excelled, and Dawn remained at home to look after Edward. Things were beginning to calm down. A sense of normality returned and a date was fixed in a month's time for the family to meet at a London hotel to discuss what was to be done with the castle that they had jointly inherited.

Dawn and Ken were not at all prepared for the next intervention in their lives. Ken's company — he was joint managing director — was offered a good deal by a German company who wanted to buy them out. Just when things were running more smoothly, a major decision was required. There were many meetings between the two parties and Ken was often in Germany with the legal team brokering the best deal. Jobs would be created in both companies and the future looked secure. The upshot was a very good deal, Ken thought it really did favour his company more than the German operation, but they were prepared to pay good money to get a foothold in the UK.

Ken was to stay on and his counterpart from Germany would run the company jointly. Ken told Dawn he felt it was a very good move all round and hoped that he could forge a good relationship with the new man. Ken was an affable, easy-going man. Very capable and able to keep his hand on the tiller, steering the company to achieve even more success. Moritz Eckhoff was from the Saxon city of Wolfsburg and was the exact opposite in every way to Ken. He was business through and through and found Ken's slightly relaxed approach to situations to be testing to say the least. More staff were employed and it looked as if another factory would need to be found to house the new labour force and the machinery. Moritz and Ken clashed over the location. There was a disused factory two miles from the existing one that Ken thought could ideally be adapted to suit their needs. It would not be overly expensive to do, but Moritz felt it more economical to move the whole enterprise to Bristol where there was a purpose-built building which could house the entire operation.

Ken was at his wit's end. He had tried very hard to bond with Moritz, but bonding was not on the agenda with the man. Ken pointed out that the workforce at presently employed in a good site, close to the M25, working at full capacity, could easily adapt to moving two miles away with no disruption to the employees. Moritz did not consider the employees in the equation. It was purely profit. It would be profitable to move to Bristol, the port was there, road and rail communication was in place and he could see no reason to refurbish another factory simply to keep the employees in one area.

The Trade Union was in favour of as little disruption as possible and came down on the side of continuing as they were. Ken was beginning to realize that his part in all of this was probably a goodwill gesture on the part of the German company who he now worked for. He was growing tired of not being able to negotiate, to broker his deal.

He talked it over with Dawn. She could see how frustrated he had become and wasn't surprised when he said he felt he could no longer continue in the present atmosphere. He felt it was a *fait accompli*. They had needed his input at the outset but now really only listened to Moritz Eckhoff. Ken's role had exhausted its reason to be.

He flew to Germany to meet with the managing director. He was sorry to hear how Ken felt but realized he was in an untenable position. He thanked him for his invaluable contribution in making the takeover run smoothly and reassured him he would be handsomely rewarded for his considerable expertise.

Ken returned home and although he would miss his old job, the camaraderie of his friends both in the boardroom and on the shop floor, he knew he could not continue being blocked at every turn.

5

Edward had made remarkable progress. The physiotherapist was good at coaxing the best out of him and he persevered through the pain and discomfort to finally walk unaided without his stick. He finally began to grieve for Anne. Luckily he was not aware of how she had died. He had been unconscious as they cut her from the car. He felt a huge burden of guilt on his shoulders. He remembered he had been shouting at her, not concentrating on the road ahead and the impact of the crash caused her death and his injuries.

He descended into a tunnel of gloom, unable to see how things could ever get better. Dawn realized he was in depression and told the physio of her concern. The physio said it was a natural progression, grief, guilt and blame. She arranged for a counsellor to visit him and by talking openly and honestly to a complete stranger he felt the burden gradually lifting, there was light at the end of the tunnel.

He was grateful to Dawn and Ken. They had been there for him through his angst, his pain and finally the recovery. He talked about Anne and that helped him. He knew she had changed into someone he could not really relate to, but she was no longer part of the equation. He felt he was ready to move on, to go back to his home and start living independently. Dawn thought it was all too soon, but Edward confided in Ken that he had to make the break now or it would be so much harder as time went on.

It seemed strange to not check on Edward automatically, and Dawn missed his company and caring for him. She felt as if her last child had left home all over again. She was relieved that Ken had settled into a different way of life. He missed going to work but he wasn't really qualified to do anything else. He could probably find work in the automotive companies operating around London, but he really wanted a complete change. He also felt they both needed a holiday. It had been one trauma after another, to the extent that they had not even thought about their inheritance. The payout from the German company was beyond generous. He was dumbfounded when he checked his account. Three million pounds had been deposited. He made Dawn count the zeros, was it really millions?

"Dawn, I think we need a break away from all of this. How about we go to Scotland, to check out the castle Mum left us, or a share of it? I have never been before and it would do us both good to get away. The family meeting has been deferred again. Wendy is still away spending all her money, and we have made it clear to her that on her return we will have the meeting within two weeks." Dawn loved the idea. It would be amazing to visit the castle her mother had brought. She found the brochure in the desk drawer. "Let's sit down and look at it together Ken. We haven't really given any thought to it and the brochure is very informative."

They sat at the table and the photo of a huge white building with turrets surrounded by farmland with the sea in the background was imposing to say the least — a fourteenth century castle with panoramic views towards Edinburgh overlooking the Firth of Forth and towards the Lammermuir hills. East Lothian with excellent transport links into Edinburgh and long sandy beaches and now one of Scotland's most desirable places to live in an area of historical significance with many ancient monuments, historic houses and castles. "I guess we can fly from Heathrow to Edinburgh Ken, I am getting excited already!"

The photographs showed beautifully furnished bedrooms, eight in total, a lower hall with the utility room and central heating boiler, open plan kitchen and sizeable dining area with gas range cooker and a large biomass stove.

A solid cast stone stairwell rose up to the first floor hallway leading to the lift and also to the drawing room featuring a great fireplace with a solid fuel stove and triple aspect views. Off the drawing room was an office again with windows on three sides and also a solid fuel stove with a back boiler. There was a spectacular painted ceiling amongst wooden beams. A door from the office led out to the second stone staircase.

At the top of the old tower there was bed and breakfast accommodation. On the third floor was the principal bedroom with a bath and separate shower and washbasins and a sitting room. A steep spiral staircase led up past a glass walkway over the old dungeon and up to a rooftop walkway with panoramic views over the Firth of Forth. The staircase also led to the Great Hall, a classic feature of a castle of this age. This magnificent old room contains an original stone built fireplace with a log-burning stove. The staircase led down to the library where there was another stone fireplace with a multi-fuel stove. There were a further five bedrooms on the fourth floor with a bathroom and bedrooms seven and eight at the top of the stairwell.

"Oh my goodness!" exclaimed Ken. "There are also two cottages in the grounds. I assume someone must be living there to maintain it, although I would imagine it would take a lot of manpower to really make it work."

"Ken, what are you thinking, make it work?"

"Dawn, I am incredibly excited. I never realized it was in such excellent condition, beautifully furnished and what a history. Can you see it as a hotel? Do you think we could make this one great big project?"

"Ken, it is not ours. It belongs to six people. Naturally I include Philipa in Australia. If you wanted to go ahead we would have to buy them out. We need to do some homework, Ken. We need to take a serious look at our finances and we would need an income while we were renovating, changing, whatever work needs doing. We would need a valuation as well. Do you know it is strange but I am thinking it is a possibility. It will be a brand new lease of life for us both. Mind you, this is the brochure when Mum bought it. I wonder if it is still in the same state. I am sure Mr Pegden would be very happy to help us out on the legal side of things. He was so thrilled to be able to administer the estate. Golly, I really do not know where to start."

"Well, first things first. Maybe Mr Pegden has information as to who, if anyone, was looking after it for Mum after she bought it. Someone may be living in it, or one of the cottages, like a caretaker. Perhaps the agent who sold it to Mum may know the current state of play."

It was getting late and they realized they were getting a bit carried away by it all. "I suggest we both make lists of what we consider is the way to go forward. We will sort it out tomorrow. All I can say is I have never felt so enthusiastic about anything in a very long time." Ken smiled at Dawn, "not in a very long time.

6

Mr Pegden was delighted to hear from Dawn. He had wondered how things were. It had been at least a couple of months since they last met and he was very sorry to hear of Anne's death. He offered his sincere condolences, privately remembering one of the most unsavoury women he had ever met.

Dawn told him that she and Ken were really interested in the possibility of maybe purchasing it to convert to a hotel. They would obviously need to view it before any further progress could be made and wondered as to the current state of the place.

Mr Pegden had contact with the agent when Estelle bought the castle and was able to confirm that a Mr and Mrs Taylor were employed as managers of the castle. They were paid via Estelle's estate to ensure it was well maintained and if major works were required Mr Pegden sanctioned the estimates and payment. As far as he was aware it was in good condition. However the property market was not as vibrant as when Estelle had bought it, and a new valuation would be necessary.

"Mr Pegden, we would very much like to view the castle. Do you know if any of the family made such a request?"

"No, Mrs Campbell, this is the first time I have spoken to any of the family. I did wonder how it would pan out but obviously with the sad loss of your sister-in-law I can see how time has passed. I have not had any recent contact with Mr and Mrs Taylor. They are paid monthly and as far as I know there is nothing major, maintenance wise, that is needing to be done. I can give you their contact details after I have contacted them to say you would like to visit. I am sure they will be delighted that a member of the family has thoughts on developing it."

"Thank you, but I would prefer you simply to inform them that we would like to come to see my mother's castle."

"Of course, Mrs Campbell. I will be in touch as soon as I have spoken to them. May I say, it is quite a pleasure to be in contact once again."

"The pleasure is mutual Mr Pegden. Should things progress I know we would like to use your services. The family meeting planned to discuss the future of the castle has been postponed, not only due to Anne's death but my sister Wendy has so far cancelled two planned meetings. However, should Ken and I decide we would like to progress the matter, I am sure Wendy will be readily available." Mr Pegden remembered yet another charmless woman as he said goodbye, and he would be in touch.

"Well, that's the first hurdle. I have looked up flights from Heathrow to Edinburgh and there is a regular service. It takes about one and a half hours direct and costs between £70 and £100. We can hire a car at the airport. Oh Ken, no matter what the outcome, it is our holiday."

"Yes, Dawn, it is and we will enjoy it very much. We will need an up to date valuation of the castle. When Mr Pegden calls after contacting the Taylors we can ask him if he knows of any other estate agents in the area. We will need three valuations at least. You can imagine Wendy in all of this. I do believe the way she has been travelling, staying in the best hotels and looking to move to a more upmarket area, that her funds may be diminishing. We also don't know what Julian may be planning, or Anthony and Madeleine. I have done the sums, Dawn. With my German pay out, my pension and our considerable savings, I do believe we will be in a strong financial position to purchase the castle. This of course includes paying everyone their share."

"Is this really happening Ken? Are we seriously considering moving lock stock and barrel to a castle in Scotland? The upkeep must be enormous, yet I believe it has been renovated to a very high standard in the most economical way. The heating bill would probably give us a heart attack, but the details show a lot of wood burning stoves and back boilers. All this has to be taken into consideration before we even think of buying it."

"Don't jump the gun, Dawn. Of course we will have an accountant look at the outgoings and the general maintenance of such an old building. I believe someone has done the hard work for us. It has been so tastefully restored. However, we will need a very rough idea of the value before we can begin to consider buying it."

Mr Pegden called to tell them Mr and Mrs Taylor would be thrilled to meet them. They said the situation was totally under control. Since Estelle had bought it there were only a couple of major works, the turrets needed reroofing and this had all be carried out with Mr Pegden's blessing. Ken and Dawn had the green light.

Dawn booked the tickets. She was in daily contact with Edward and was so pleased he was doing so well. He had not returned to work yet but was doing some paperwork at home and felt he was on the way to getting back to his old self. Dawn told him they were going to Scotland to see the castle and he was pleased. He told them to take lots of photos, every room, the grounds and surrounding countryside. Like them he had never been and was looking forward to hearing how they got on.

The flight was smooth and Dawn had booked the car to be ready at the airport. They had arranged to stay in a small hotel in the local village and had pre-ordered supper for their arrival. The owner welcomed them, they had heard they were going to look at the castle (word travels fast in a small community) and hoped they would enjoy their stay. Dawn wasn't sure if they were aware of their connection to the castle and it was not necessary that they did.

Mr and Mrs Taylor were delightful. So pleased to see them and so happy they were going to see how well they had looked after it. They met them at the gate to the driveway. Behind the arch of the gate loomed an enormous white building with black turrets that glistened in the sun. They followed the car to the main front door. First impressions thought Dawn — imposing, grand, maybe a little austere but so well maintained. They entered onto the flagstone hallway and were struck by the vast space that opened up before them. They remembered details from the brochure and as they were pointed out to them they felt an almost instant familiarity. The castle did not seem cold, almost the opposite, it seemed welcoming and friendly. The rooms were spotless, well, no one lived there, and Dawn thought the kitchen itself was a work of art. Ken couldn't believe the ornate ceiling among the beams in the office. He was mentally looking at the bedrooms, working how to knock through to en-suites and the two bedrooms at the top of the spiral staircase could be changed to house an en-suite shared between them.

The tour of the castle took over an hour and Mrs Taylor had prepared some tea and cakes in the kitchen. They had yet to explore the grounds and see the cottages. They knew one look would not be nearly enough and after the refreshments, which were delicious, they set off again on their own.

"Okay, Ken, what is the verdict? Are you as thrilled with it as I am?"

"Dawn, even more so. It needs no work as it stands. However, if we are going to make it a hotel we will need an architect to plan how to change the bedrooms into en-suites. We could either knock through or use one bedroom as the bathroom to the existing one. I would also like an opinion as to the space taken up by the hallway on the second floor. It is quite large and I feel we could make use of it. Another bathroom? Also I would like to make more of the ceiling in the office. If it were a hotel the office could become a lounge so that the guests would be able to appreciate it. It is an amazing feature. The bed and breakfast accommodation could become a self-contained apartment, maybe a suite. I know so little about the hospitality business but I am very willing to learn."

Dawn wrapped her arms around him. It was strange. She'd never been here before but felt so at home. She felt it was theirs for the taking. She loved to see Ken so positive. The last few months at the factory had changed him. He was no longer in control and although his input was valued, as demonstrated by the pay out, it was not his baby any more. The German vision was obviously new and adventurous, but it wasn't his vision. Now he had a purpose, a very positive vibe and she thrilled to his enthusiasm.

They thanked Mr and Mrs Taylor, complimenting them on their wonderful care and attention maintaining every aspect of the castle. They had put their own stamp on it and it was faultless. Ken and Dawn decided to leave the viewing of the cottages and exploring of the grounds to the next day. They drove down the drive, out through the gate and as they looked back the castle seemed to whisper, please come back.

7

They were both on a high, almost jubilant. Neither had believed they would have found the castle to be in such wonderful condition. Obviously a full time job for the Taylors, yet they made it seem as if it was a pleasure, never a job. They went to their room and Dawn opened the notebook of "things to do". "I am sure we will find the cottages to be in good condition and the grounds appear to have been well kept. Be lovely to see them tomorrow, I just couldn't take it all in in one visit." Dawn looked at Ken. "I haven't seen you this happy in a long time, Ken. I do believe we can do this, if only because the work I had envisaged has been done for us." Ken smiled. "I am so hopeful, Dawn. I know it's all very new and daunting yet we can afford to do this. The next step will be to get the valuation done. Mr Pegden has emailed me the three agents he feels would be suited to value such a property. They are based in Edinburgh so I will contact them first thing in the morning."

They both went over the figures again. In Scotland the price of property was far lower than in London. They knew their house would sell for at least £700.000. It was in a desirable area. A village within commuting distance to London and it had been well maintained. Strangely, neither of them felt sad to be selling it. Mind you, it would depend on the valuation of the castle. That was pivotal to any decision they had to make. Dawn felt her mother would be so happy to think that she and Ken were considering making it their future. An architect would have to be employed to draw the plans from Ken's rough drawings. He was an engineer and had a good eye for change, but the architect was the person who could transfer his dreams to paper. Ken didn't think planning would be a problem. Change of use from a residence to a boutique hotel he felt could be achieved with just building regulations. He made a mental note to check the fire regulations, he had not actually looked for smoke alarms but felt they would be there as part of the modernization.

Dawn ran a bath and enjoyed a good soak while Ken went over the figures again. The estate agents would know a local architect in Edinburgh and that would be the next step after the valuation. Dawn emerged from the bathroom wearing the hotel bathrobe. She felt relaxed, warm, and she wanted her husband. She pushed the paperwork away from him, turned his chair towards her and let the robe slip. Ken was surprised but in a receptive way. This hadn't happened in quite a while and he found himself wanting her as she wanted him. They went to the bed. Ken hurried out of his clothes and embraced her as she nestled into his arms. They made love slowly. Not urgently, the old familiar rhythm taking over, they knew how to please each other, to tease each other and they reached the pinnacle together in a wonderful haze, completely sated. They lay, their arms entwined. It was as if this was the stamp of approval, the conclusion they both wanted. Together they would go forward, onwards and upwards to cement their dream.

The cottages were delightful, lattice windows, a good-sized kitchen and lounge with a log burner and two double bedrooms. They had been modernized in keeping with the castle and brought a new dimension to the whole estate. Appointments had been made for the estate agents the next day. The first early appointment did not take that long. The agent was familiar with the property and offered a conservative estimate of £1.5 million. The second agent was more mature in years and considered it a valuable property with great potential as a hotel valuing it at £1.7 million. The third agent arrived in the late afternoon, a young energetic and to say the least very enthusiastic man, and suggested £1.2 million.

Ken was suitably impressed and happy with the estimates. "Do you think £1.6 million would be a fair figure, Dawn?" He really had no clue as to the actual value and had expected a higher valuation. "I am sure that is very fair, Ken. They all said they would get the written estimates to us within two days. Can we afford it taking into account the cost of the alterations?" Ken had asked the agents to recommend an architect and two had come up with the same name: Andrew Fairburn whose office was in Edinburgh. "We can definitely afford it, Dawn. I had expected a much higher figure. A rough calculation, dividing it by six to include all the beneficiaries, would be £268.000 per person. We would have to pay out about £1,340.000 to include the five people apart from ourselves. We have the £3 million plus the money from the sale of our home and Mum's inheritance. We will be in a very good position to carry out the alterations required. Yes, Dawn, we can do this, with money to spare."

They hugged each other. They could achieve what they had only dared to hope for. Ken contacted Andrew Fairburn who could meet them at the castle the next day. He was a charming, confident and efficient man. Looking at Ken's rough sketches and measuring the various rooms he could see the possibilities of knocking through and creating the en-suites as Ken had envisaged. He was amazed by the magnificent painted ceiling and agreed with Ken it had to be made a feature of the lounge rather than the office. They went to the local pub and had a ploughman's lunch, sharing a bottle of wine as Andrew Fairburn drew a very rough idea of what was possible and attainable. He could sense their excitement and it was palpable. He said he would have some ideas on paper for them to check over and considered that building regulations would be all that was required to carry out the work.

The estate agents submitted their valuations and Andrew Fairburn met them two days later with the draft of the alterations. Ken and Dawn had decided they would ask Andrew to project manage the build from the conception to completion. He was pleased to accept and his rough estimate was that the work, including labour and materials would amount to roughly £400,000. His professional fee would be eight percent and the amount was therefore £432,000. The creation of the en-suites was a small proportion of the costs, the main expense being in creating the lounge in place of the office. Ken was pleased with the drawings, they were really as he had roughly sketched his ideas and the fact that Andrew would project manage the build took a huge amount of responsibility off his shoulders.

They contacted Mr Pegden who was delighted they were able to go ahead with the purchase. He knew Estelle, Dawn's mother, would be very pleased her legacy was to be in such capable hands. They decided to return home the next day, as Dawn's 'to do list' grew longer by the hour.

8

Dawn was delighted to see Edward and he was thrilled to hear their plans. He had been making good progress with his walking and was so excited to hear about their complete change of lifestyle. He made them smile when he wondered just how Wendy would take the news. They all realized there had to be total agreement and two weeks after Wendy returned home from her travels all the family, except for Philipa, met in a pub to discuss the inheritance of the castle.

Ken came straight to the point. He and Dawn would like to purchase the castle. He showed them the estate agents' estimates of its worth. "Ridiculous" was the word uttered by Wendy. "You are trying to tell me that a castle in Scotland, with all that land and cottages is worth less than an apartment in London? What planet are you on? I shall get it valued by my own agent. You are trying to do us out of our money, Dawn." Ken took a deep breath. "Please feel free Wendy to do whatever you feel is necessary to secure a correct valuation. Naturally if anyone in this room is in a position to buy the castle we will negotiate. At the current estimate, we are going with £1.6 million, we will pay each of you £268,000, which is one sixth of the price."

"Do not tell me one sixth. Obviously you are including Philipa and she is not part of this family. My mother would never have agreed to this." Wendy turned on Ken. "Actually Wendy, she is our mother, not just yours, and you have obviously forgotten, or chosen to ignore, that our mother left her inheritance to all of her children and Philipa as the widow of her son, is entitled. It is written in the will."

Although Julian and Cynthia, the eldest son and his wife had very different ideas of how they would spend the initial £500,000, Julian made it very clear to her that he needed to sort out some financial commitments before anything else. Cynthia was surprised. She thought that they were in a good financial position. Her father's legacy had paid off the mortgage and she thought Julian was happy and secure in his job. Of course she knew nothing of the gambling debts he had accrued or that he had taken a loan with the house as collateral to pay off the initial £200,000 of debt. He then needed a loan to pay off the interest that was growing daily and he was in a huge downward spiral. He had used the inheritance to clear his debts, leaving about £75,000 and for the first time in his life he was in the black.

Anthony and Madeleine lived near Harwich and his first thought was to buy a boat. Madeleine was already planning to visit a travel agent to sort a trip to New

Zealand. She had always wanted to visit and of course that money could be spent on the most gorgeous designer shops. A kind of compromise was agreed in as much that Anthony purchased a smaller boat (the marina fees were prohibitive so something had to give) and Madeleine agreed to postpone New Zealand but on the condition they could do a world cruise.

Edward had not used any of the money. He had invested wisely and right now all his energy was taken up in getting his health back on track. He had been very grateful to Dawn and Ken, taking him in, nurturing him and picking him up when he felt so low. His old job was kept open for him and it was his secretary Jeannette who brightened his days. She brought the paperwork to his home and typed the manuscripts. She did the spreadsheets for his calculations and after a quite detailed account had been closed she suggested they celebrate by going to the local pub.

Edward was really rather smitten by this woman. She had just sort of eased into his life, just by being there. She had the most beautiful smile, and as heads turned when she walked in front of him in the pub, he realized she was quite unassumingly attractive. Jeannette had met Edward's late wife Anne at the dinner dances organized by the firm and she had never liked her. She gave the appearance that she was so much better than everyone else, whereas Edward was the complete opposite. Jeannette had kept in touch with Dawn, checking on Edward's progress after the crash and was so pleased he had finally turned a corner and she was able to resume her secretarial duties.

Away from the office environment she relaxed and was great fun to be with. She pulled a face at a rather haughty woman trying to squeeze into a long booth beside them that made Edward laugh out loud. He actually heard himself laugh for the first time in a very long time. He thanked her so much for all her help both professionally and personally and told her how grateful he was. She loved his earnest blue eyes, his generous mouth and finally his smile just seemed to grow and grow. Of course she had been in love with him forever. You don't work for someone as long as she had and not develop some feelings. Many times she really had to check herself, hold back, he was not your husband. The year before Anne had died, wait, that was now only fourteen months ago, she had seen a kind of sadness take over his warmth. The banter ceased and he became absorbed in just working. No laughter. Now he was alone and she thought, thankfully not struggling quite so much.

He was pleased he was able to walk without a stick as they made their way to the car park. The next day was a Saturday and he turned to her and asked if she was busy at the weekend. She had nothing planned and he asked if she would mind doing the driving and they could go to the sea. He hadn't really been anywhere lately and he always felt so relaxed breathing in the sea air. She brought a picnic and the two-hour drive seemed five minutes as they both chatted and laughed. He had not felt like this, in a long time and never with Anne. Possibly in the early days, first flush and all that, but this feeling had so much depth.

They ate their picnic on a bench on top of the cliff. There was a gentle slope down to the beach and she took his arm as they walked down, taking care not to go too fast. That's actually how he felt, mustn't go too fast. Must not screw this up. Jeannette got two huge ice-creams from the kiosk and the chocolate flake tipped out of hers on to her blouse. She roared with laughter. He gave her his flake and she bit it in two and he felt this woman was his destiny. Just like that. They walked on the beach and she paddled rolling up her jeans. A wave came far faster and bigger than the one before and she slipped and was up to her waist in water. Edward was horrified because he couldn't move fast enough to reach her but she rolled on to her knees and crawled out of the sea, laughing so much she got a mouthful of salt water.

They found a bench and she sat in a huge puddle while Edward took off his sweater to put round her. Luckily, the sun was warm and although she was wet through she snuggled up to him and they sat drying off, and his eyes gradually closed. She looked at him. This was all she had ever wanted. She had had relationships but deep down she only had ever wanted Edward. He opened his eyes and she smiled at him. She went to say, you sleepy head, but he took her face in his hands and very gently kissed her hair, her nose and her mouth. She kissed him back. She melted into his arms and it seemed to all the world they were two lovers, so happy, so obviously in love.

He kept looking at her as she was driving back. He couldn't stop smiling and she was laughing and talking all at the same time. He opened the front door and pulled her inside. He tugged at her jeans and pulled them down and she opened his shirt and undid his belt, yanking his trousers down. He stepped out of them and they lay down on the rug. When you have wanted something for so long, dared to dream how it might be, it is as if it is the most natural thing in the world. He was not in the least bit hesitant. He knew he was beyond any holding back. It was probably one of the most wonderful times of Jeannette's life. Everything she hoped it would be. Edward rolled onto his back, a little out of breath, but completely wholly, truly wonderfully happy.

They both lay there. Edward looked at this stunning woman, capable of bringing him such enormous love and he felt his chest swell and his heart beating so fast. She kissed him all over, just couldn't stop. He got to his knees and pulled a throw from the settee over them. They didn't need to say anything. They had made a commitment far deeper than any words could possibly begin to say.

They eventually went to bed and he took her coffee and they finally got out of bed to go to the pub for lunch. Her jeans had dried out and he lent her a sweater and they enjoyed a delicious lamb roast with a couple of glasses of good red wine. They couldn't wait to get back and it was with a huge reluctant sigh he let her go, after all they both had work the next day so it wasn't too long to wait.

9

Edward waited until they were driving to the pub to discuss the castle before he told Dawn and Ken about Jeannette. Dawn squealed with delight, she was absolutely thrilled her favourite brother had found love. "We must meet her Edward, I am just so happy for you. You have been through so much and this woman seems such a wonderfully kind and good person. Actually, I haven't asked you if you would want to buy the castle, or be a part of it."

"Dawn, I am fine about the castle. I wouldn't know where to begin and now that Jeannette is in my life I am in a bit of a spin. We both cannot believe how lucky we are to have found each other and we will be making plans. She has her own flat that she may rent out. She is virtually living with me anyway. We have hopes and dreams and with Mum's money, the opportunity to fulfil them. You and Ken have found your special project, and I am so happy for you that, Wendy permitting, you can go ahead. Needless to say, bit jumping the gun here, it would be a very special honeymoon rendezvous." Dawn squealed again and Ken roared with laughter. "So thrilled for you Edward, you deserve it, mate."

Ken had no idea of how any of the beneficiaries had dealt with the initial £500,000. He guessed Cynthia was one of the "spend, spend, spend" variety. He had a feeling Julian had had some problems financially. About a year ago he had asked Dawn if it would be possible to get a loan from his mother. Dawn had told him to approach her directly, saying that she felt sure their mother would want to help if she could. No more was said and he didn't know if Julian had actually spoken to Estelle or not. Regarding Anthony and Madeleine, they were, or thought they were, part of the elite "set" in Harwich. They were always going to dinners at the yacht club (Madeleine's brother was the president of the club) and he knew they had bought a boat but had no idea how much they were actually worth. He felt that this was all within his grasp.

"I will appoint my own agent to value the castle. That has to be done before any decision regarding it can be made. I may be interested in purchasing it myself." Wendy knew how to twist the knife. "That's fine Wendy. Can I ask all of you, are any of you, apart from Wendy, interested in purchasing the castle?"

Julian looked at Cynthia. "To be fair Ken, we have made other plans for the investment and would welcome being bought out by whoever makes the successful bid."

He was mentally calculating how to use the £268,000, or whatever the percentage of the final valuation turned out to be. He also knew that this time around Cynthia was fully aware of the financial situation and gambling was completely out of the window.

"I am committed to my boat and the life that goes with it. We are also going on a world cruise and that would leave very little to afford the castle and renovate it." Anthony smiled at Madeleine who knew they didn't have the money anyway but the thought of £268,000 coming their way enabled her to smile winningly at her husband.

"I am personally so thrilled that Ken and Dawn are hoping to buy the castle. I know Mum will be so proud that someone in the family is going to take on her dream and make it work. Good luck to you both, I am very happy for you." Edward hugged Dawn and Ken, smiling as he spoke.

Ken turned to Wendy. "Well, that seems about all we can do for now. Wendy will you be able to organize an agent as soon as possible? I know Mr Pegden is aware of agencies in Scotland, indeed he gave us some names."

"Oh, I shall not be using anyone recommended by that funny little man. I have fingers in many pies Ken. You are not the only one who has an eye for a bargain you know." With that Wendy left the room. Dawn and Ken both thought that actually said it all. Ken did say to the rest of the family that as far as they knew the sale of Estelle's bungalow was going well. The prospective buyer had the cash and was anxious to complete as soon as the searches had been done. It would amount to roughly another £50,000 for each beneficiary.

They all hugged and said goodbye and Ken told them that as soon as he heard from Wendy he would email everyone so rather than another meeting it could be done electronically from now on. So it was agreed, and once again, everyone was waiting on Wendy.

It was strange that six children from the same mother and father could vary in so many ways. Why was Wendy so vindictive, so selfish and unkind? She would never admit it but it was the green-eyed monster. She had never found happiness in any relationship. Her marriage failed at the first hurdle, her husband lost his job and then Wendy. She needed status. Estelle had always told her children that the most important things in life aren't things. That went straight over Wendy's head. With the divorce settlement she bought a flat in Wimbledon. She was an attractive and personable young woman (if you didn't know her) and easily found a job as a receptionist in a solicitor's office in London. It was her intention to find herself someone with money. She really didn't want to work, she was destined for better things and Charles Kestle was the tool she would use.

He was a regular client of Noel, the head partner of the firm who was administering his estate. It was considerable. His wife had left everything to him, and there was no inheritance tax on the first death. It was quite straightforward and Charles enjoyed his trips to

London, getting him out of the house, a sense of purpose to settle outstanding money matters. He had spent time talking to Wendy, mainly because he arrived early for his appointment in order to do that. Come into my parlour, thought Wendy, as she dazzled him with her smile and made sure her legs looked their best in the highest of heels as she came around the desk to shake his hand. No fool like an old fool. Charles wasn't actually a fool, or old. He was fifty- years old, he had made his money working for expats in Europe and his offshore account was secure. He was simply very lonely. Before she died he and Diana had a large social circle that had rallied around him in his time of need. His daughter and her family lived in Spain and although she stayed with him after the funeral, she had a family and her commitment was to them. He appreciated the help and offers of dinners out from his friends but he didn't have the heart to go where he always went with Diana.

The stage was set. Noel told him it was all but tied up, one more appointment to sign off the paperwork. This spurred Charles to ask if Wendy would be free for lunch on that day. She checked her diary and was able to say yes. She had to play this carefully. Against the rules she had read the file, she knew his worth. She chose an elegant two-piece suit that accentuated her figure in the best possible light. She was eager to hear all that Charles had to say. She expressed her sorrow at his loss. She made him laugh, exactly at what was a mystery, but he was hooked and anything she did or said was perfect.

He invited her to his house in Surrey. She did her best not to gawp at the size of the rooms and the gardens. His housekeeper was discretion itself and although she thought this woman was there for one thing, that was none of her concern. Wendy was there for one thing. She had never enjoyed sex but obviously it was necessary to completely draw this man in. He knew she was divorced with no children and he certainly did not want any more, not at his age. Everything seemed to be falling into place.

He asked her if she would move in with him. There really was no need for her to work and he had approached Noel for his opinion regarding this. Noel told him she was efficient and capable and he was happy for Charles. Wendy excelled at doing not a lot. Charles invited his daughter and family to come for a holiday in the summer and although Holly thought it was all a bit sudden, she could see how happy her father was and she was grateful for that.

When things are going really well and you have managed to get what you want, you do not expect anything to change. Charles was content, amazed that this woman could share his life and be there for him. The dreadful pain that seared through his chest, made him grab at his arm, caused him to fall and crash to the floor came without any warning. He didn't make a sound. The housekeeper found him in the study. She ran to his crumpled form and his blue lips told her he was gone. Wendy was shopping in London. When her mobile rang she could not believe it. He was a fit man, how could this happen?

She was in shock. What now, what about her, where did she stand? Of course, common law wife — wasn't she? She googled it on the computer. No, that cannot be right. She thought that if you lived with someone you were a common law wife. This was a common misconception apparently. Unless you have married you have no legal entitlement to anything, unless it is decreed in a will. Oh my God. Holly was distraught. The happiness she had felt for her father turned into a gulf of sorrow. He was so young. First her mother now this. She knew from helping her father with her mother's funeral what was necessary to be done. Wendy seemed totally preoccupied. Grief affects people in different ways, thought Holly.

The funeral came and went. Holly tried to reach out to Wendy, who certainly had nothing in return for Holly. She stopped dead in her tracks when Wendy asked her where the will was kept. Hindsight is a wonderful thing. Wendy had worked for the solicitors holding the will. Holly needed to get home to Spain. Luckily, she knew Noel from when her father used his services and Noel, although in shock with the loss of his friend, offered to administer the estate. Charles had appointed him executor and if there is anything that could salvage such a tragedy it was a relief to know that Holly would be taken care of. Noel organized a meeting at his offices. Wendy felt nothing as she entered Noel's office. He went forward to hug her. She stood resolute, not giving one inch. Holly on the other hand dissolved into tears. In truth there had been no one in England who had shown her any warmth and this triggered a flood of tears.

Noel stated that the will was perfectly straightforward. Holly was the only beneficiary. The gasp that emitted from Wendy's mouth was audible. Not possible. She was the only beneficiary? Who had been the one to pick him up, take care of him, be there for him? The word love was not included in the diatribe. At least this stopped Holly's tears. She assured Wendy that she was grateful for how she had cared for and loved her father. She asked Noel if there was a codicil, a legal document that would have added Wendy to the will. Noel had been fully aware that the only will Charles had drawn up was this one. No codicil of any kind.

Holly and Wendy returned to the house. Holly did her best but she could not break through the icy shell Wendy had around her. They barely spoke. It did not occur to Holly to suggest that provision must be made for Wendy in all of this. That was mainly because money was never a motivation to Holly. Her parents had loved her and she loved them back. Her husband was extremely successful. Money had never been an issue. She told Wendy she must stay in the house for as long as necessary. She had no idea at this time how things would pan out. Wendy said that would not be necessary. She would return to her flat in Wimbledon. At least that was hers. Charles suggested she rent it out when she moved in with him. At least that's something he did, she thought, not to mention the generous cash allowance and exquisite wardrobe. It never occurred to Charles why on earth she wanted all these clothes when they didn't really go anywhere.

She hired a car and drove back to London. To say she left with far more than what she came with was an understatement. Although cut short, her main aim had been achieved. She had money, albeit not as much as she wanted, a home to live in and good clothes to wear. The human cost to her was nothing. Charles had served his purpose, time to move on.

Wendy knew she could not afford to buy the castle. She had managed to 'spend' all of her inheritance. Not by wisely investing in property or the stock market, purely indulging herself in whatever took her fancy. She had hoped the money would enable her to move in expensive social circles, dine in the best restaurants, enjoy cruising. The money was the enabler but it didn't bring a new man who would adore her. The money was gone and she had maxed her credit cards. The £268,000 from the sale would clear the cards, not leaving very much in the bank.

She called Ken. "I have decided I do not want to move to Scotland, which is where I would have to spend time in order to renovate the castle. Therefore I believe you will be able to buy it yourself. In this regard I do hope you proceed as quickly as possible." Ken was relieved. He didn't argue the toss, simply phoned Mr Pegden instructing him to go ahead with the purchase.

Andrew had finalized the drawings and was making plans to begin the work as soon as the materials could be sourced. Mr Pegden thought it would take about a month to complete the purchase. Ken put their house on the market and didn't haggle with the cash buyer who offered £5,000 less than the asking price. The sale could be hurried, the searches completed in a month.

The move to Scotland was happening. They had decided to sell the furniture to the buyer, so Ken recouped the £5,000 that had been knocked off. Really there were only a few items to transport. Ken suggested that for the small amount they could hire a van and do it themselves but common sense prevailed and two removal men and one small lorry set off ahead of them to the castle.

It was strange that neither of them felt their old home to be tugging at the heart-strings. It had been a happy home with wonderful memories, but new ones were about to be made. Dawn looked at Ken. "I do not regret one moment Ken, we are on our way to a new adventure, a completely different way of life. I had one thought. I wondered if we could name the castle The Sycamore Boutique Hotel, after Mum's nom-de- plume. I think she would like that." Ken smiled and patted her hand. "That is a wonderful idea, Dawn, The Sycamore Boutique Hotel it will be."

They both knew this was totally new to them, a completely different challenge, but challenges were set to be overcome and they had every confidence that with luck and a fair wind, and a lot of elbow grease, they would get there.

10

Amanda Barrett, formerly known as Andrea Harrison, decided she would need to get a flat in Amsterdam. She couldn't stay in the hotel, it had been a month now and she needed to sort out a base for herself. Money was not a problem. Her bank account in the Cayman Islands had been regularly topped up as arranged by Alessandro Degan. She had left her life working for the John Bartlett Corporation in London and successfully adapted to her role as Amanda Barrett. Her ambition was to run a successful business using sex workers, and she would be the madam.

She chose Amsterdam because prostitution is legal in Holland. Her original plan had been to recruit women to work as high-class sex workers. She was disappointed to find that legally sex workers can only solicit for sex from behind a window. Many women rented a room, with basic furniture, and worked independently.

The cost of property with windows fronting on to the streets of Amsterdam was prohibitive. She decided to look further afield, to find a property set in its own grounds and an estate agent in Rotterdam offered four properties within her budget.

As she was from a country in the EU she did not need a visa to live or work in the Netherlands. Once she had purchased the property she would have to apply for a residence permit and a national identification number called a BSN.

The Ringvaartweg is known as the Golden Mile of Rotterdam. It is one of the most popular and most exclusive residential locations in the city. Residents can enjoy a quietly pleasant existence only a short distance from all that Rotterdam has to offer. The bustling centre, the beautiful Kralingse Plas, a lake mainly used for water sport and recreational activities, can be reached within ten minutes.

The first property had six bedrooms with a very representative entrance foyer with stylish settees and a guest toilet. The living room had an open fireplace and the dining room was magnificent and Amanda fell in love with the huge open spaces in each of the rooms. The dining room with a huge marble table that would seat twelve led to the immaculate steel grey kitchen with all the equipment imaginable. Off the kitchen there was a utility room with a shower.

The 'Underfloor' as it is known was, surprisingly, extremely luxurious with day lighting and an adjoining patio. A huge hot tub was bubbling near an open fire-pit and lawns led down to a swimming pool complete with changing cabins. There was a lounge area annex with a sitting room. This led to a bar. A professional cinema was beyond the bar that led to a fitness room with an adjoining spa. An office housed all the technical data necessary for any business.

The first floor had a spacious landing off which there were three bedrooms and two bathrooms, one with a Turkish steam bath. The second floor housed the master bedroom with dressing room annex with a walk-in closet. A huge bathroom completed the suite. Two further en-suite bedrooms completed the tour.

The garden was spacious and was transformed into a beautiful Italian-style garden with cypress trees, olive trees, extensive lawns and spacious terraces.

Amanda was enthralled. The price was 2,900,000 euros. She would offer the asking price. She had just seen this one property but it ticked all the boxes. She was excited and so pleased she could afford to buy it. It was in immaculate condition and being on the Ringvaart Canal ensured privacy of the highest standard.

The agent was surprised that she didn't try to reduce the price. He had been given authority to drop 50,000 euros to clinch the deal but it was an added bonus to be able to accept the asking price on behalf of his client. Before the viewing she had shown her accounts, ensuring her credibility and to her it was a done deal.

She was a cash buyer, no need to get an appraisal report. She did not consider it necessary to have a structural survey. It was a beautifully maintained property in every way. The agent earned his commission. He hired the notary used by his company to act as the legal mediator between Amanda and the seller. He would investigate the registration in the Land Registry and update it with the name of the purchaser, Amanda Barrett. There was a seventy-two hour cooling off period, in case either party should change their mind and this was the most nervous part of the whole process for Amanda. The date was set. Funds were transferred and within a period of two months she was the proud owner of a very special property, yet to be registered as a brothel.

She registered herself in the Municipal Personal Records Database and received her BSN, Citizen Service Number, enabling her to run her business. She applied for a license to run a brothel from the City Council in Rotterdam. It was a straightforward process and so the Cypress Herenhuis, being the Dutch word for mansion, evolved.

She created different themes for each bedroom. One she called Gypsy Rosaria, with vintage bohemian décor. The centrepiece was a large round bed, covered with sumptuous velvet cushions and throws with a lace pelmet above. Arabia featured an Arabian bed with theatrical curtains in golden silk and the Moulin Rouge was in decadent purple and red with large settees and a four-poster bed. A totally modern twist was Digame, translated to 'tell me' in English. It was stark, grey and white, wooden floors with white rugs and a large bed with a mirrored ceiling. Sunset Boulevard was the complete opposite with floor to ceiling pink shag carpets with a huge fireplace and a gold plated heart shaped bed. The master suite she called Aphrodite after the ancient Greek goddess, which was decorated with ornaments of doves, swans and sparrows with four pillars around the bed.

It took workers two months to achieve the reformation and she used the time to source and interview her high-end call girls. She was surprised at the response to her online advertisement. She knew exactly the type of woman she was looking for. No one under twenty-five years old, with a limit of thirty-five years was the range. They had to like men. It was a common myth that sex workers were lesbian. In fact it had been written that men had greater satisfaction if they could bring the woman to orgasm, as well as themselves. The women would need to be experienced. They would have learned how to deal with clients who fell in love with them, which often happened. They had to be intelligent. Some clients simply wanted companionship and good conversation. They would make it clear how they intended to offer their services. Amanda didn't entertain bondage or sadomasochism. She wanted those who would work for her to celebrate sex through enjoyment, making sure the clients were satisfied. When you are charging upwards of one thousand euro an hour you didn't clock watch. She also told them that the biggest sexual organ in the body is the brain.

She knew she was offering a workplace like no other. She had invested a lot of money and time in paying attention to detail and it showed. The women, she called them her ladies, appreciated the décor and trappings that would enable them to show themselves in a good light and were eager for the 'Cypress' as they called it to be open for business.

Amanda also advertised for cleaners, laundry workers and two chefs. The latter were employed to create intimate dinners or alfresco lunches, as well as hearty breakfasts to be served either as room service or in the dining room.

She organized the creation of her own website and it was here that she announced that the Cypress Herenhuis was open for business. The photo gallery was one to behold and the tariff would attract only the clients who had the means to enjoy the experience of such luxury.

She had created her own apartment on the underfloor of the property by turning the fitness room and spa into an en-suite bedroom off the lounge annex. It was completely private and unobtrusive. She had been mindful that hygiene was vitally important and each week a visit from her private doctor ensured her ladies were always fit and healthy.

In six months she had recouped her outlay. 'The Cypress' was fast becoming the best brothel in Rotterdam, not least because she had made sure the surroundings lent themselves to suit most tastes. The grounds were exquisite and the clients would often arrive in the afternoon to enjoy the privacy of the grounds before their evening entertainment.

Amanda had worked tirelessly to make sure her investment would work. She realized she had not taken a break or indulged herself in any way. She had distanced herself from her ladies. You cannot mix business with pleasure, although that did sound ironic in her situation. She was surprised by a knock on her office door one Friday morning. It was the time for the visit by the doctor who normally would just set himself up in a side room to see the ladies. She opened the door and could not believe her eyes.

Kevin Whittaker smiled at her. He was the cosmetologist who had been blackmailed into working for the Ellenburg Corporation. It was the very same corporation that had funded her. She recovered her composure sufficiently to usher him inside.

11

Her mind was going into overdrive. How on earth had Kevin Whittaker, the best cosmetologist from the John Bartlett Corporation, been able to find her? She had not used any photos of herself in her publicity for the brothel. She was not Andrea Harrison as Kevin would have known her. It was nearly a year since they had both, through very different means, left that life working for the corporation behind. The common denominator was obviously Allesandro Degen, the owner of the Ellengburg Corporation based in Switzerland. He had blackmailed Kevin. He threatened to expose his gambling habit to John Bartlett, forcing him into moving to Switzerland to create another 'Impactus' from the formula in his head. Only he and John Bartlett knew of the secret ingredient. It was so simple yet so elusive.

Amanda felt he must have put two and two together and realized it was she, on her frequent visits to the lab where he worked, who had passed his laboratory test results to Alessandro. What now? She looked at him and actually realized that the old Kevin Whittaker was a shadow of the man in front of her. This man was self-assured, beautifully dressed and with his well-groomed hair and face down to his manicured nails the epitome of a successful businessman.

What a transformation, and how was it achieved, she wondered. "Andrea, allow me to introduce myself. I am Adam Jones and I work for the Ellenburg Corporation."

She extended her hand. "I am Amanda Barrett, Madame of the Cypress Herenhuis." They shook hands and laughed out loud. "How on earth did you find me, Adam Jones?"

"It was never going to be easy. I realized that your visits to the lab gave Allesandro the information he needed to know. In other words how the formula was progressing. He knew, obviously, of the launch date and he acted with speed. He was true to his word. I have access to all the racetracks in Switzerland and a salary to allow me to play. I thought gambling was my reason to be. However, when it is offered to you on a plate you lose the rush of anticipation, the thrill of backing a winner, it all seemed to fade into insignificance. I think Allesandro was as surprised as me when I stopped going to the track. I knew I didn't owe John Bartlett. He had sold me short. I had no compunction in completing the formula for Ellenburg. They launched 'Catalysis' three months after 'Impactus' and it was received with great success."

He looked at Amanda quite aware of how stunningly attractive she was, so self-assured in her own sexuality. "The next product Allesandro wanted was the reduction of age spots on the areas of the body exposed to the sun, hands, face, neck etc. Hence they are often called sunspots. They are a type of hyperpigmentation, a common skin condition, where melanin is overproduced causing dark spots and uneven skin tones. I am currently experimenting with a concoction of mandelic acid, glycolic acid and kojic acid, well known ingredients currently available in cosmetic creams. However the very common hydrogen peroxide is the catalyst and I am nearly there."

Sitting in her lounge she realized the catalyst in all of this was Allesandro. "So, why are you here Adam, what brings you to Holland and to my door?" He turned to face her. "Allesandro gives me a very generous salary and my accommodation is beyond adequate. The Ellenburg labs are superb, allowing me to conduct my research in relative serenity compared to Bartletts. To apply for chemical products, equipment, I go through my friend Matteo. We became friends when I first arrived, he too being a gambler, and we enjoyed visits to the track together. We socialized, something I never had the time to do in England, being so focused on the horses. We went to the highest train station in Europe, on the Jungfraujoch, near Interlaken and to get to it we went in a tunnel right though the mountain!" He was obviously completely in awe of this feat of engineering. "Anyway, we were talking and he just happened to say that I wasn't the only person that Allesandro had on the books from Bartletts. I do think he was totally going against all protocol but he didn't seem to think it was a problem. He asked if I knew a woman called Andrea Harrison. I said of course, I knew her very well. He told me that Allesandro had rewarded her in much the same way as myself. She had worked on his behalf and he honoured his pledge to handsomely reward her. As I had become Adam Jones, she had become Amanda Barrett."

Amanda jumped to her feet. "Oh my God, Adam. This man has a very loose tongue. What if he tells other people about me, what if John Bartlett finds out who and where I am?" He also stood. "Amanda, who on earth is going to care? We are both out of the Bartlett equation now. He knows Allesandro blackmailed me and why. To be fair I don't care about what he would think of me. I was the best cosmetologist he could ever have had and he overlooked my skill in so many ways. I owe him nothing and I am sure he doesn't even think of me at all. I know Sarah Cook ruffled your feathers to say the very least. Yet it was Bartlett who cast you aside and still expected you to be loyal to his selfish endeavours. You have nothing to worry about Amanda." She sat down. "How did you find me, I could have gone to any country in the world, or have remained in England?"

"I knew you wouldn't have stayed in England. Too much water under the bridge and I had time to do my research. I wasn't looking for Andrea Harrison, thanks to Matteo I was looking for Amanda Barrett. I found the hotel but then you disappeared off the radar until two months ago. Matteo told me he had visited the most amazing brothel in Rotterdam. Brothels were his first port of call on any trip, which was why he came to Holland. Pillow talk and compliments lead to many secrets. He told his lady he had to meet the Madame, to compliment her on such an amazing experience. He preferred the Aphrodite by the way. The lady was not at all forthcoming. Business was between her and her client and her client would not be able to meet the Madame, it was not possible. Matteo didn't give up. He wondered if there were other places of this unique quality in Holland. He went to the City Council and checked out the licence. Amanda Barrett. Now where had he heard that name before?"

Amanda sat back in the soft cushions, trying to make sense of all of this. Why had he wanted to find her? She didn't think he held any animosity. He had chosen his own path. She hadn't made him into a gambling addict. Allesandro was meticulous in covering his tracks though. Obviously she wasn't.

"Adam, I am at a loss. Why would you find it necessary to try and track me down? We didn't have any kind of real relationship did we? I always thought you were almost reclusive. You were certainly not in any way sociable or amenable. I am quietly stunned to hear of your trips out with Matteo. So why, do you have a hidden agenda?

"I am a considerably wealthy man. However, I realized that for all I have, I do not own anything. My home is lent to me. The company hire my car. Now that I am no longer gambling, and by the way not lining the pockets of the bookies, I have amassed a considerable fortune. I also have an account separate to my salary in Switzerland. Naturally it is tax free. When Matteo told me about Cypress, how impressed he was, and he is a connoisseur, believe me, I did some investigating.

"It is totally unique. It is the decoration. The presentation, your exquisite attention to detail that ensures the brothel's success. You are the high end of the prostitution business. The girls are absolutely first class and the whole business states professionalism as well as being so personal. Amanda, I would love to replicate this brothel. I can buy outright, but I would need you to do it all over again. What do you think?"

Amanda did not know what to think. She felt his reason for tracking her down was without malice or revenge. She didn't think those two sentiments would have ever crossed the old Kevin Whittaker's mind. This was the mind of Adam Jones, a far more sophisticated and energetic man. Charismatic was an adjective she would never have applied to Kevin Whittaker, but most definitely to Adam.

She was flattered. It was quite something to hear such praise from someone who, though not exactly one of her peers, was someone who knew her before. Someone who could see how far she had come. Her business empire, for that was what it was fast becoming, was gaining a first class reputation. She had done it all on her own. It was her dream and she had done her very best to reach her goal.

She was beginning to feel that old excitement, like the thrill of the chase. When you have done what you set out to do it can become not exactly boring, but the feeling of what's next hadn't so far crossed her mind. Adam Jones had turned her attention to a totally new venture. This time round she would know exactly what was around the corner. She had the blueprint, the wherewithal to do it all again.

"I have to say I am interested Adam. I can create another Cypress, I know the ropes and I have the license. Your money will finance the deal. It can amount to quite a few million, depending on the property and where it is. What do I get out of this? Do we form a partnership? If I am going to be managing the décor, staffing and the day to day running of the enterprise it would seem to me I am going to be far more involved than you."

"First, Amanda, I am so thrilled you will consider this. Naturally it will be a legally drawn up contract. It could be a partnership with a fifty-fifty share of the profits. I know the tax bill will be huge but this oldest profession in the world isn't called that because it's not lucrative. It is a huge money-maker. I know this has all been a bit of a shock, me turning up out of the blue and my proposal, but may I take you to dinner this evening? You will have had time to absorb what I have said and it will be good to meet socially and relax. Shall I pick you up at seven?"

"Seven sounds fine, Adam, thank you. I look forward to discussing your proposal in more detail, and over dinner will be perfect."

Adam left the Cypress in a far more buoyant mood than when he arrived. He had not known what to expect at all, but he could see how professional Amanda was, her attitude seemed to be complicit with his suggestion and he looked forward to an evening which could bring about a huge change for them both.

12

Adam had booked a table inside the restaurant known as FG Food Labs. Amanda was charmed by its trendy ambience and its location in an old train tunnel. The hams hanging above the bar added a Spanish feel creating a relaxed atmosphere. They were shown to a high table for two, and the waiter asked what they would like to drink. "Would it be presumptuous of me to order champagne?" Adam asked. "That would be lovely," said Amanda. She looked around the restaurant that was very busy. "I think we are lucky to have been able to get such a good table Adam." He looked a little abashed. "I was presumptuous yet again and reserved it two days ago!"

"Two days ago, but we hadn't even met then." He looked straight at her. "I had such high hopes and I am not disappointed." She laughed. I, too, have high hopes, she thought.

They began with a vichyssoise with sour dough croutons, coupled with tobiko caviar that made a wonderful crunchy texture. A falafel ball with roasted onions, anchovy and chive gave a tangy spiciness to the meal. Amanda was impressed by the choices, so diverse and interesting. She had always loved fish and wasn't disappointed in the halibut with watercress, fennel and sour sea lettuce with broad beans. Adam chose the tuna ceviche with Japanese mayonnaise, hoisin with spicy tomatoes and sweet and sour celery with tapioca.

They were happy in each other's company, the champagne flowed, and they were more interested in their personal lives than the proposal on the table. They both thought this was something for another day, the restaurant was not the place to discuss business. They chose beef topside with artichoke in hollandaise sauce with crispy oven chips and mace and while Adam ordered a strong red wine, Amanda was happy with champagne. The dessert didn't disappoint. It was an adventurous mix of caramelized macadamia and foie gras in breadcrumbs with vanilla ice-cream. They were both too full for the cheeseboard but when the waiter appeared with a mini barbecue with lavender marshmallows they enjoyed a wonderful aroma with a refined flavour.

Adam suggested a walk to a bar where all kinds of coffee were served and Amanda was impressed by his knowledge of Rotterdam when he had only been there for two days. He took her arm and guided her across the street to the bustling bar and the coffee was delicious with the brandy liqueur. Neither of them had noticed the time and when Amanda excused herself to go to the restroom she was stunned to see it was one-thirty. "Goodness, Adam, look at the time." He laughed. "Well you haven't turned into a pumpkin and you still have both your shoes!" She loved his humour and dug him in the ribs. "That's as well as maybe but I have a business to run and I really ought to be getting back."

The taxi dropped them at the gate and he walked her to the door. The entrance to the underfloor was a discreet black door to the side of the steps leading to the main front door and she got her key from her bag. She turned to him, "Adam, thank you for a wonderful evening, it was a delight and very special to spend time together. I would ask you in but I really do have to prepare for the day."

"My pleasure and I do apologise for keeping you out so late. I will call you later this morning so that we can discuss the project in hand. Once we have settled on a plan of action we can organize a notary to complete the legalities. I feel sure it will be a formality but everything must be clearly set out. Goodnight, Amanda and thank you for a wonderful evening." He kissed her hand and she turned the key as he made his way to the gate and the waiting taxi. At least he wasn't that presumptuous, she thought, he hadn't sent the taxi away.

Although she was tired she couldn't close her eyes. Her mind was turning over and over, things he had said, things she had wanted to say but hadn't. Hold steady, she thought. This has all happened in twenty-four hours, one day, and yet she felt she was on the verge of a new beginning. This could be a life not all about work, but a hope for something more. It was a reason to understand that not everything is rational and purposeful. Allowing feelings, sentiments, giving yourself time to relax and realize that you do have a life outside work. When she finally closed her eyes she felt a huge weight had been lifted. She could see the direction she wanted to go and she had a feeling she would not be alone in her ambition, both personally and professionally.

13

Julie Samson was lost. She was grateful that her husband Dave was making such good progress physically after the accident. It seemed that mentally he was not firing on all cylinders, unless he knew about her and Gary. Maybe he was perfectly clear in his mind that she had cheated on him.

Dave Samson was drifting in and out of consciousness. He felt as if he was floating high up on a cloud. He was weightless and he could see the people around his bed and his body with all the tubes coming out of it. He felt as free as a bird. He saw Julie enter the room and he felt so happy, then he felt so dreadfully sad. She had made him the happiest man and now she had crushed him, more than the impact of the crash. She had taken his trust, his belief in her and given it to another man. He hadn't believed his daughter saying mum hasn't been right since Cyprus. She had seen Gary, the neighbour from Cyprus leaving the house. He couldn't contemplate it, out of the question.

The question had to be faced. The evidence shown to him by the investigator proved that the woman he held in the greatest esteem had taken his life and trashed it. He didn't care if he lived or died. He wondered if he could make the decision whether to go back into his body or if God did. God did. He felt himself falling back down and his body gave a jolt as his soul returned.

The nurse saw his body jolt and checked for vital signs. All was as it should be. This poor man had been in agony when he was brought in and she knew there was a lot more pain to come his way. At least he had a pretty wife who cared about him. That would help him in the dark days ahead.

The operation to reset the hip was a success but the healing process would be slow because he couldn't bear weight on his injured foot. Julie was able to visit the next afternoon. He was wearing the pyjamas she had got him from Marks and Spencer. He didn't own a pair himself preferring to sleep in his shorts. He looked okay, Julie thought but when she moved to touch him he stared straight ahead. "Dave, it's me, Julie." No response. She started to cry. The nurse led her away from the bed. "Mrs Samson, don't expect too much too soon. He hasn't spoken to anyone yet, he is taking fluid intravenously, still nil by mouth. Don't upset yourself. You have to be strong for him. He doesn't know why he is here or what happened. All I can say is that he is doing well. His vital signs are strong and for the moment each hour he gets through this is an hour to the good. Now go and get a cup of tea. Mr Burgin will be in touch with you shortly, he knows you are here and will want to speak to you."

Julie brushed away her tears and thanked the nurse. She texted the kids that he was looking good and she would know more when she had spoken to the consultant. Wayne and Charlie texted back, nothing from Suzie. "Your husband is a strong man Mrs Samson. We have been able to reinstate the hip and that is the main thing. When it's more settled we will be able to deal with the foot."

"He doesn't seem to recognize me Mr Burgin, he doesn't know it's me."

"He has been through a dreadful ordeal. It is amazing he has coped so well with the operation. The fact that he hasn't communicated in any way is normal. Once the body settles down he will be in a better position to communicate and believe me that is a vital part of his recovery. He is being monitored twenty-four seven and we will detect any change in his condition immediately." He got up to leave and Julie concluded that was the end of the discussion. "Should I stay, do you think it will help if I do?"

"I really don't think your being here will make much difference at this time. He really needs to rest, that is the best healer you know. Call any time but I suggest you go home now and try to go about your normal routine, that will help you to be more settled yourself."

She thanked him and texted the kids. Once he had started to take food she felt he would be ready to see them. She stopped short of telling them he didn't recognize her, wasn't aware she was his wife.

It struck her as she put the key in the door, what if knows them and not me? The thought filled her with dread, a feeling deep down that turned her stomach. That would mean he knew.

She hated coming home to an empty house and regretted her decision to let the kids stay at their mates. She called Wayne and said maybe they could all come back tomorrow, as she needed them to be with her. Wayne said he would organize it and hopefully they maybe could see dad as well.

Gary couldn't speak for long. He was obviously in a meeting, but just hearing his voice calmed her and she set about sorting her beauty products and began the assignment she should have handed in on Monday.

The consultant seemed pleased with his progress when she saw him the next morning. "He is taking a little nourishment now and as long as he keeps his fluids up he is on the road to recovery. He does seem reluctant to communicate though. He seems withdrawn. We may do a brain scan tomorrow but for the moment the rest is doing him good. Hopefully he will recognize you and open up. Possibly it would do him good for the children to come, would that be possible, say this evening?"

"Yes, I would think so, or rather I don't see why not. I will get them after school and bring them on here."

"Good, I feel sure that will do him good." She stood by his bedside, talking to him, stroking his hand, silently pleading with him to acknowledge her. He didn't. This time he didn't even turn his head.

The kids were so excited they were going to see their dad. Suzie wanted to stop at the newsagents to get some of his favourite toffees and Julie warned her he will not be able to eat them yet.

She was filled with a sense of foreboding as she took the children into Dave's room. They were all tense, looking so anxious and worried. Suzie went straight up to him, ignoring the tubes and buzzing machines. "Dad, dad it's me, Suzie. I love you dad, you will be fine. You will be just fine." Julie watched, looking for any sign and there was none. Thank the Lord for that, she thought, but then — "Dad, you squeezed my hand, you squeezed it, didn't you, dad?" He very gradually turned his head to see his beautiful daughter, tears rolling down her cheeks. He tried to speak and he hoped he was smiling. She wouldn't let go of his hand. Wayne and Charlie both kissed him, they were crying too. "Dad, mate, it's us, me and Charlie. Got to get well dad, big game on Saturday, we can watch it with you, can't we Charlie?" He was so happy to see his little family. He hoped his head was nodding yes. He just wanted them to stay there. Suzie started rabbiting on like she always did and the boys raised their eyes to heaven because once Suzie was off on one, no one could get a word in.

"Come on mum, we have taken all the room. Suzie step back so mum can get in." She went to move back but Dave held on tightly to her hand. "It's all right, love, it's you he wants to see. I can see him any time but right now you are doing him the world of good."

The nurse came to check on the machines and Charlie's anxious face looking up at the dials and tubes touched her heart. "Your dad's a trouper, he has rallied and these machines tell us that everything is as it should be."

Except it's not, thought Julie. Her worst fears had been confirmed. He must have known. Somehow he had found out about her and Gary. Never before in the marriage had he held back, but never before had she cheated. She didn't know which way to turn, what to do. She resolved that whatever happened between her and Dave and Gary, the kids had to come first. Right now they were there for their dad and he knew them — and he knew me and he hates me.

The consultant saw Dave's positive reaction to his children. Reluctantly he told them they really should leave now, Dave needed to rest. They all kissed him and he eventually let go of Suzie's hand. He was so proud of his kids. They had turned out all right hadn't they? Julie kissed his head and they left the room. The consultant turned back to Dave and saw the tears running down his face. Finally, a reaction, thank goodness. There was no need for a brain scan now.

They went to McDonalds and they were all so much happier. "Mum he looks okay, doesn't he? Bit pale but I think he is going to be fine. Do they have to do the foot operation now? Can't he come home and get strong and then go back in?" Wayne so wanted his dad back home. "I don't know, son, I really don't. It's good he has reacted to seeing you, knowing you. Maybe that means he is healing inside and out. I will ask the consultant tomorrow because he did say it will depend on how well the hip settles as to when they can operate on the foot."

The next day Julie sat with Dave and he did not acknowledge her. The consultant was puzzled, but it was not his place to interfere and he was far too busy to try. The accident had drained their resources and his fellow doctors were exhausted. Julie asked about the foot operation, could it be delayed, could he come home? No, they needed to monitor progress on the hip without disturbing it. He was mobile however, they had got him into a wheelchair, elevating his foot, and he had gone through the general ward and come back to sit by the side of the bed. Progress indeed. The staff were relieved. They had seen too many fatalities that week and a result like this was a much-needed boost to morale.

Julie returned home totally deflated. It was virtually impossible to get hold of Gary in the day and now the kids were home and the weekend would be the usual rounds of football, ponies and mates staying over. She had to leave it until late in the evening to call Gary. She told him about him loving seeing the kids, so happy to be with them, not wanting them to go. He knew about her and Gary, it had to be faced. His coldness towards her was palpable, yes, he knew.

She had organized that the boys could watch the match on Wayne's computer and she was touched that

Helen wanted to go with Suzie to see Dave and support her best mate.

Dave was able to nod and he was smiling. He could say yes and no to questions and was making good progress with the physio. The progress wasn't quite as good hip-wise because he couldn't put weight on the damaged foot. As the days went by he was able to speak a little more and it was two weeks to the day of the accident when he finally acknowledged Julie.

She had pushed him to the dayroom and they sat by themselves, her eyes imploring him to speak. He did. "Julie, I know you are cheating on me. I have had you followed and I know you meet this man who I think is the bloke from Cyprus." Julie went to speak. He held up his hand. "You'll have your chance, girl. I don't know why you did it. I know I wasn't around much but I didn't go and fuck about. I was working for you and the kids. I got that villa so you and the kids could have good holidays. I didn't expect you to end up screwing the bloody neighbour now, did I?" Julie just stared at the wall. It was out now, no more secrets. Her voice sounded so timid. "Dave, I am so sorry, I got carried away. He cared about me you see, he thought I was special."

"And I didn't — you don't reckon that I didn't rate you as right up there? I was bloody smitten, girl. I thought the world of you. Didn't have all the fancy words, just took it for granted we was married and that's it. No mucking about. What about the kids? Did you ever think what this is going to do to them? They love you and they love me and now you've thrown that down the tubes."

Julie was sobbing, heart-rending sobs, but she knew she had burned her bridges. Dave was a proud man, rightly so, and he couldn't take betrayal. She realized at that moment she had destroyed faith, trust, everything on which a marriage is built. Eight, possibly nine weeks of being adored, of putting herself first, above her own morals, and for what? She had brought havoc and destruction, despair and hate to what was once a beautiful and happy marriage. She knew what she was doing when she went to Gary, but she didn't realize what she had actually done. She was in despair, so ashamed.

"I don't want the kids knowing, although I think Suzie has sussed it. When I am stronger, after the operation and out of here we will have to split. Won't be easy, but who says life is easy. As you sow, so you reap. Remember that one, do you Julie? Well you have your harvest now, don't you, girl? Push me back now. Bring the kids when you can but don't come on your own. We don't have anything to say any more, do we?"

Julie somehow got to the car before she completely collapsed. Her world was upside down and there was no one to blame but herself. Strangely the thought of being with Gary had lost its appeal, even though there would be no strings attached. She realized she had left a very good man in a very good marriage. Her selfishness, her pursuit of lust, looked very tardy now. She would lose any respect the kids may have had for her. No excitement, no fulfilment, no future, nothing any more.

14

Mark Bartlett knew just how lucky he was to be alive. If his father had not been able to get him released he would not have survived for much longer in Kerobokan Jail in Bali. It is one of the worst prisons in the world. He had stolen a fish from a market stall and was immediately arrested and put in prison. No trial, no quarter. He had broken the law in one of the most corrupt countries in the world.

John Bartlett was fortunate to have had enough money to be able to hire a lawyer who needed an enormous fee to source a 'judge' who could be bought. It took time to negotiate and all the time Mark's condition was getting worse by the day. Eventually a deal was reached and John was able to get his son out of prison. With his two backpacking mates they made it to the airport and finally home.

He was emaciated and his face looked almost ethereal; the weight loss was huge. Gradually he started to recover, course after course of antibiotics finally killed the infection from where a piece of coral was growing in his foot. He did his exercises with the physio religiously and his muscle tone began to return.

He wasn't academic like his siblings. He had achieved his A-levels and while he was studying for them his aptitude for maths became apparent. His mate Jonathan's older brother was working overseas in Saudi Arabia, under the wing of an investment manager. On a visit home Mark met him and was fascinated by his knowledge of the financial markets, how he was buying and selling stocks, trading on the markets. Damien was very good at what he did and was making a lot of money. Mark was eager to learn and Damien was a good teacher. He perfected the core skill of reading stock charts. He understood the trend line, one of the tools used when making investments. He learned that the trend is your friend, never trade against the trend. If a stock is moving higher as is the trend, the stock is making higher highs and higher lows, then why suddenly think this is going to move lower?

Ongoing, chart patterns are only a useful tool to give an idea of what the price action is likely to do next. He saw that history tends to repeat itself over a longer period of time and most stocks are cyclical. He realized it's important to understand stocks tend to react around certain times of the year, possibly the company's quarterly earnings report, etc.

He became engrossed, looking and learning about a lot of different factors such as the company's current trend, trusted areas of support and resistance, potential for the stock to breakout and move higher. The implied volatility of the stock and the volume of shares trading was a factor. If the stock is trading above its two hundred day moving average, that was a pointer and when earnings are due and how the company tends to perform after earnings becomes a pattern.

Damien was impressed by Mark's thirst for knowledge and how quickly he absorbed and reacted to the world of trading. He suggested when he had done his A-levels he would be interested in offering him a job with the guy he worked for.

However Mark had always wanted to travel and with his like-minded friends opted for a year out to do just that.

Now, he knew he owed a huge debt to his parents, both of whom had stood by him, saving his life. He knew he should start to find a way to repay them both spiritually and financially.

He contacted Damien who was delighted to hear from him and so glad that he had made such a good recovery. Mark told him he intended to invest in the stock market. Damien was curious. To invest you needed capital not only to invest but also to build up an emergency fund that could cover expenses for a minimum of three months if you lose all sources of income. He told him over the long run investing isn't worthwhile if it puts your financial safety at risk.

"Mark, I do believe you are cut out for this. Your brain is quick and you have learned the basics, I saw that when I met you. What would you say if I took you under my brokerage to place your trades? I would advance twenty thousand pounds of my own money for you to invest in your first few stocks. I would like you to compile a list of companies you have considered. It's best not to get too complicated with your first investment. That's why putting money into companies you know and understand will yield an important advantage. For example, you may invest in Walmart but over time you realize store traffic is dwindling, that's an indicator to inform your decision to buy or sell more of the stock."

Mark was completely taken aback. He had no idea that Damien had such faith in him, so much so that he was prepared to invest money in him. "Damien, that is incredibly generous of you, to finance me in that way."

"I suggest, at the outset, we operate on a fifty- fifty basis for the first six months. Once you can double your investment, you are on your own. You will be able to repay my advance and you are a bona fide trader under my brokerage." Mark could barely conceal his excitement. Damien told him he would have to research the competitive moat. In investing the moat is what protects a company from competition. It is the sustainable competitive advantage that keeps customers coming back year after year, while holding the competition at bay for decades. He explained he would have to ease himself into stocks, focussing on what he is familiar with and make his decisions with the long term in mind.

He said he hoped to hear from Mark within a week to know which stocks he had chosen and why. Mark didn't waste any time, determined to show Damien that he would do his research and choose his first stocks. Finally he had a purpose, an opportunity to strive for success and the bonus in all of this was that he enjoyed the challenge enormously.

Damien was impressed with the selection of companies Mark had made: Alphabet, Amazon and Facebook and two from the biotechnology sector, although Prolific Pharmaceuticals was a new one on him. Mark explained that his father's laboratories had created a cosmetic using living systems and organisms and this was a subject close to his heart. Damien knew about the enormous success of 'Impactus' and could see where Mark was headed. Mark, with Damien's blessing, began his introduction to the stock market.

15

John Bartlett settled back, Scotch in hand, gazing at the fire. Finally he felt he could relax. He and Victoria had come through an emotionally draining time.

He found out that any stress caused by business-related problems was nothing at all in the grand scheme of things. The terrifying thought of losing a son, in possibly the worst prison in the world, was right up there in the bizarre stakes. He thanked God every day that they had managed to get Mark home, out of the jaws of filth and corruption. He had made a remarkable recovery, obviously he had youth on his side, and the doctor felt sure there would be no underlying health issues as a result of his experience. He smiled when he remembered Mark's determined promise to get a job and try to pay him back. John was pleased he felt that way but in truth it would take a lot of time to be able to accumulate anything near what he had paid. He didn't tell him that. Just encouraged him to find work which hopefully he would enjoy.

He was pleasantly surprised when Mark told him about his hopes of investing in the stock market. He knew he had been researching the ins and outs, so many pitfalls and so much to learn, but he had a quick mathematical brain. His love of figures, equations and quite often knee jerk reactions would stand him in good stead. He offered to back him, to speculate to accumulate as he put it, but Mark told him of his arrangement with Damien and John was suitably impressed. So, finally, his boy was on the road of making something of his life.

'Impactus' was the best product to come out of the John Bartlett Corporation. He didn't dwell on his disappointment, anger even, that someone could betray his trust. Everyone has issues, he thought ruefully. He knew that Kevin Whittaker had been blackmailed to join the Ellengburg Corporation in Switzerland to replicate the product for them. His assistant, Andrea Harrison, was the go between, giving information from the labs to Alessandro Degen. Maybe not to him personally but to the corporation as a whole. Industrial espionage in this instance was not a crime punishable by law. It was a disgruntled employee, Andrea, being rewarded for passing information to his competitor. Kevin was probably ignorant of what she was up to, mainly because his focus was on his gambling addiction. It was that addiction and his huge losses that made him the prime target, a sitting duck, ready for the taking. John knew the cosmetic to emerge from the Ellenburg labs three months after 'Impactus' was a copy. 'Catalysis' was launched and was doing well.

He felt that at least he had had a head's start. Sales were going through the roof and his new cosmetologist, Dominic Kelly, was earning his money. He had used Kevin's basic notes on the elimination of 'sunspots' on ageing skin as a basis for his research. It was at the patent stage and this time nothing was left to chance. A registered design protects the external shape and design of the product, as to how it will be presented at launch. The design team was hard at work creating a unique presentation package, the first in its field.

Victoria entered the room, smiling. "Just guess who is coming to dinner, John." He smiled at his wife. "Oh now let me see, the King of Siam?" He laughed and she sat next to him on the sofa. "Very funny, it's Samantha." John looked surprised. "Really, our long lost daughter has agreed to grace us with her presence?" Victoria had hoped he might have been a little more receptive. "John, she has been very busy travelling for her work. Her diploma from the Taylor Institute opened so many opportunities she was spoiled for choice. You know that and you know how busy you were when you were starting out trying to establish yourself in a competitive market." She knew he was upset that she hadn't kept in touch, not even the odd phone call. "Why now, I wonder?" Just thinking about her made him realize how much he had missed her. Admittedly he had been working incredibly hard himself, trying to keep on top of things in London he had his work cut out. Giving time and thought to the New York office was time consuming in itself. "I am sorry Victoria, of course I will be so happy to see her. When is she coming?"

"She picked up a hire car from Heathrow and should be here by four."

"Great, I will freshen up and look forward to giving her a hug. Just hope she is okay."

16

Samantha eased the car down the drive. She knew she had to see them. She loved them so much. Her mum and dad, they had given her a wonderful childhood, growing up in a house filled with fun and laughter. Her two older brothers would tease and cajole her, but she loved it. She was so glad she could be there for Mark in that dreadful time when he was desperately ill. Yes, a family home with wonderful memories. She wondered how they would receive her news.

John flung open the front door and bounded down the steps to grab her into his arms. In that instant he knew how much he had missed her. She hugged him back, tears streaming down her face. "Oh Dad, I am so sorry I haven't been in touch. Every time I thought I must call, something cropped up. No excuse I know." John hugged her so hard. "Samantha, you are here now and that's what is most important." Victoria was in tears too, just so thrilled to see her daughter again. "Welcome home, Samantha, to say we have missed you is an understatement. Come here," and mother and daughter walked with their arms around each other into the lounge.

Mrs Johns, the housekeeper, came in with a tray of tea and as soon as she put it down she hugged Samantha. "My goodness, girl, you look good. Just look at you! You look like someone off the cover of a magazine. Beautiful." She turned to Victoria. "Got a lovely leg of lamb on the go, have a feeling that was one of Samantha's favourites." Samantha laughed, "you know how to spoil a girl" and she hugged her again. John asked her about the flight and had she been working in Spain again? She told him she had been promoted to be the business consultant for the whole of the Venidero Holdings Group. She had been analysing its existing practices for weaknesses. She was creating solutions to help the group more efficiently meet its goal. She was specializing in human resources. The group had hired her specifically to deal with issues associated with hiring new full time employees. They were going to establish a company in America.

John and Victoria were both amazed and thrilled that this young woman, so confident, so self-assured, was their Samantha, their "magnificent afterthought". She had come along when they thought their family was complete, and she made it so. "You have been hiding your light under a bushel, Samantha! Well done, so proud of you. Does this mean you have to go to America?" John was really excited at the prospect. "The groundwork, the office accommodation has already been done. They are taking a suite in the Chrysler

Building in Manhattan, it's opposite Grand Central Station on Lexington Avenue."

"I know exactly where you are Samantha. What a great opportunity. They must have pretty deep pockets to be able to operate from there. Mum and I absolutely loved our time in New York, that's where Paul was born. It is an amazing lifestyle, you will love it. Oh, I am so happy for you." He jumped up and hugged her. "Dad, they are a pretty major player, that's why they want to go to New York. The offices are being furnished as we speak. The Spanish HR team is organizing the recruitment of staff. That is they are advertising for about ten sales personnel as a start-up. I will be going out in about a month's time. Initially I will be staying at the Fitzpatrick Grand Central hotel. It's nothing grand but very convenient for the office. To be honest it has all been a complete whirlwind of dates and times. I hadn't realized they would want me to recruit in America. I had been brushing up on my Spanish, but I guess that will still come in handy."

Mrs Johns had set the table in the dining room and told Victoria the lamb would be ready in about thirty minutes. The vegetables were roasting and there was an apple pie for dessert. She said goodbye to Samantha and said she would call in tomorrow to see her. "How long can you stay with us?" asked Victoria. "Mum, I wish it could be longer but I have to fly back in two days." She really did wish she could stay. She missed this lovely home, and her mum and dad. "We will make sure we make the most of it." The lamb was delicious complemented by the roasted vegetables and a sliver of apple pie and hot custard topped it off.

John was wondering if he could help out in any way. His office in New York really ran itself, he had enormous faith in his vice president and staff, but he did love going there. "I can help you source accommodation when necessary Sam. In fact, we could do with a break and New York fits the bill, don't you agree Victoria?" She didn't need any persuading. She had enjoyed their time there, obviously the freedom before children was very special and they had done all the touristy things before settling into an 'American' way of life. Samantha was thrilled at the prospect and once she knew a bit more about the timescale they would be able to make plans.

Paul and Mark freed up their diaries to spend time with their sister and Victoria was grateful they could spend precious family time together. She and John stood arm in arm on the steps as Samantha waved till she was out of sight down the drive. "I will miss her even more now, not seeing her for so long and now just that brief visit." Her eyes were full and a tear splashed down her face. John hugged her tight. "It would seem all our children have finally found their niche, more in the case of Mark really. Paul seems to be doing really well and now Samantha is starting her new adventure. We are lucky we can play a small part, it will be so good to be in New York again and this time we will be together."

John made some business telephone calls and Victoria arranged some counselling appointments. All back in the old routine, except they could now focus on a trip to New York. It was always so special to have something to look forward to.

17

It was a year since James Hardcastle had lost the woman he wanted more than anything in the world. She had died in an accident on her way to meet him at the car hire office in London Heathrow airport. The accident itself was horrendous and she was one of the many casualties. She never knew that he was going to take her to Paris, to their favourite hotel and he was going to ask her to marry him. She thought she was returning the car and they were flying to Edinburgh where her fashion business was situated.

Hindsight is a wonderful thing. You look back and think, if only, why didn't I? It is all a negative energy. He had told his wife he had met someone. Their marriage was a sham and he wanted a divorce. After all this wasted time of worrying about the effect divorce would have on his sons, twelve and fifteen. They were in boarding school and had become independent from family life. What family life, he thought to himself. Boarding school had become their family. Who could blame them? Michelle really found that her sons interfered with her social life. She said to James that it was impossible for her to have them at home, especially as his work took him away for a lot of the time. Joe was eight when he left home and hated it. Eddison was enrolled and although at first he had missed his brother the three-year gap at aged eight was vast. James hated the fact that Joe was so unhappy but in truth he was establishing more and more retail outlets throughout the country and he could not be in two places at once.

Michelle loved the social climbing, the ladies who lunched, the gossip and scandal. She didn't miss the boys at all and managed to get them places in adventure holiday parks in the summer. She found her niche in the golf club. She was a good player, and didn't take prisoners. Most of her peers had children and they were all at boarding schools so really there was everything to play for. James came home less and less. He visited the boys whenever he could, either at school or at home, but the guilt he felt over them being there meant he could not be guilty of leaving them for another woman.

Michelle had insisted the divorce was to be low key. She was going to tell her friends that James was basing himself in France for the foreseeable, to enter the haute couture of Paris. That would explain his absence. James was not to tell the boys. She had a very good settlement — well she was entitled as the mother of his sons albeit a mother who had never had a job and was that person in name only.

James had to tell them. He had not been a good father. Of course he loved them, kept up with their progress, but hands on he never was. He felt he owed it to them to tell them that he and Michelle were now divorced and he was moving to London. Considering they felt their mother had never really wanted to be in their lives they didn't seem at all perturbed. James hugged them and said he hoped it wasn't too distressing for them, particularly as Joe was at a critical stage in his exams. Joe told him 'no worries', two of his mates had stepmothers and no one seemed in the least bit bothered. Eddison seemed distant, almost embarrassed that his dad was there. "I will always be here for you both, I know I am not physically in your lives but my house in London can be your home too. I would be so happy if you can come for the holidays." As he said it he did wonder how on earth it could be arranged, but even if he had to employ a live-in housekeeper he would do it. He was sad it had come to this and told them so.

Children are far more resilient than people realize. In the first term Joe had cried himself to sleep so many times. He was in the changing rooms after rugby when he heard sobbing from one of the cubicles. He called out, "are you okay?" and the sobbing stopped. He got down on his knees and saw a pair of feet in the middle stall. "My name is Joe and I cry a lot too. I don't like it here. I miss my brother and this place is so big and so cold." Torquil Grainger pushed open the door and stood awkwardly wiping his face with a grubby handkerchief. "I hate it, too. My parents are abroad and they can't come to see me. My uncle is supposed to be coming but he doesn't turn up when he says he will. My name is

Torquil and I am glad we have met." They stood looking at each other. A smile gradually crossed Joe's face. "Well Torquil, looks like you and me are going to be really good friends." He put out his hand and they solemnly shook hands. That was the beginning of a beautiful friendship. They each had each other's back and together they found a kind of inner peace.

Joe made sure he was there for Eddison three years later. It was so much easier for Eddison. No two children are the same in one family and Eddison had an air of confidence that attracted friends from all quarters. He was good at sport and also enjoyed most subjects and although he was glad Joe was there if he needed him, he was glad he didn't.

What you have never had you don't miss and the two brothers hadn't really known a mother's love. It was Mrs Hawthorne, the House matron who first showed any kind of loving care. She knew Joe was unhappy at the outset. It was her rule to never favour one pupil more than another but in Joe she saw such sad insecurity. She had met his mother and father who were chalk and cheese. The mother was all for keeping up appearances, asked hardly any questions regarding Joe's care whereas Mr Hardcastle was warm and wanted to know exactly what would be expected of Joe. He asked to see Joe's dormitory, the food hall and where he could spend his free time. The grounds were maintained to a high standard with tennis courts, rugby and football pitches and two Olympic sized swimming pools. All the facilities ticked the right boxes that she thought tended to ease the feeling of guilt she sensed he felt.

She was so pleased to see a change in Joe. He was a far happier little boy who had made a friend of Torquil. The two were inseparable and their friendship was heart-warming. She was always there if one or other of them needed to talk, making sure they could enjoy tea in her apartment and the odd cuddle didn't go amiss.

She wasn't surprised when James Hardcastle told her about the divorce. She did need to know how the practicalities would work. During term time, things would continue as normal. Joe and his friend Torquil would be sharing a room now they were sixth formers and Eddison was happy in his dormitory. James knew it was down to this woman that the boys had been able to settle into the daily routine and told her he hoped to employ a full time housekeeper in his London home. He didn't think they would want to go to their mother, or rather she didn't want them there was more the truth of the matter. He said he intended to cut his hours during the holiday period to be there for them. He had neglected his responsibilities for too long and really hoped that they would come for the holidays.

James settled into his new home, totally new, no memories of Jane. He was both surprised and pleased when he had a call from Penny, Jane's sister. She was so sorry to be the bearer of bad news but sadly Doreen, Jane's mum, had passed away. James was mortified. He had only met her on a few occasions, it had been too painful to visit so soon after the accident, but he remembered a very gracious and charming woman. "Penny, I am so dreadfully sorry. What happened, are you okay?"

Penny told him it was very quick. A missed diagnosis of breast cancer meant that when it was finally found, there was so little time. She died peacefully at home a week ago. "Penny, I am so sorry I haven't been in touch. I have been struggling and the only way I could get through was to keep busy with work. I cannot bear to have time on my hands, time to think, time to dwell. How are you coping with this so soon after dear Jane?"

"Like you James, we both found it very difficult. We had each other and for that I was so grateful and I was pleased that I could be there when Mum passed. The funeral is in ten days."

"Would it be possible that I could come? I didn't know Doreen well, but I loved her daughter and having met you I can see she was a very special person to have two such daughters." He hoped he wasn't intruding, but Penny's reaction made it clear that wasn't the case. "That would be wonderful James, I would so appreciate your support and it will be good to catch up. Are you able to come the day before?" James felt the warmth of her welcome. "As I recall you live in that pretty village called Braughing. Are you still there?"

"Yes, mum has lived there since she and dad retired. I have booked several rooms at the local inn and I can reserve one for you if that would suit." While he was talking he was looking at his diary and there was nothing that couldn't be rearranged. "Please book me in for three days Penny. Can you give me the dates again?" Penny confirmed and she was surprised at how relieved she felt, and happy, that James was able to come to the funeral.

18

This was the third time in Penny's life that she had suffered huge personal loss, her mother, her sister and Derek, her lover and best friend. They were madly in love. They had met quite by chance. She had got on the train at Winchmore Hill and was balancing her briefcase in one hand while trying to hang on to the overhead strap. The train lurched and she swung around, trying to hold on. Her briefcase fell out of her hand and landed on a young man who was intently studying an open file. "Oh I am so sorry, did it hurt you?" He looked up to see a worried face searching his. "No, not at all. I was so absorbed I didn't even see you standing there. Please have my seat." She tried to protest but he stood and virtually put her on it. He gave her the briefcase." I am Derek by the way." He held out his hand. "Penny, pleased to meet you."

It took thirty-five minutes to King's Cross during which time they established they both worked in offices in Holborn. They changed onto the Tube and two stops down the line they went up the steps to Kingsway. "This is me," Derek said. "Where?" Penny asked. He laughed. "Right here, number eighty-eight Kingsway, above the station." The building was on the corner of Kingsway and High Holborn. "I am just up there, Templar House, who would have imagined that?" She hoped she hadn't sounded stupid saying who would have imagined that, but who would?

"Do you break for lunch?" Derek asked. "Sometimes I do. I can work through my lunch hour and build time so that I can take a day's holiday." That arrangement didn't exist in Derek's office. "Well, could you make an exception and meet me for lunch today? There is a little place just down the road from here." He pointed to some bright parasols outside a restaurant across the road. "I usually take twelve-thirty to one-thirty if that is any good for you." Derek said it was fine with him and he would be outside the restaurant at twelve-thirty.

Penny hurried to work. She wondered if he was a regular on the train. She had been making the journey for about two years now and thought she might have noticed him. Mind you it was rush hour and the train was always full at that time of the morning. The short Tube ride was standing room only and quite often she was mindful of someone's hand trying to touch her bottom that made her furious. No chance to see who it was, crammed in like sardines, just a blur of faces. He would have gone straight from the Tube into his office so she wouldn't have seen him walking along. Gosh, and I am going to meet him for lunch. She knew he worked for an estate agent as she had told him she was a personal secretary to the senior partner of an accountancy firm. She had worked on the agenda for the partners' meeting and emptied her briefcase to do the final tweaking.

She walked as quickly as she could and saw him waiting by the bright red parasols. He smiled and had reserved a table just inside the window because although it was fine and dry a chilly wind could creep up from around the corner. It was an Italian bistro and she ordered pasta carbonara and he had mussels in white wine. They both had a glass of red wine and a deliciously strong coffee that came with a macaroon. He asked her where she lived. Did she take that train most days because he felt sure he would have remembered her? She was renting a flat in a small block on the Broadway in Winchmore Hill. He was the next stop on, Bush Hill Park, where he shared a flat with his friend Stu who was a chef at the local pub. They both kept very different hours and that was a bonus as they were hardly ever there at the same time, other than after the pub closed.

An hour was never going to be long enough. "I don't keep regular hours at the office. If I have a viewing it can take up to two hours, but most mornings I am on the same train." Penny smiled. "Likewise. I usually know at the beginning of each week if there will be evening meetings. My boss is very fair, his meetings are normally in the city or clients will come to our office." Derek settled the bill and she thanked him so much. It was delicious and she hoped she might see him on the morning train. He watched her walk away. He hadn't noticed she had such gorgeous long legs. He would make absolutely sure he would be on that same train the next morning.

A kind of ritual was established. She would stand in her usual place and he would be by the door as she opened it. They rarely got a seat but were happy to chat and get to know each other. The journey was over far too soon. The weekend was looming and she knew it would be a very long one without him in it. "Are you busy this weekend Penny? I wondered if we could meet. There is a lovely old pub right on the New River. Perhaps we could go there for lunch, if you have no plans?" She hoped she didn't sound too eager as she immediately said "that sounds great, Derek, thank you." He kept his car in garages at the back of the station. "Is eleven too early? I don't usually get up that early on a Saturday but if you have things to do I can make it later, whatever suits you."

"Eleven is fine. I go to the supermarket on the Broadway and stock up for the week." She didn't mention that her shop this week would include a fresh chicken and some vegetables, just in case.

The weather was warm for early April and the daffodils were showing their trumpets in the garden that went down to the river. They had their drinks outside and the sun had some heat so they stayed there for their lunch. It was an extensive menu and she had plaice stuffed with prawns and he had the game pie.

All the while she felt so comfortable with him. He was tall, which was good because she wasn't short at five foot eight, and his eyes were almost startling they were so blue. His easy smile, which always seemed to be present, lifted his face. She was smitten. So was he. Her hair had a kind of reddish glint, piled on top of her head that accentuated her neck. She had an open cream silk shirt tucked into brown slacks, with a jacket to match. They both started to speak at the same time, sorry, no after you. He told her he was twenty-eight and enjoyed his job, especially when he was given *carte blanche* to promote a new office block coming on to the market in Camden Town. She was twenty-five and was happy working for her lovely boss who was really old school, and she respected his knowledge. He had a good client base and was known for his integrity in the city.

Derek suggested they visit Forty Hall, a Jacobean Manor House in Enfield, that was about twenty minutes' drive away. He pulled out her chair and held her hand while she collected her bag and jacket. It seemed so natural, to walk hand in hand, as though they had known each other forever. The daffodils were magnificent, a golden carpet under the trees leading down to a huge lake where swans glided effortlessly by. Penny gasped. "Derek, its amazing, I never knew this was here so near to where I live." He pulled her to him. "I never knew that you were so near to where I live." The kiss was gentle, not demanding, and she returned it. She hoped he wouldn't see her heart was thumping under the satin shirt. She didn't want it to end. They parted but he held her hand so tight, as if he would never let her go.

The house had many additions made by the different families that had lived there from when it was first built in 1632. There was the great hall opening up to a series of rooms that led from one into the next. The grand staircase, crafted locally from oak they were told, led to two more suites and the top floor was where the servants had lived through the centuries. They were both very impressed and it would be hard to discern whether it was the building or the fact they were so together.

They enjoyed a coffee and shared a pastry before making their way to the car park. He stopped as they got to the car and kissed her again, this time a long lingering kiss, although they both felt a sense of urgency. "What would you like to do now Penny? I am certainly not hungry and we have walked our legs off." Penny turned and kissed him. "Perhaps we could go back to my flat and I can rustle up something for when we are hungry." He opened her door for her and said he thought that was a very good idea.

There was space outside her building where he was able to park and she was very glad she had left the flat looking as good as it could. She led him through the front door to the lounge and the late afternoon sun had warmed the room. "I have wine, red or white?" Derek kicked himself. "Penny I don't expect you to provide wine."

"Oh really? You have treated me for the second time to a great meal and a wonderful time at Forty Hall. I hardly think offering wine is out of the question."

He laughed. "Red then, please." They sat side by side on the sofa. The wine was good, they both felt good. He put his glass down and put his arm round her. She put her glass down and stood up. She went to the bedroom and turned to him. He was right behind her. He held her so tight and kissed her so hard. She kissed him back. They undressed very fast, she turned back the bed but he pushed her down and kissed her mouth, her neck. She arched her back as he sucked her breasts and licked her stomach and her wetness. She moaned, he stroked her and she reached for him. He was so hard and she guided him inside her. A gentle rocking became a strong demanding need. They reached a kind of waiting, a moment before they were both ready, as if this moment was so precious, it had to be perfect. It was. They both lay there and got under the covers, just holding each other.

"Well that was something else." Penny laughed, it was magical, the icing on the cake. She pulled on her dressing gown and went to get the wine. He got the glasses and they enjoyed the moment. "Are you hungry? she asked. "Funnily enough, I am starving." They went to the kitchen and she made cheese on toast with tomato on top and they opened another bottle. It was getting dark when he said he thought he ought to go. "It's Sunday tomorrow, must you go?" She hoped she didn't sound needy. "I don't have to go and I really don't want to. Would it be okay to stay?" She kissed him and the dressing gown fell to the floor. They wasted no time, yet this time they were more relaxed, it wasn't so urgent and if you can replicate something perfectly, they did.

It had been a long time since Penny had invited a man into her home. Her previous relationship was all a bit predictable, it became routine, the excitement had gone. She knew you had to work at a relationship, if you wanted it to work, but she lost the impetus. They didn't hurry to get up, the rain was pouring down the windows and it was not conducive to going out at all. They made love and talked, asking all sorts of questions about each other. Derek's previous relationship ended six months ago, it had run its course and he was relieved that there was no one special in her life. "Well actually there is someone special." He sat up, resting on one elbow, looking intently into her eyes. Penny's heart skipped a beat, was all this too good to be true? "You, gorgeous girl, you are the special person in my life."

They showered and had some toast and marmalade and thought they should make an effort to get some fresh air. The rain had stopped and they walked to the local park. The air smelled so fresh after the rain and it wasn't cold. "I can make us roast chicken for supper if you would like." They went into the local pub and had a glass of wine and Derek bought a couple of bottles to have with supper. While the chicken was roasting they went to bed and thoroughly enjoyed each other and a perfect chicken dinner. "I have to drive home so I will leave the wine for you to enjoy," he told Penny. "I will make sure I am on your train in the morning, stand in your usual place gorgeous girl." He kissed her goodbye, said he had had the best ever time and she agreed. She was clearing the dishes when her mobile rang and he told her he missed her and the night would be too long without her.

Their busy work schedules meant they could only meet on the morning train, but they made plans for the weekend that would start Friday night. Derek's friend Stu actually said to him he hadn't seen him so happy, this girl must be special. He confided that he had never felt like this before. She was beyond special. She was a keeper. From their past loves they both knew that this was the first flush of love, a heady time, discovering new things about each other, learning how to please, how to complement. They were always laughing, talking, holding each other tight, never wanting to let go or say goodbye. Unlike a first love, this feeling had tenacity. They knew what they wanted and it was on a summer's evening, walking back from the pub that Derek said the words she hoped he would. Men never say what you would have them say, but then they say something wonderful. "Penny, I have never felt this way before, I love you. I am in love with you. I hope you feel the same, that we have a future together." She flung her arms around him. "I love you so much, I can't believe the happiness you have brought me. I cannot imagine my life without you Derek."

Derek had managed to save a considerable amount and Penny couldn't match it but her contribution enabled them to have enough money for a deposit. Her tenancy agreement was a month's notice and Stu was happy to take on the flat on his own. He had had a good promotion and could afford it. They found a maisonette in Enfield. It was a little further out and was therefore in their price range. Derek's salary covered the mortgage repayments and the excitement they both felt when he carried her over the threshold of their first home was palpable.

The maisonette needed work doing on it. Structurally it was sound but had been left in a pretty poor state and they set about rubbing down and painting skirting boards and doors. Derek found out he was good at tiling and retiled the bathroom and kitchen. Penny could hang wallpaper and in six months they had achieved a makeover of which they felt very proud. A very pleasing two-bedroom ground floor maisonette in the leafy suburb of Enfield. "You sound like an estate agent," laughed Penny and he chased her round the hall and into the bedroom.

Their lives were idyllic. A happy routine of work, meals out, visits to the beach in the summer. Frinton-on-Sea was about two hours' drive away. They went to the theatre after work, watched films in Leicester Square and filled their leisure time with busy activities.

There are no symptoms of a brain aneurysm unless it ruptures. Derek collapsed while he was cutting the grass. He felt a searing pain in his head and fell unconscious on the grass. Penny was hanging out the washing and screamed as she saw him go down. She rushed to him, calling his name. She called the ambulance on her mobile. He wasn't moving. She was trying to get him onto her lap, trying to make him more comfortable as the ambulance screeched to a halt. Two paramedics gently moved her away. She didn't realize Derek had died. They asked if there was anyone they could call, to be with her. She didn't move. He cannot be dead. He was cutting the grass and he must have tripped. The paramedic called the deputy. He arrived to conduct his own investigation.

Penny was numb. She felt nothing. This is ridiculous, her lovely man, her soulmate, her reason to be, cannot be dead. Why isn't he moving though? The paramedic asked her the name of her surgery. It was on her phone and he called the number. He needed the doctor to come, to pronounce the death, but also to see Penny. She was in deep shock. She tried to get up off the grass but her legs gave way. They asked her again as they led her inside, who can we call, who can be with you? She looked at her phone. Her mother was an hour away and she told the paramedic they would be there as fast as they could. He told her to drive safely, no rush, someone would stay with Penny until they got there.

19

That was six years ago. The pain was no longer so raw, whatever coping mechanism you can find, you use. Her parents were able to take over because at the time Penny was not functioning. Their sorrow at Derek's death was doubled as they tried to care of Penny. There is no right or wrong way to grieve. It takes so many forms from the fear of being alone, the sleepless nights, the dreadful wrenching sobs, the complete despair. There is nothing that can offer hope. All hope dies with the person you love. No future and you are not able to grasp the memory of the past. Those amazingly wonderful happy times, dashed into oblivion.

She gradually managed to reach some kind of normality. She got through the first year of 'firsts', anniversary, birthday, death day. Her boss was keen for her to return, he felt routine would help settle her. He didn't know she could never get on that train again. They were opening a branch in Amersham. Did she think she might be able to organize the office? She knew she had to do something and this would be a completely new situation. She set about it with a determination that surprised her. Her boss, dear old Mr Parkes, was so pleased to see a little bit of the old Penny coming back. That was the start of the healing process. Keeping busy, having a purpose. It doesn't get any better but you get better at it.

Her parents were finally able to relax. The haunted look left her face and she had been able to buy a flat in Amersham. There was no memory of Derek there. No, all the memories were in her heart and she knew she had to succeed. She had to because Derek would hate her to not make the effort. She needed him to be proud of her, to see that she could achieve again. Little by little, things became less of a struggle. She could survive and when you actually take stock you realize everyone has to. You can't just give up. You have a life and you must do something with it.

She had created a good workplace. The articled clerks were quite fun, cheeky young men doing their articles. They would say to her if she knew they were paid hardly anything and Mr Parkes charged them out at twenty pound per hour? They did lift her spirits, quite dauntless but they knew this was the best way to learn the ropes. Three new partners were recruited and Parkes and Co had a good client base that would ensure the viability of the branch for a long time to come.

She didn't really have a social life. She worked long hours and that was fine. Most weekends she would go to her parents, company for her and for them. She was able to take them out and about and she loved the way they cared so much for each other, and for her. She was really weaving a cocoon around herself and her parents were secretly worried that she didn't seem to need any company other than theirs. They were a generation away from hers and it bothered them. Penny knew she was relying on their company a bit too much, but she found that there was security in routine and she wasn't interested in making friends or joining clubs. She enjoyed walking and Braughing was a pretty village surrounded by lovely countryside which she loved to explore.

She felt she had reached a major goal when Mr Parkes invited her to London with her colleagues for a celebration to mark the success of the Amersham office. She went on the train. It was a different route into Marylebone Station and although she felt a wrenching feeling in her stomach, she did it. The icing on the cake was a generous bonus, which Mr Parkes told her she had more than earned. It would be paid each year.

There is no one like your mother. Her death affected Penny differently than Derek's. They had been able to prepare themselves. They had been given notice. So little time but the palliative care team was wonderful. They cared for her as if she was their own mother, carefully washing her, laughing with her and one of them would always be holding her hand. They arranged for an adjustable bed to be set up in the sun lounge. Head and foot areas could be raised or lowered. It was possible to raise the whole bed to facilitate washing by the health care workers. Doreen was really quite lucid.

Penny would read to her but gradually Doreen needed oral morph at more regular intervals. The doctor told Penny that a syringe driver would best manage any pain. A concoction of drugs decided by the doctor was administered and Doreen slipped into a deep sleep. The doctor urged Penny to talk to her, read to her. Let her know she was there because hearing is the last sense to go.

The Marie Curie nurse was possibly one of the most compassionate people Penny had ever met. She came so that Penny could get some rest at night, but quite often Penny would sit and talk with her into the night. Doreen finally breathed her last breath and with a kind of sigh she was gone.

Penny was in full control this time. Not shell shocked like she was with Derek and she knew from her experience of Jane's funeral what needed to be done. Doreen had wanted a cremation and the service was at twelve in the main chapel. James had driven up the day before, it wasn't too long a journey and he and Penny had supper at the pub in the evening with some of the other mourners.

As funerals go it was a smooth transition from the entrance of the coffin to the curtains closing around it as *Amazing Grace* played the mourners into the fresh air. Penny and James stood together remembering a year ago when Jane was laid to rest. James wept as he remembered her, and his tears were also for Penny for her great loss.

The wake was well attended, and it seemed as if everyone was more relaxed, they had said their goodbyes and there was a steady buzz of conversation. Old friends reunited, cousins who hadn't seen each other for ages catching up and dear Uncle Bill recalling with relish how he and his sister used to scrump apples from the next-door garden. Reminiscing, in a nice way, helps calm a situation and Penny was finding herself able to let go for a little while.

She and James spent the next day trying to cram a whole year's events into twenty-four hours. He told her about the divorce and that the boys seemed so well adjusted. He was hoping to organize a housekeeper for the holidays so that the boys could be with him. She thought that was very commendable and was happy for him. She told him about Derek. It had never come up before but she wanted him to know that once she had been very happy and she hoped that he would be able to move on to better times.

James was in denial. He hadn't really grieved for Jane. He was keeping so busy, filling his days with appointments, almost to the extent of neglecting himself. He needed to be busy, anything to get through the day, the week. He often worked through weekends until his friend and greatest support told him he would burn out.

Keith had been the first one to get to him at the hospital when he went to say goodbye to Jane. He was shocked at the effect it had had on James. He didn't know he was taking her to Paris, to ask her to marry him.

All he saw was a shadow of a man who had aged overnight. He had supported him throughout, and he knew that work was the only way he could cope, at first. Not now, not after all this time.

James didn't have many hobbies but Keith introduced him to playing squash. It didn't matter what it was but he needed to get him out of the non-stop work routine. Gradually James seemed to be more attentive, noticing things other than his workload.

He told Penny he owed so much to Keith and she said she felt the same way about her parents. Her dear dad had dementia and hadn't known her mum or her for a long time. She had stopped visiting because he just didn't know who she was and that killed her. She rang the home each week, always asking them to give him her love, but she knew it wouldn't mean a thing. That is one of the cruellest illnesses she thought.

They said their goodbyes and hugged each other for a long time, both grieving but hopefully healing. She promised to visit him in London, it was quite near where their old maisonette was and she had always loved going to London.

20

Once he returned from the funeral he seemed to have more energy. He made space in his diary for two games of squash a week. Keith had introduced him to Rupert who had been a member of the club for ages but like James was single so they played on a Sunday morning and had a few drinks followed by a roast dinner. Some kind of system was working out for James. He enjoyed the break from office work and Rupert was good company. He had never married, never felt the need and was very happily single.

The summer holidays were approaching and he went to see the boys one Saturday morning for a long overdue meeting. They were pleased to see him. Joe was enjoying sixth form and Eddison, who now wanted to be known as Ed, was a good all-rounder as his report said. James asked if they had given any consideration to coming to stay with him in London. To his surprise they both said of course they would come. Be great, said Dad. Joe asked if it would be okay if Torquil came too. His family was abroad and no one seemed to be around for him. James told him it would be no problem at all and Ed was fine with anything. He had been thinking and wondered if they would like to have a real vacation, abroad in America. The hugs said it was a definite yes and James left the school thinking at last he had a chance of a relationship with his long neglected sons.

Linda, his secretary, had suggested various agencies that supplied live-in housekeepers. She offered to do the initial interviews on his behalf. After all this time she knew the man inside out. She created a short-list of three very different personalities. They were all given the same criteria: When the boys were home their wellbeing was paramount and when they were not they would run the home in a professional and efficient manner.

James was happy with the high standard of candidates. It wasn't rocket science but there had to be a certain demeanour, a warmth, as well as the ability to work hard to make the house a home. He settled on Mrs Bailey. She was a widow who had lived in with a family whose children had now left the nest and her references were impeccable. He guessed she was around fortyish, which he thought was sadly young to be a widow, but they connected and she was delighted to be offered the job. She had her own set of rooms on the top floor, bedroom, en-suite bathroom and a small living room. Joe and Ed's rooms were down the hall from James and there was a guest room available should it be needed. He thought Torquil would want to share with Joe as they did at school but there was the guest room if not. Each bedroom was en-suite and a large lounge and separate dining room on the ground floor had a delightful aspect with two huge bay windows. The kitchen was well equipped and Mrs Bailey, Kirstyn from now on, was delighted with her new surroundings.

He collected them from school and Torquil couldn't stop saying thank you so much, he was very grateful and so happy. James thought to himself, we pay all these fees and they have a two-month break but not from the fees. Never mind, he was glad he could afford the school and the prospect of a real vacation was a bonus. He had asked people at work about teenagers and holidays and learned that they needed space and don't expect them to get up early. However a holiday in America would count for a lot and he wanted their input, where they thought they should go and what they really wanted to do.

His sons were thrilled with the house. London was a twenty-minute train journey and the suburb was a stone's throw from the countryside. Kirstyn told James they were delightful boys and made sure there was an ample supply of cupboard love, as well as warm hugs. They were not at all self-conscious about showing her affection and she was secretly very pleased. They soon settled in and Joe and Torquil included Ed in everything, including games on their computer although Kirstyn wasn't too sure about Grand Theft Auto — the language was not what she was used to at all.

James suggested that at the weekend they could go to London, see the sights and act like tourists. In the evening they were going to plan their holiday in America. He had got some brochures from the travel agent he used for work and they really were spoiled for choice.

How did they feel about Malibu Beach? Living for most of the year in the country surfing was never thought of. However, they were keen to try anything and a kind of three-phased trip was planned. They would fly to Los Angeles, stay for a couple of nights in the Malibu Beach Inn. Then fly to Las Vegas to stay one night at the famous Bellajio Hotel and then fly to Arizona to see the Grand Canyon. The boys' minds were boggling. Fly back to L.A. then to San Francisco, home of the Golden Gate Bridge and Fisherman's Wharf, the location of Pier 39, a great tourist destination. James was particularly keen to see the Giant Redwood trees, telling the boys some of the trunks were wider than a car so that was a must. They must factor in a ride in a cable car as well. Then he planned to rent a car and travel down the coast towards San Diego. Their final destination would be San Clemente with its famous surfing beaches, before driving back to L.A. to fly home.

He felt it best to take three weeks and handed their plans to the travel agent who said he would organize the flights, hotels and car hire. The excitement was almost too much. James suggested they go to London on the Monday to organize a summer wardrobe, most importantly to include beachwear, the proverbial boardies being top of the list.

He met them for lunch in Covent Garden and when he got back from work Kirstyn was roaring with laughter as the lounge was littered with beach shoes, beachwear, shorts and t shirts. They were having a ball and this was all before the actual adventure. All passports were in date and travel documents complete. James held all the paperwork in his hand luggage and the boys had their backpacks.

Kirstyn waved them off in the taxi and with a slight sigh of relief set about clearing up the havoc wreaked by three young boys who didn't understand the importance of putting clothes away and hanging up shirts.

James had such high hopes for the holiday and they were surpassed, big time. The accommodation was superb, he was particularly proud of the boys and their behaviour. He couldn't help notice how the young girls congregated around them, and although it was just to hear them speak — oh my God you are so English — it gave their confidence a bit of a boost. Malibu Beach was a great success. The locals set about teaching them to surf and after one day they could just about stand up. The second day was a breeze and they looked quite the part carrying their boards in their boardies down to the waves.

The stay in the Bellajio Hotel in Las Vegas was pure indulgence. The boys shared a room and James had an adjoining suite. He extended the stay to two nights mainly because they needed to experience everything they could in this award- winning hotel including five swimming pools, amazing dining at any hour of the day and the incredible fountain shows. They couldn't believe how the fountains played in different colours with different moves and each display was different throughout the afternoon. At night it was even more magical, a very special memory.

The Grand Canyon in Arizona was a complete contrast to the opulence of the hotel. The agent had booked them on a flight to fly from one end to the other and to witness the boys' faces as they gazed down at the Colorado River was a highlight for James. This was nature in the raw as Joe put it.

There were several tours operating in San Francisco and they had opted to drive over the Golden Gate Bridge and on to the Giant Redwoods. Before the bridge the guide stopped so that they could see Alcatraz, the prison known as The Rock in the middle of Frisco Bay. It was built in 1934 but closed permanently in 1963. It was now a tourist destination. He told them there had been several attempts to escape but the most famous was when three inmates vanished in 1962. They had used sharpened spoons to bore through the prison walls and left papier-mâché dummies in their beds. They floated away on a raft made of fifty raincoats. Their bodies were never found and there was much speculation as to whether they had perished in the icy waters or made it to land and freedom. It was open to debate, the guide told them.

Driving over the Golden Gate Bridge was another tourist dream and they were very lucky that on this clear blue day they were able to look down and see the bridge from where the guide had stopped the bus, high above, almost in the clouds. More often than not the bridge is shrouded in a hazy fog.

The Redwoods were stunning. You could drive a car through the huge gaps in their trunks and they felt enormous respect for the majestic branches reaching higher than the eye could see.

James recalled the films he had seen where the trams rattled over the rails down to Fisherman's Wharf. It was like being on a big dipper and it was great to be experiencing it in the flesh so to speak.

Before picking up the hire car he rented boards for the boys because the last leg of the journey was really all about them. Each cove they came to out came the boards and they persuaded James to have a go. He was happy just to paddle out and ride in on his stomach but the boys 'high fived' him for that. They had all really caught the bug and the week was spent finding a beach, booking into an inn and just surfing. The agent told James about San Clemente, that it was a delightful town with two great surfing beaches and he wasn't wrong. It was brilliant surf and the perfect end to a wonderful holiday. They got back to L.A. and flew to Heathrow.

Kirstyn had cooked a beef wellington that was very well received and they all flopped into their beds. James had tried to beat jet lag, adjusting his watch to British time, but he found that travelling east to west was not as bad as the other way round and his body clock just needed one day. The boys could sleep it off and still had two weeks of the summer break to enjoy. They discovered another kind of board to ride. James took them to the local skate park. Maybe it was because they could surf that they found it was easy to skate board. A trip to the local sports shop sorted out the skateboards and there was a bus they could catch most days to the park. It became a daily ritual, no lazing in bed, up and ready for the bus with the packed lunch from Kirstyn.

James still played squash in the week but as the weekends were reserved for the boys he asked Rupert if he would like to join them for a Sunday roast after his game. Delighted to accept, Rupert was a great guest, regaling them all with stories of his various exploits when he was a young man.

The boys were making the most of their last week when James arrived home from work to be met by a rather agitated Kirstyn. "James, I am so glad you are here." He was not used to seeing her disturbed in this way. "Kirstyn, what's wrong — is it the boys?" She ushered him into the kitchen. "No, it's not the boys, well in a way it is." They both sat at the table. "It's Torquil. His mother is in the lounge. Apparently the father has gone off with another woman. A total shock to her of course. Things hadn't been right for a while, she told me, but a bolt from the blue to be sure."

"Has she seen Torquil?" he asked. "They aren't back from the park yet. They called to say they had missed the bus but would get the next one so don't worry."

James was aware that Torquil hardly ever talked about his parents, except that they were abroad and couldn't visit. He wondered how he would take it, maybe like his own sons, nothing really to miss if you haven't had it — a kind of self- reliance, your virtual independence.

He was completely taken aback as a tall elegant woman extended her hand in greeting as he walked into the lounge. "Mr Hardcastle, I do not know where to begin, to be able to thank you for all I know you have done for Torquil." He shook her hand. Sometimes you meet people and you have to force yourself not to stare. Her face was exquisite, framed with jet black hair pulled away from her high cheekbones in what he thought might be a French pleat. Her eyes were a warm brown colour and her mouth was a beautiful smile. "James, please" he managed to say. "Charlotte." They sat in opposite chairs in front of the mantelpiece. "Please forgive the intrusion. I got back to England two days ago and it's been a whirlwind. The school gave me your address and told me how you had invited Torquil to spend the summer break with you and your sons. My husband and I are to divorce and I do not think there will be any problem at all with me getting custody of Torquil.

After all he will hardly fit in with the lifestyle my husband is about to embark on."

It had been a long time since he had been affected, startled even, by a beautiful woman.

"I am so sorry, Charlotte. I am divorced and I know it can be a painful journey." He didn't tell her that to him divorce was a blessed relief, although what he had hoped would be a happy outcome didn't materialize. "It was a shock in a way. My husband is a very successful, charismatic man, and I had known of two of his affairs. This was just a step too far. I think in my heart I had been bracing myself that this time it was different." Hearing the words spoken out loud, "I love someone else, I am leaving you," her voice faltered and she reached for her bag. James stepped forward, he could feel her sadness and he touched her arm. He looked at her. "I do understand. It is so distressing." It was ironic that he had said similar words to Michelle, but the fact was that their marriage was in name only. She dabbed her eyes and sighed. "I do apologise, James, you really don't need to hear all this."

He smiled. "No apology necessary. Can I offer you a drink, gin and tonic?" He went to the sideboard. "Gin and tonic would be wonderful, thank you."

He poured her gin and his Scotch and soda. "How do you think Torquil will react?" He hoped he wasn't interfering. "I am not sure. I hate the fact that the marriage has failed and that I couldn't make it work but there is only so much you can do. Both partners must want it to succeed and obviously that isn't the case here." There was a banging of the front door and any peace that had been before was shattered as the boys came through into the lounge. It was as if it would be totally impossible for them to do anything in a calm, quiet way. James stood. "Hi guys!" Torquil had stopped dead in his tracks. "Mum, what are you doing here? Where is Dad?" Joe and Ed had the same reaction on seeing his mum as James, except that they stared. "Joe, Ed, come with me, let's leave Torquil and his mother alone for a bit."

"Dad, she is gorgeous isn't she. Is she a model? Torquil never told us she looked like that." James smiled. In his experience children didn't really look at their parents in that way. It was more a begrudged hug or just a look of not wanting to do what they had just been told to do. "Joe, you really mustn't speak like that, especially to Torquil. Her name is Charlotte and I do agree, an attractive young woman. The sad part is that she and his dad are divorcing." Joe sat down with Ed in the kitchen. Kirstyn put the kettle on and offered some cake. "Oh, sorry, Dad, I didn't mean to be rude. Poor Torquil, I wonder how he will feel. He never really talked about them." Ed spoke with his mouth full of chocolate cake. "I am sorry for him too but at least he has us." Just like that, James thought. He guessed that they were comparing his divorce to what Torquil would have to go through. "Well I hope he is okay. Not being rude Dad but we didn't see much of Mum ever did we? It didn't hurt us. It was more kind of a normal situation.

We didn't feel sad, did we Ed?" Ed managed to put down his cake. "All I can say is we are lucky because we have each other and Dad, and Kirstyn," he added with a broad grin.

James was surprised and pleased that he had scored some points with the boys. He had done his best to make up for not being there before, but the holiday had created a bond between them all and that included Torquil.

The kitchen door opened and they all looked expectantly at Torquil. Joe and Ed hugged him, and that in itself tugged at James's heartstrings. "Are you okay, mate? Dad told us and we are here for you, if you want." Torquil looked a bit shocked, they didn't think he had been crying. "Let's go and check out the computer. Last I saw I was beating both of you." Joe laughed and they didn't really give Torquil any time to protest as they kind of marched him out of the door. "They are good boys, James." Kirstyn said as she cleared the cups. "I have beef casserole and it will stretch loads." James thanked her and went into the lounge.

Charlotte was standing looking out of the window and when she turned he felt his heart skip a beat. She seemed so vulnerable. "How is Torquil? The boys are on their game right now. He looked shocked, I guess it's a bolt from the blue for him." She seemed distant, a bit shocked herself, he thought. "I hadn't seen him physically for about two years. We facetimed but it's nothing like actually being able to hold him and he is so tall now. That stopped me in my tracks, he has grown into a charming young man." James knew exactly about stopping in your tracks. "He was so sweet, he wanted to know if I was all right. He and I had a rapport and although his dad loved him, he wasn't that good at responding to him. He didn't really mention his dad, just hugged me and said he would be there for me. I forget he is almost an adult and he seems very confident for a sixteen-year old. I guess all this must be a lot to do with being with such a happy and settled family. I really am so grateful James." He took her glass. "Can I refresh this for you?" She nodded and they both settled in their chairs again while he moved a table for her to put her drink on. "I have parked my car down the road as I wasn't quite sure which one was your house. I should be going soon." James looked at her. "Where are you staying in London?"

"I have booked into a Premier Inn because I wasn't really sure how long I would be here."

"Do you have to get back for anything? Kirstyn has dinner for all of us. It would be lovely for both you and Torquil to spend a bit more time together before you have to go." She smiled. "That is so kind of you and I would love to stay for dinner, thank you."

Torquil was so happy to see her, he positively beamed. The meal was delicious and instead of bounding off to their game they all went into the lounge. Torquil chatted non-stop, telling her all about his amazing American holiday with interjections from Joe and Ed. James sat watching them all, and enjoyed all the tales, albeit some embellished, about how big the surf was and the girls really loved their accents. Charlotte looked at James. "I had no idea you had done all this for Torquil, treating him to such an adventure. I must make some contribution, you have spared no expense." He laughed. "It was our pleasure. We consider Torquil to be one of our family, he is great fun and I am glad he was able to come with us."

Charlotte looked at her watch. "I should be going. I know you only have a few days before you go back to school and I would love to spend that time with you." James stood up. "We have a spare room, you would be more than welcome to stay here. In fact, I insist." Torquil hugged her. "Please Mum, it would be great to be with you for a few days." She nodded. "In that case, how can I refuse?"

James walked her to her car. She opened the door and turned to him. "I never realized just how much I have missed him. I have never been in a family environment and he has flourished in the warmth. Thank you so much." She kissed him on the cheek and he closed her door. "I am owed some time from work so we can spend the time altogether. I will clear it in the morning and be back for lunch. You come over whenever you can." He watched her car lights disappear and as he walked back he felt something he hadn't felt for a long time. He felt really alive, but more importantly he was alive to his feelings.

21

James got home earlier than he thought and Kirstyn told him she had prepared the guest room and the boys and Charlotte had gone to the skate park. He drove to the park hoping to catch them and was totally blown away to see Charlotte balancing on a board, scooting along as if she was born to it. The boys were skating beside her with Torquil shouting "go girl," running along cock a hoop. She came to a stop and he clapped her as she came towards him. "Not going to do the ramp just yet," she said laughing. "Where did you learn to do that then?" Torquil took his board back and demonstrated how they could all do the ramps. "In Dubai. I learned to surf and so I guess it came easier than if I hadn't." They watched the boys for a bit and walked towards the café. "Kirstyn has done all of us a packed lunch. Let's have a coffee, my treat."

He asked what her plans were. Did she intend to stay abroad? She told him she had a few loose ends to tie up and solicitors had been appointed to sort the divorce. The villa was rented so there was nothing to sell and she knew she would be treated fairly moneywise, but not in any other way, he thought ruefully. The divorce was uncontested. He had left her and had agreed a fifty-fifty split of their assets, which were mainly his earnings. They had sold their house in Surrey and there was money from that so she had no money worries. He would pay school fees and maintenance for Torquil until he was eighteen. Strangely, she felt no emotion. No anger. She wished she could get angry, she thought it might help. Maybe that was an indication that in her heart a love had died. Give a flower no water and it will die, she thought.

They all ate their sandwiches and the boys wanted to stay on at the park. James asked Charlotte if she felt like a walk, the park had a bandstand and quite beautifully tended flowerbeds and it made a change from just watching skateboarders. They walked past some swings and she swung really high and James found himself doing the same. She was having a good time. James was the tonic she needed to let go, to enjoy herself once more. They found an ice cream van and sat in the bandstand while they ate, watching children feeding the ducks.

Kirstyn had done a midweek roast with all the trimmings and James got the game of Monopoly from the sideboard. They all entered into the swing of it and started to buy houses. Ed was the first to get a hotel in Bond Street that really wound Joe up when he landed on it and had to pay one thousand four hundred pounds. If Charlotte hadn't landed on his Park Lane where he had four houses he would have been bankrupt. James was quietly accruing quite a lot of rental income owning King's Cross and Fenchurch Street stations plus the water works and electricity company. All in all everyone was just about even until Torquil landed in jail and couldn't throw a double for love nor money to get out. Lots of laughter and it was a lovely end to a good day.

Two days before they had to drive back to school Charlotte surprised them with a trip to the Warner Bros Studio. They went behind the scenes and on to the sets where the Harry Potter movies were filmed. It was a magical experience and they saw the actual props, costumes and special effects in creating the films. Strolling through the Great Hall, seeing Diagon Alley, Dumbledore's office, the Gryffindor Common room and Hogwarts Express was amazing. Gringotts Wizarding Bank was the latest addition to the tour and inspiring to say the least.

She had reserved a table in a nearby hotel where they enjoyed pasta and pizzas of every description followed by multi-coloured ice cream. A great day out and an outing never to be forgotten enjoyed by all. James was very impressed that Charlotte had done all of this and thanked her. "James, it is the very least that I could do, and I thoroughly enjoyed it. It is a special day to end so many great times the boys have had."

The last day was spent packing. Not a happy time but Kirstyn had laid out the clean pressed clothes for them to put in their cases. James had created an album of their American holiday and they each packed a copy. Kirstyn took a photo of them all sitting around the supper table which she printed off.

They all hugged her as they went to the cars. Torquil would travel with his mum and Joe and Ed got in with James. When they arrived James was surprised they were not in the least embarrassed to give him a kiss and hug. Before it had been don't kiss me, don't hold my hand. They unloaded the cases and finally went in; three brothers who had had the very best of times.

Charlotte and James stopped at a pub on the way back. They both enjoyed ham, egg and chips that oddly seemed fine with a glass of wine. Charlotte was going to collect her things and then go to London Airport where she would leave the hire car and go on to Dubai. She was totally unaware that the hire car office was where a year or so ago James should have met Jane. Where his life had ended, or so he thought. He had never expected to feel as he did now. Sad that she was going away and he hadn't even told her how he was feeling, hoping she may be felt the same way. The coffee was strong and he felt the end of the meal must not be the end of them. "Charlotte, I have really enjoyed the very short time we have spent together. I am going to miss you very much." She touched his hand. "I will miss you too, James. I feel so happy in your company. I love that you care so much for the boys, for my Torquil equally with your sons. When you say my name my heart sings. It means so much to me. I will keep in touch, I promise.

I am not sure how long it will take to sort things in Dubai but I will keep you in the loop. I feel strongly that we have a future." At those words James caught his breath. "You do?" She kissed him, full on the mouth and he kissed her back. She laughed at his reaction and this time he kissed her. His heart was soaring, a surging happiness engulfing every part of him. "I had dared to hope you might have felt what I feel. I know we have only known each other for a very short time but that time has been the best of times. I cannot tell you how glad I am. I believe we have a future Charlotte and I cannot wait to make it our adventure." They kissed again, both wishing this didn't have to be goodbye.

She collected her things and said goodbye to Kirstyn. She thanked her for her kindness, her fantastic cooking and for making her so welcome. Kirstyn looked at them both and she felt what she had hoped might be, possibly was.

They walked to her car. "This isn't goodbye. It's see you soon. Take very great care Charlotte, I will miss you so much but we will keep in touch." She kissed him. "Every day, James, every day." They held each other tightly and reluctantly he let her go. As she drove away she could hardly believe how her life had turned around from despair to a kind of fulfilment. She could face the future with a confidence that had been lacking, a new beginning. James was thinking the same thing as he went back inside the house. He could never have imagined that this vibrant beautiful woman could feel about him as he felt about her. A new chapter, a whole new story, with, please God, a wonderful ending.

22

Sally Harvey Smart was getting concerned. Her mother's death meant that she no longer had anyone fighting her corner. The inherited wealth from her father passed to her mother who had bequeathed it to her, the only child of Oswald and Harriet Harvey Smart. The cause for concern was the fact that Harriet had made Oswald sign his will leaving everything to her and ignoring the children of his first marriage. They were contesting the will and Sally was horrified by their sheer greed. How dare they think they were entitled to anything from her parents, Daddy signed the will and it was therefore her right, her inheritance.

Bridger, Tamarind and Georgina Harvey Smart passionately hated Harriet. She was like a terrier chasing a rat. Not that their father was a rat, far from it. They loved him and he loved them, very much. She just wouldn't let go. Their mother wasn't really much of a mother to them. She herself came from a wealthy family. It was a natural progression to meet and marry Oswald, a very wealthy landowner and well respected in Cheltenham society. When the girls reached the age of ten they entered Cheltenham Ladies College as daygirls.

Oswald fought his wife tooth and nail to stop them boarding. Evelyn thought it would make them 'more rounded', more independent if they boarded. What she really meant was she would have more time to pursue her social life without having them 'under her feet'.

Oswald won that round and Bridger was not at all fazed to be a boarder at Boyne House in Cheltenham College. He didn't miss his sisters' persistent nagging that he was boring and silly. He was neither of those and excelled at making friends in his new environment without the Misses bossy boots as he called them.

Evelyn was good at entertaining. She would make lists of guests and came into her own hosting events in the National Hunt Festival week in March. Their house would be open to so many from what she called the rich set, like minded, high flyers from all walks of life with the common denominator of money. One such guest was Harriet Bramley; quite ironic that she was on the hunt in National Hunt week. She had done her research. Oswald was quite a catch and she knew his love of horses probably outdid any love for his wife. They appeared to be happily single in their different pursuits but nothing seemed to spark when they were together. Evelyn was so at home chatting to her peers while Oswald would top up his whisky and talk to his estate manager rather than any 'fluff' as he called her guests. That was until Harriet cornered him, flattering his unassuming soul. How marvellous! What a wonderful gathering, he must be very proud of his stables and the runners he produced. He demurred, saying it was down to his equestrian trainer, Solomon, who was responsible for all things stable-related. He and Joseph, his estate manager, ran the estate like clockwork. She said she would love to see the stables, would it be possible? He couldn't take his eyes off her plunging neckline, her gorgeous legs and jumped at the chance. She flirted outrageously, and this didn't go unnoticed by Tamarind and Georgina who thought she was a complete tart. Well, Tamarind did, Georgina was quite in awe of her, a bit like a film star, so glamorous.

Harriet tottered beside Oswald in her ridiculously high heels. Fine for a social event but not much good for walking. He took her in his Land Rover and she arranged her legs at their best angle. She hoped he would actually look at the road rather than her breasts because it was quite a narrow lane. The stables were immaculate and she was genuinely impressed. She told him she loved horses, had two of her own and complimented him on the high standard that Solomon had maintained.

It was getting dark and he couldn't resist touching her bottom as she got into the Land Rover. She hesitated, turned and smiled at him and put his hand on her breast. A Land Rover hasn't got that much room in the back seat but there was enough for her to undo his belt and release his throbbing manhood into her mouth which didn't last long before it spluttered into life. He got out and managed to sort out his clothes and she kissed him on the mouth. He was used to the stable girls. They were very giving. They thought this may be a way into his heart, but really he just enjoyed what they had to offer. They were not in his class. Harriet was. God he wanted her. He told her he had to see her, had to have her again. She invited him to her flat. Luckily he didn't query where were the horses? She gave him all that he had never had. She was good, she knew just how and when to tantalise and tease. He was beyond any going back.

Evelyn wasn't surprised when he said he wanted a divorce. Although he thought he was being very discreet Cheltenham is a small place big on gossip. She didn't care about the stable girls but vowed if he wanted to go he would have to pay. He did. She didn't know about various investments he had overseas so whereas she thought she had him over a barrel, the settlement was easily absorbed by the money they brought in.

23

The solicitor's letter was brief and to the point. Tamarind, Georgina and Bridger Harvey Smart were contesting the will of Harriet Harvey Smart on the grounds that the will of Oswald Harvey Smart was signed when the deceased did not have the required mental capacity. All his worldly goods passed to his wife on his death, totally ignoring their existence, the children he loved. Now the bitch was dead and they needed to act immediately to prevent the money going to her only daughter.

Sally got in touch with the solicitor her mother had used when she made her will. He said the claimants were still within the twelve-year time limit since the grant of probate. They were contesting the will on the grounds that the deceased did not have the required mental capacity. He suggested negotiating some kind of settlement would prevent court proceedings that were always expensive and lengthy.

The thought of money being spent on trying to disprove a fact infuriated Sally. Her mother was obviously only concerned for her daughter's welfare, leaving her a financially secure future. The witness to her father's will had died. There was no living soul to confirm or deny that there was anything illegal or wrong. In her head she felt that her mother would not have deliberately blindsided her father, but in her heart she knew she would stop at nothing to make sure she was the only beneficiary at the time of her death.

The estate comprised the house, where Sally lived, the stables and cottages plus the offshore investments. The tenants of the cottages were wondering what would happen if they were to be sold. They worked at the stables that also could go if Sally opted to sell up. Only she was aware that the will was being contested and this was a huge thorn in her side.

The forty odd thousand pounds she had left from her mother's provision for the funeral was dwindling. She had sold two of the paintings in the study which had made sixty thousand, but that had gone on indulging herself holidaying in Mauritius, after all she deserved a break. A new BMW Sports sat on the drive. She had expensive tastes, only the best labels hung in her wardrobe and she needed the money now. The contesting of the will was going to prevent her getting her hands on the fortune. It irked her that the three of them would also inherit from their mother. Why should her father have to provide for them when they were out of his life.

Gregory Argyle, the solicitor, arranged for an appointment to see her to discuss the options available. It was the responsibility of those contesting the will to raise a real suspicion that the deceased lacked such mental capacity. If they achieve this, the burden passed back to those seeking to prove the will. They would have to prove that he did have the capacity.

He was hopeful. Oswald had signed the will quite early on in the marriage. This in itself was a huge factor in Sally's favour. She would have been about ten at the time, and Gregory himself was often in his company. He knew he idolized his daughter, possibly to the exclusion of his other children. The fact that Gregory was more often in the company of Harriet in Oswald's absence at the stables was neither here nor there.

He would be willing to state that Oswald was in good health, firing on all cylinders so to speak at the time he would have signed the will. Sally was elated. She asked him to put the wheels in motion. Speed was of the essence. She thought the "other side" would have a hard job to contest that fact, put succinctly by her own solicitor.

The solicitor acting for the now grown up children knew it would be a hard one. There was no one around to prove one way or another what had taken place. He urged them all to reconsider. Gregory had contacted Solomon, Oswald's equestrian trainer. Although he was now retired he was able to recall quite vividly how proud Oswald was of his daughter. He was fit and well when he brought her down to ride. Solomon was particularly pleased at how she excelled under his training. She wouldn't slacken and when she fell off, which happened a few times, she would get straight back on and urge the horse to go faster.

It is strange that when you have money, you want more. The three siblings could easily afford any costs incurred by challenging the will. The allowance from their mother was generous and having a financial cushion, they had known nothing else, enabled them to pursue their future careers. Tamarind wanted to study law at uni and had applied for a vacation scheme in her second year. It would stand her in good stead for a training contract. She would need a good academic record and an abundance of commercial awareness. She spent each summer vacation working through different departments of the firm, making a positive impression on the graduate-recruitment team. She was one of the best candidates selected from the scheme to attend a training contract interview, so she was pleased to get her degree and then be offered the contract. Her hard work was well rewarded and she was on her way to a career in law.

Georgina was not that academic but had a flair for all things theatre-related. She joined the drama group at school getting involved in productions and her teacher recommended she apply to do an acting foundation course. It was an introduction course that lasts for one academic year and helps to build acting skills. She joined an amateur dramatic group, taking all the parts offered, and this stood her in good stead to get through the highly competitive audition process to get into drama school. She had attended a summer school programme at the school that eased her passage. It wasn't RADA or the Bristol Old Vic but it was a start and she loved the interaction with like-minded students. The school organized showcase performances for its final year students, inviting agents to come and watch. She was one of the lucky ones to get an agent and was pleased her friend Joanna got one too. Look out Broadway, here I come!

The work ethic seemed to have missed Bridger. After a good first year at college he seemed to lack motivation. He knew he could never achieve at uni like Tamarind and he opted for a course in business studies. Eric came to the college for the last year due to his parents moving house. He was an enthusiastic pupil and some of his exuberance rubbed off. Bridger and he struck up a friendship and spent weekends going to parties and getting stoned. Unfortunately getting stoned encroached into the week when they had targets to meet, projects to hand in and they were called to the Head. He told them he was very disappointed they were not making the effort and consequently the deadlines. One teacher had smelled weed and they both knew it was a matter of luck they were not actually stoned at the interview. He made it very clear that drug use was a cause of instant dismissal and expected them to take this as a warning it would not be tolerated.

Money wasn't a problem for Bridger. He could get the weed, and supplied Eric. Eric saw a business opportunity, using Bridger's money. The downside of weed, apart from losing its appeal and progressing to stronger drugs, was the coming down after the high. They were not so addicted that they couldn't realize they could buy and sell. After all they were doing business studies and the irony wasn't lost. Bridger's mother had no idea of what he was spending his money on, or that he was earning a considerable amount from drugs. She never thought to check his bank account. Her money went in each month and she felt that more than covered anything he would need to buy. Bridger and Eric were surprised just how many students wanted it. Cocaine was cheaper but this was skunk and it always hit the spot.

The guy supplying them couldn't get enough so they looked elsewhere and cut a deal with a more efficient operator. They were making a serious amount of money. Who needed qualifications when you could do all this without them? Eric's parents realized he was not achieving like he had before. The Head had written to them, requesting an interview, he really wanted to help. He told them that there was a suspicion earlier in the year that he and another pupil were smoking weed. Horrified looks, no, not Eric. However, any drug taking seemed to have stopped to be replaced by a lethargic attitude that precluded any interest in academic achievement. He hated waste. Eric had the ability to do well but was choosing not to.

Eric's parents were at their wits' end. You can lead a horse to water but you can't make it drink. Eric was that horse. He hated college. He had no interest in learning and he could not legally drop out. He should not legally be selling drugs either. Bridger on the other hand was making some effort to just try. He had to be at college for two more terms. After that the Government had no say. He decided it was better to suck it up than not. The drug supplying was easy. What wasn't apparent to him was the fact that Eric was concentrating solely on 'the business'.

The college registration system was electronic, meaning students were registered for every lesson they attended but Eric was not attending the lessons he should. This was flagged up to his parents who once again had no idea he wasn't at college. Where was he if he wasn't there? There is very little parents can do if their son doesn't want to learn. The college can suspend a student, only for five days, but that seems to be defeating the object when not attending college is the problem.

Eric solved the problem. He had been withdrawing cash from Bridger's account over a period of three months. He packed a bag and took a train to London. He knew no one there. He didn't have a passport or any identification, just a holdall full of cash. He wasn't streetwise but he would learn. He was now on the road to becoming a full time criminal. He was ignorant of the consequences of his actions, not only of the total devastation felt by his parents, but of what would actually happen to him. He was as green as grass.

Bridger was totally dumbfounded when a sign "insufficient funds" appeared on the ATM. He checked his pin and tried again. Same message. There had to be some mistake. He called the bank and they suggested he make an appointment to review his finances. Putting two and two together came as a sharp shock to him. How on earth had Eric managed this? Easy-peasy. He knew the pin number and often asked Bridger for the card so that he could pay the supplier. Bridger couldn't let his mother know any of this. She certainly wouldn't grasp the seriousness of not having the funds to pay the supplier. He thought on his feet. He withdrew the remaining amount and closed the account. It was all kind of falling into place. The supplier sent a couple of "heavies" to get the money from him. He didn't have it. He was beaten black and blue. This was a warning. He had one week. The sight of his bleeding broken nose and black eyes frightened the life out of Evelyn. How could this happen to her son? He told her he had withdrawn a considerable sum from his account. He wanted to show her he had been saving for a car. He was almost seventeen. Someone was watching and followed him. They beat him up and took all the money. His account was empty. She said she would call the police. He begged her not to. He had seen the thugs hanging around the college and if they could do that to him in broad daylight they could do it again. They could find out where he lived.

She was mortified. This was Cheltenham after all, that sort of thing didn't happen here. He asked if she would give him the money to replace his savings. Of course, that is the least she could do. She also told him although she thought it was very commendable he wanted to independently buy his own car, she would do for him what she had done for the girls. On his seventeenth birthday a brand new car would be on the drive. She didn't want anything too powerful. Just a new set of wheels waiting for him to pass his test.

He paid his dues, his face was healing but he was angry. He thought he and Eric were mates. How could he have done this? They had a good thing going and he had taken a beating that ensured he would not pursue this line of business ever again. He knew how lucky he was. It was a massive wake-up call. No one knew where Eric had gone or where he was now. Bridger had no intention of trying to find out. He had learned his lesson and would finish college and then find something he wanted to do. If his sisters ever found out what he had been doing they would be horrified. They had been born into a very privileged lifestyle and his abuse of it was despicable.

Eric became one of the six to seven percent of children and adolescents who run away to London each year. He turned up at a direct access hostel and was offered a space. He didn't need to pay a deposit or rent in advance and shared a room with Gerald who seemed far too posh to be homeless. He slept on his holdall. It was never out of his sight. He made a few enquiries, so far so good. The thing he couldn't see was how people perceived him as a very wet behind the ears kid, obviously with money, all pot noodles and no common sense. He was about to learn a very hard lesson, after which he would need to make a core decision. Did he want to live or die?

24

Although Bridger wasn't going to uni, he wanted a gap year. Everyone leaving college, those whose parents had deep pockets, were going to travel. What the gap was between didn't arise. He thought it would be best to make plans on his own. He knew only too well how you could have faith in someone. To build trust only to have it dashed away. A lot of the students were going to Asia. Europe didn't hold the same fascination and they had heard so much about Indonesia and Bali, they were on a route well-trodden by previous gap year students. He opted for Australia. He was eligible for the working holiday visa that permits both work and travel within Australia for the one year it is valid.

Marketing was the sector he most enjoyed in his business studies course, with Human Resources a close second. He would have enough money to cover his expenses for a month. His allowance from his mother would still be paid into his English bank account and depending where he chose to stay he should be okay financially. Obviously not the dizzy heights of an apartment in Sydney, but hostels on the Gold Coast were a popular starting point. Also he would meet fellow travellers and he was very personable and socially outgoing. Bar work was the most common form of employment and after meeting all the criteria and requesting his visa it came through in three days.

The family rarely got together. Their mother with her social butterfly attributes was hard to pin down and Tamarind and Georgina were quite often in two different parts of the country. The three siblings managed to meet in Covent Garden to say goodbye. They were by no means close but felt a bond as they met, each hoping to make something of their lives not knowing when they would all be together again.

Bridger achieved more in two years in Australia than his whole life. Bar work led to meeting people from all walks of life and he excelled at getting people to talk about themselves. Australians don't suffer fools gladly and he gravitated to front of house in a hotel. No more hostels, but meeting people with money. His own resources had enabled him to cope pretty well. He hadn't needed to touch the money in his English account and his flair for spotting a business opportunity led him to sales. The chief executive of a relatively new catering company saw his potential as a salesman. Not just any salesman. Promoting a brand as yet unknown in the country was a challenge, and the guy had put great faith in Bridger. He recruited his own group of agents, training them in all aspects of selling. They learned people skills, how to be a team player, learning when to walk away and roll with rejection. Honesty was vital and on closing the deal always seek referrals.

When he got the call informing him that there were no legal grounds to contest his father's will it didn't bother him. He knew how hurt they had all felt, and it was a lot of money, but he was doing very nicely thank you. He was promoted and was charged with opening a new branch in Sydney. With promotion came a house in Manly, a beach side suburb of Sydney. It was where the first surfing contest was held, a submerged reef creating the waves that inspire the world's best surfers. He felt he could relax the pressure a little bit by not working weekends and resurrecting his social life.

Georgina had pinned her hopes on getting the money. Treading the boards wasn't the most lucrative way of earning a living. She learned the meaning of "resting" between roles. Basically being unemployed. She asked her mother for an advance on her allowance but her mother thought she had paid enough. Tamarind offered to help her out but that didn't go far enough. Some of her theatrical friends went on the game. She wouldn't do that.

Instead she researched sugar daddies on line. Her friend Barbara had managed to find a man who "looked after" her. Sex was an option but not everything. She told Georgina to make a connection with a guy. Don't mention money. Tell him of your acting career. Barbara had found her sugar daddy that way. He loved the theatre and wanted to help in any way possible. She met him outside the theatre in London and it was chemistry from the start. Well, good luck with that, thought Georgina. What are the odds of that happening to me? After a week of looking and hoping she thought it was a lost cause.

However, Barbara's sweetie, as she called him, knew several people in the theatre and introduced Georgina to Brandon Foyle. She knew she had to be subtle and told him of her time in the amateur dramatic society, progressing to touring around the UK, acting in regional theatres. She particularly loved the theatre in Frinton and stayed there for six weeks. The play was a sell-out. He was fascinated by her. Her love for all things theatre enthralled him. Right now she was auditioning for a part in *Little Women*. She wanted to play Jo, an outspoken tomboy with a passion for writing. In the book Jo says she would like to try *Macbeth*, she always wanted to do the killing part. She made Brandon roar with laughter as she rolled her eyes saying "is that a dagger I see before me?" Her sister's reply, no it's the toasting fork with mother's slipper on and caused him to smile whenever he remembered it.

Brandon asked where she lived and she told him she had a room in a boarding house in Soho. He was quietly appalled. He suggested he had a spare room in his apartment and it would be so much better for her there. She told him she could just about scrape by paying the rent for her room. He didn't expect any payment, or anything else. He would love to be able to say one day that the great Georgina Harvey Smart stayed in his house. An obvious romantic with wild hopes, thought Georgina, but although he was not a fully blown sugar daddy, she was on the way to making him one.

26

Gregory Argyle was pleased to tell Sally that her inheritance was intact. She was the sole beneficiary of her mother's will. There were no grounds to be contested. It was a *fait accompli*. The total sum of all the assets would be in the region of several million pounds, depending on whether or not she wanted to stay in the house or move. The cottages used by the stable workers could be sold as a package including the stables. He suggested this would be the best option. It would also hopefully allow the current tenants to stay on, working for whoever bought the stables if that was their wish.

Sally had no interest in what would happen to the cottage tenants, it wouldn't affect her in any way. She needed the cash now and the prospect of having to wait for things to be sold was not on the cards. She asked Gregory if she could get a loan, offering the estate as collateral. He said his knowledge of finance was non-existent. He knew everything about the legality of owning the assets but not how they should be handled. He suggested she used an independent financial adviser and recommended a firm known to his.

Sally was surprised at how young Ross Smythe was when he introduced himself to her at his office. He told her Gregory had recommended he get in touch regarding the handling of the financial affairs she had inherited. Sally hadn't been in a relationship since the death of her mother. The holiday fling had been flung and she was more concerned with surviving than finding a man. Now she was confident she could inherit she looked at this young man with different intentions.

When she wanted she could be charm personified. Ross in turn was single, and after a long-term relationship ended he had concentrated on his work to help him forget her.

The file on Sally's assets was considerable. He had already been in touch with a possible buyer for the stables. The Cotswolds are well known for the many livery stables and the one Sally now owned, with its cottages and tenant stable workers, was a very desirable prospect. He had a contact at a bank in the British Virgin Islands who was able to reveal the extent of Oswald's, now Harriet's assets, held by them. He didn't realize just how big the investment was. Sally was going to be a very wealthy young woman.

He asked her if she intended to stay in the house. At the moment she wasn't sure, she felt she needed a base while she decided how she would manage her wealth. Gregory had suggested she could market the stables and cottages as a complete package and she felt this would be a good idea. She was impressed when he said he had made enquiries and there was a potential buyer ready to do business if it was her wish. She concurred and that would be the first piece of asset management he would undertake.

She wondered if there was any way she could get an advance on the inheritance, everything seemed to be taking so long and although she was asset rich, she was cash poor. Ross assured her she was not to worry. It was quite easy to arrange such a transaction and he would put the wheels in motion. How much did she think would be a reasonable amount, she could get up to sixty percent? Her eyes widened. He told her that could be in the region of several million pounds.

She asked Ross if he would like to come and see the house and stables, give him an idea of how it had been maintained. He had to admit he found her quite appealing. He had no romantic thoughts, he had only just met her, but money was a heady aphrodisiac and he had to be professional. He said that was very kind of her and they arranged for him to go in two days. By then he should have feedback from his various enquiries. She suggested he could stay for lunch if he had the time. He said he would check his diary and get back to her. He thought that sounded better than have I died and gone to heaven?

First impressions count and she was very impressed by this smart suited and booted young man. His dark hair was combed straight back accentuating his chiseled features and warm smile. A firm handshake, not a bone crusher was another plus and she wondered if he was gay, married or in a relationship.

Two days later she opened the door to her handsome Ross Smythe. He had a way about him that made you feel as if you have known him forever, she decided. He had accepted the invitation to lunch, after consulting with his associate, and handed her a beautiful bouquet and put a bottle of wine on the hall table. Actually you could hardly call it a hall. It was an enormous rotunda with various passages leading from the centre. She told him that the house had been designed by a sea captain. He had created a ship's wheel with the hall being the pivotal point.

She showed him around. It was all on one floor, the different passages leading to the kitchen (she had organized a caterer — well she couldn't cook) off which was a dining room. The next passage led on to a huge living room, with two open fires surrounded by different sets of sofas and chairs. All together there were six passages. Apparently a ship's wheel can have from six to ten spokes.

Her bedroom with its en-suite bathroom and dressing room was almost as big as the living room. There were two other suites in two of the remaining three passages and the final passage was for the utilities. In the main hub there were two oak panelled doors each housing a toilet and shower. He hoped he didn't look completely awestruck. He was no estate agent but he felt it was a very special property and would need to be marketed to a select group of purchasers. It was unique in its design.

She suggested they had drinks in the living room and he opted for a lager while she poured a strong gin and tonic. She told him on reflection the house was far too big for just her and she would be selling it. With the advance she could find something smaller. She would show him the estate after lunch but felt that maybe she would be better suited to an apartment in Cheltenham. She wasn't a gardener (she wouldn't know what a spade was for goodness sake) and it sounded a good idea.

Melon followed by roast lamb was a far cry from his packed lunch and he allowed himself two glasses of red wine, he was driving after all. She asked him to tell her all about himself. Not much to tell really. He lived in a flat in a block near his office. His parents lived on a farm in the Cotswolds and had been disappointed he hadn't wanted to take it on. He had witnessed it first-hand. It was a roller coaster, hoping for a good harvest, dependent on the weather. He considered it all a bit hit and miss and his heart wasn't in it. He went to university and studied for a Bachelor's degree in economics and accountancy. He was now an independent financial adviser after completing his training with his current firm.

She asked him if there was anyone special in his life and he told her he had recently come out of a long-term relationship. He didn't elaborate and she volunteered that she had had no time for a relationship with all the stress of contesting the will. She was so glad there had been a successful outcome and that it was all behind her now. He told her he was hoping to have a portfolio prepared for her within the next week and would contact her when it was complete. She really didn't think she could go a whole week without seeing him again.

He was bowled over seeing the estate and cottages. The stables were beautifully kept with some horses in their stalls and others exercising in the yard. Solomon had retired as stable manager. She told him he was a lovely man and had taught her to ride and now Jensen was the manager she introduced Ross to.

He thanked her profusely for lunch and the tour and she thanked him for the flowers and wine. All quite ordinary really except he was now in the presence of a multi- millionairess and that in itself was extraordinary in many ways.

Finishing school had been the icing on the cake for Sally. She had been taught social graces and upper-class cultural rites as a preparation into society. The primary goal was to teach students how to acquire husbands. She didn't want a husband. She enjoyed all the trappings of wealth and concentrated on improving her sexual prowess. Sadly this had been enjoyed by young men of a completely different cultural background, but maybe that suited her. She was not looking for a husband. The thought that she would see Ross again soon cheered her.

Husband material he was not, but who really knows what that material is?

An appointment was arranged for the following Wednesday to carry out the necessary formalities of Ross acting as her financial adviser on behalf of his firm. A basic written contract had been drawn up between the two parties. The client agreement would continue to govern the relationship between the IFA and the client until ended by notice. There was no charge for the initial meeting. It was regarded as a chance for the client to see how the IFA worked, how much they charged and a sense of whether or not the client felt comfortable with the situation. Ross suggested they negotiate a set fee for a piece of work, the creation of the investment portfolio. He would need to have a complete picture of what was involved and the amount of work that would be required. He thought it was a fairer way than charging an hourly rate. A fee of 0.75% was written into the contract that Sally found to be acceptable. After all, the full extent of her inheritance had not yet been established and she felt that Ross had acted with integrity with her best interests at heart.

27

She had wasted no time in getting in touch with Gregory Argyle asking him to suggest an estate agent who would be in the best position to value and sell her house. He gave her the names of two agencies. One valued it at a conservative two point five million pounds and the second thought it would fetch three million. She went with the cheaper valuation, mainly because the agent himself was extremely handsome. She thought he was around forty-five but grooming counted for a lot with Sally and she didn't notice him wearing a ring. She didn't know it was in the glove compartment of his Range Rover. He would get the brochure prepared as soon as possible. The photographer was available the next day, if that was convenient. Had she any thoughts as to where she would like to live?

She didn't want to move away from what she knew and had discovered Charlton Kings, a beautiful village adjoining Cheltenham. There was a large building that had once been a private residence and now offered some very desirable serviced apartments one of which was available to view. Desmond Johnson knew the property. It was with another agent. He wished her good luck with the viewing and said he would be in touch in a day or so.

She met the agent, a charming middle-aged woman, who showed her a raised ground floor apartment with floor to ceiling windows. It was beautifully furnished, both bedrooms had large en-suites and walk-in wardrobes. The kitchen had all the latest "must haves" and the lounge had a double aspect offered by sash windows. She was impressed but had not really given much thought to the fact that it was a village and although bordering Cheltenham, it was rather out on a limb.

Desmond accompanied the photographer to show him the various places he wanted to take precedence in the brochure and asked her what she thought of the apartment. She told him she had decided she would prefer to be in Cheltenham itself. Perfect. A new listing had come in last week and he would be able to arrange a viewing, if it suited her plans.

As soon as she walked through the porticoed entrance into a grand hallway she felt at home. The ground floor apartment sold itself. It was one of twelve empathetically constructed living areas in what was previously a hotel. The Grade Two listed building had retained the tall sash windows from the Regency period and the lounge had the double aspect with generous drapes held back with double tassel tiebacks. It was similar in design to the one in Charlton Kings, serviced and tastefully furnished, but being in the centre of the town tipped the balance. She was sold. Desmond was delighted. It was an impressive apartment and she was more than impressive.

He suggested they go back to the office to sort the paperwork. She told him she was a cash buyer and subject to the relevant searches she would be ready to move in straight away. He was good at what he did. It wasn't very often that sales just fell into place, no chain involved and cash to boot. He said he would instigate proceedings and would keep her in the loop. He knew he had the confidence and experience to take this situation to another level. He also felt she was open to the same idea. Wouldn't rush, they would be in touch throughout the sale anyway. Half the fun was the thrill of the chase.

Things had certainly moved on a pace. She was so pleased she had settled on being in the centre of town. She had grown up in Cheltenham. She took a trip down memory lane and went to see Kit Williams's iconic wishing Fish Clock at the Regency Arcade. As a little girl she had been enchanted by the fish blowing bubbles out of its mouth as it played its signature tune at the turning of the hour and the half hour. Now of course it was the draw of the shops in the arcade: High-end retailers interspersed with delightfully unique boutiques. She had to be in the mood to shop and today wasn't one of those days. She found a table outside in the sunshine at a bistro in Montpellier Terrace. She ordered a white wine and some bread and olives. "Well, hello Sally," a familiar voice sounded in her ear. "Ross, how lovely to see you. Please join me, are you on your lunch break?" He pulled out a chair. "I can be," he replied and they laughed. He did wonder if she could ever be anything but beautifully dressed with her warm smile and upswept hair. He ordered a coffee and croissant. He was on his way to meet a new client, but rest assured he had almost completed the work on her investments. He had no idea if she knew of the investment in the Virgin Islands or not. Her solicitor would have had that information. However, he would be in a position to disclose all in a day or two. She told him about buying the apartment and he was happy for her, telling her they didn't come on the market very often so she had been in the right place at the right time.

He looked at his watch. "Well, it's been lovely to see you but I have to dash." He stood up and pushed the chair back under the table. "You too, Ross, look forward to hearing all about my wealth!" He smiled. You don't know the half of it, he thought, as he walked away, turning to wave as he disappeared around the corner.

28

Sally had not expected to hear just how much she was currently worth. It was all from "old money", inherited wealth from her father who had inherited himself. Landed gentry, or the gentry were a largely historical British social class of landowners who could live off a country estate. At least this is what Ross perceived when he had researched the Harvey Smart family.

He presented the portfolio. He had been helped by the senior partner in the firm and was grateful for the input. It was a life-changing amount of money and every effort had been made to ensure good practice. It had proven its strategic relevance as the most effective way of achieving the specific objective, a positive impact on Sally's inheritance.

Sally was quietly amazed at the way Ross had constructed such a succinct and thorough presentation. He was judged to be able to handle the portfolio, an accolade in itself. He in turn felt privileged to be given the opportunity. The senior partner congratulated him and said he spoke for the whole firm, including the branches throughout the country. He thanked him for introducing such a prestigious account. Ross in turn contacted Gregory Argyle and thanked him for his recommendation.

It didn't occur to Sally that she had never done a day's work in her life. She had not needed to. Not sure if that is always a good thing, her father had thought. He didn't work nine to five. His love for horses and presenting them at races had been the nature of his work, and he knew he was lucky to have such a lifestyle. Unlike Solomon, his wonderfully wise old trainer, who had once said to him the biggest thing you should wish on your children is difficulty. That way they will learn how to handle adversity, preparing them for the future.

In that way Sally was totally unprepared. Having money meant you never needed to need. You didn't have to learn the difference between a want and a need. You had a protective shell that would repel all boarders. Security is a luxury that very few are given. It has to be earned. It comes through endeavour, not complacency. It was hard to ascertain if she actually felt lucky. She didn't expect because she was always given, so she wasn't at fault, possibly just unaware.

Desmond arrived with the brochure that really showed just how unique the property was. Offers in excess of two point five million pounds had already attracted viewings. There were clients on the books who were on the lookout for such a property and Desmond said he would be pleased to show the prospective buyers around, if that was all right with Sally. She didn't want to be there anyway, seeing strangers peer into rooms that had once been her home.

The contracts on the apartment had been exchanged and it was two weeks to completion. She had already been sorting through her wardrobes. Whoever bought the house could make an offer for the furniture. Some of it was worth quite a bit. The marble fireplaces were fixtures, but the exquisite dresser with dovetailing indicating quality craftsmanship was antique. Desmond told her there was no market in second hand furniture but he would call in an expert to value items like the dresser and glass cabinets. He would sort the wheat from the chaff.

It hardly seemed worth the cost of producing the brochure when three days after it went on the market an offer of two point eight million was made. They wanted to exchange and complete as quickly as possible. The buyer had already sold and was in rented accommodation that was proving a nightmare, being far too small. Coupled with this all their furniture was in store. They would consider keeping some items and their bids were successful for the antiques. Desmond would organize the house to be cleared and contracts were exchanged. A very happy family, complete with two dogs, moved in just two weeks after Sally had taken over her apartment. All in all a good day at the office, thought Desmond.

29

Sally was extremely pleased and happy to be living bang in the centre of town. She could walk to the shops and restaurants and the theatre was close by although nothing being performed appealed to her. She could garage her car in the underground car park provided for the apartments but she had no need to drive anywhere.

She began to relax, it had been such a busy time and she had time to think. She wasn't lonely exactly, but she didn't have any real friends. Never having worked she had no colleagues to chat with and now Harriet wasn't around, no one to shop with. Apart from Ross managing her portfolio, no other person was aware of how wealthy she was. Obviously Desmond would be aware of the money she made on the sale of the house but that was personal and confidential.

She realized she was getting bored. She had no qualifications per se. A diploma from finishing school didn't equip you for a commercial career, or any form of employment. She did have a flair for design. Desmond had called her because the company who serviced the apartments was moving and a new contract had to be drawn up with the people taking over. She really didn't want to go back into town again and suggested he bring the contract to her at the apartment, if it wouldn't be too much trouble. Excellent, thought Desmond, any opportunity to impress her, just being in her company was more than pleasant.

He arrived at six prompt. "I hope you don't mind but I have taken the liberty of bringing champagne. The sun is over the yard arm and I think you have much to celebrate." She had not parted with her mother's collection of Jamesse Prestige Grand Champagne crystal flutes. It would be criminal to drink Moet from anything else. Naturally Desmond had ensured it was chilled and he expertly popped the cork and poured.

They sat on the Italian leather sofa with its u-shaped corner she had bought from a furniture shop in Chelsea. It enabled them to be opposite each other and she put a table for his glass and one for her. "Can I offer you any nibbles? I have some blinis and could easily serve them with smoked salmon." He thanked her but he was fine, this is perfect on its own. He looked around the apartment and asked her who had designed the layout. The furniture was exquisite. She told him it was all her own work and he was suitably impressed. "You could make a living doing this — not that you need to work of course, but you have a gift. I know some interior designers and you put them to shame." Mind you, having bottomless pockets ensured the very top end of the market.

She thanked him. She really had enjoyed doing it and was delighted he was impressed. He refreshed the flutes and settled back, sank back really into sheer comfort. Right out of the blue she asked him if he was married, shouldn't he be getting back to his wife? He told her it was a marriage in name only. They led separate lives. He told her he had a boy and a girl at boarding schools in Bath. Not a son and a daughter, she thought that sounded quite odd. "May I ask if you are single, Sally? I would find it very difficult to believe, you are very beautiful." He was staring at her so intently she had to avert her gaze. "I am single, I haven't really had much spare time, why, are you open to offers?" He hadn't quite expected that. Was it the champagne talking? He sipped his drink and smiled. "That would not be at all professional now would it Sally?" She held out her glass and he topped it up. "I am sorry, I didn't mean to offend you. Of course this is a purely business situation." She crossed her legs showing them at their best and tilted her chin, a mischievous grin displaying her perfect teeth.

He opened his briefcase and showed her the contract. It wasn't very different from the other company. They would use the same laundry and would do the linen change on the same day. There would be two employees for each clean and he knew they came highly recommended. She said anything he felt was good enough was fine by her and signed it witnessed by him.

"Desmond, did you mean what you said about interior design? I am finding the days stretching ahead and I need to be busy. Can you help in any way, introducing me to the people you know?" He felt she was sincere. "I can for sure, you could get an insight as to how they work but I honestly think you will have more to offer them than they can offer you."

She stood up. He kind of uncurled from where he was sitting. He was quite tall and quite beautifully dressed. She liked that in a man. She was disappointed that he felt it would be unprofessional to be anything but business-like. Still, he would need to be in touch once he had made contact with the designers. "Leave it with me Sally, I will put feelers out and source the best two companies to introduce you to. You will be in at the grass roots, a good place to start." She thanked him. He put his glass down and put his hands on her shoulders. "Give me a couple of days, I will call you." With that his lips brushed her cheek and she had to steady herself. Why on earth did he do that? "Thank you so much, I look forward to hearing from you soon."

Desmond was pleased with the way things had turned out. The kiss on the cheek was a taster of what he felt sure was going to come. Of course he bloody well wanted her, and if it came from her so much the better.

She took the glasses to the kitchen. Totally unaware of what they actually cost, she put them in the dishwasher. Harriet would turn in her grave. Now she had a purpose. She felt she could really achieve, find her niche, and all of a sudden having to wait two days was almost unbearable.

Rosemary Macmillan of Macmillan Interiors was charm personified. She said how Desmond had sung her praises as she ushered Sally into an enormous office with sofas and a huge dark wooden desk. "Please sit down Sally, can I offer you any tea?" Sally said no thank you. "Desmond said you designed the interior of your apartment without having done anything like it before. He said you have a flair for it and I would love to show you how we work here." Sally turned to face her. "Rosemary, I enjoyed doing it. Things just seemed to fall into place. Now it is finished I would love to get involved in another project." Rosemary stood up. "There are basically seven interior design elements. I can outline them briefly and cover them more fully later. They include space, line, forms, light, colour, texture and pattern. Keeping them balanced is the key to creating an aesthetically pleasing interior." Sally was thinking that pulling all those design elements together really seemed basic common sense. "I have an idea. We have a new client on the books. Beth, one of our top designers, is meeting them for the first time tomorrow. Would you like to go with her, see how she works? Normally the designer is the contact from inception to completion. It is their personal work, showcasing their ideas, that will gain the confidence of the client."

Beth was excited to be in the running to get the new client on the books. She explained to Sally as they drove to the venue that there were approximately twelve similar apartments owned by the client. Impress with this one and the rest should fall into place. Sally had chosen a pin striped trouser suit with a white blouse and heeled boots. The black Saint Lauren envelope medium bag in embossed leather was the perfect accessory. She looked professional and when you power dress it shows.

Some men are beautiful. Exquisite features, incredible dress sense with effortless confidence and an air of perfection enhanced by very expensive aftershave. Craig Lawrence always made such an impression. His almost casual manner disarmed many admirers and Sally liked what she saw as Beth introduced her. He had earned his money by investing in property. In 1996 he bought a large apartment near Old Street in Central London for £218,000. He had earned the £25,000 deposit working as a lawyer in Iran. He was thirty and it was a huge gamble after the recession a few years earlier. Three years later he was able to release £100,000 equity to invest in his property business. He was now a very successful property developer and was keen to present his latest investment in the very best light.

He had acquired Prentice House on the outskirts of Cheltenham. It was a rundown Regency house with three floors, three sets of stairs and it was ripe for renovation. It had pillars in front of the house with a fan light window above the panelled front door. It was symmetrical in design with classic proportions, huge sash windows although they were smaller at the top of the house. He had converted it into twelve apartments. They went up the steps through the entrance into a large vestibule. The ground floor apartment he showed them was spacious and he had retained the huge sash windows as a feature. Beth immediately began taking measurements with Sally taking notes, recording the vision Beth dictated: Light is important, lines, the trajectory of the rooms leading one to another.

Sally was aware that Beth was using the design elements Rosemary had told her about: Forms, colour, pattern and more importantly how they could come together. She was caught up in her enthusiasm, examining the different angles and how this would reflect on that.

Craig was impressed at how thorough Beth was and how eager her assistant was to please. He hadn't expected it to take so long and asked if they would need to come back another time, as he had an appointment he had to keep. Beth said could they take just thirty more minutes and that was fine. They shook hands and Beth said she would have the basic plan ready in three days and that suited him.

Sally was impressed. Beth was certainly good at what she did and she really hoped she would be able to include any input or ideas of her own. Rosemary was delighted they gave such positive feedback and Beth said she would get the draft plans on paper that night.

There was a message on Sally's answerphone. She thought it prudent to turn off her mobile while working. Desmond was asking how she got on. She called him straight back and couldn't stop talking. He said, "Hey, wait up, why don't I take you to dinner and you can tell me all about it?" He collected her an hour later. She had showered and changed from her business clothes to a soft woollen dress that clung to all the right places. He gave her coat to the waiter who was discretion itself as he did a double take while the restaurant captain showed them to their table.

The table was in an alcove and the attention to detail from the drinks menu, to the selection of food placed on the crisp white tablecloth was not lost on Sally. This is fine dining, she thought. Desmond was a very good listener, managing to keep his eyes focused on her face while making a mental note of her curves. He was pleased she seemed so genuinely interested and told her again he thought she would be a natural. Rosemary had already phoned him saying she had great hopes for her.

Coffee was served in the lounge accompanied by a very fine brandy. She was still talking about light, colours and material texture when he pulled up outside the apartment. She thanked him so much, would he like to come in? She had some brandy if he would like to drink some. It took all his will power to decline. Perhaps another time, at the weekend, they both had work in the morning. She hadn't realized that she was quite tired. Her first-ever day of doing anything resembling work

197

had exhausted her but it was a good feeling. She was finally making a difference, contributing rather than taking. That was a first.

30

Sally was in the office before Beth and was eager to learn from the master. Beth had begun the design process by creating mood boards. They enable you to swiftly pump out concepts without worrying about the execution. She had collected photos that best described her idea and had arranged them in an aesthetically pleasing way. Design taste is a matter of personal preferences, she told Sally. You need to be sure your vision matches the clients.

Sally grasped the creation of mood boards and set about creating her own from the Sample Board library on Beth's computer. Although similar to Beth's ideas, Sally saw a different angle, creating colours and materials based on a huge water colour painting on the main wall of the lounge. It was not a busy painting, more a mutation of different colours, Wedgewood blue standing out as the colour to go with. She reflected this in the sofas, the texture of plaid contrasting with the large cream Italian leather sofa. She brought it all together with the pale cream drapes hanging beneath a dark blue leather pelmet. She chose a soft grey wooden floor and the navy rug spread in front of the mantelpiece complemented the pelmet.

Beth was impressed, she really had a flair for this kind of work and she certainly hadn't played safe, her design was edgy yet casual. Between them they created four different mood boards. These would empower the client to get involved in all stages of the process ending up being more satisfied with the results if they felt their contribution was invaluable.

Craig Lawrence studied the mood boards. They were laid out across his desk and he picked one up, then the other, taking them to the window then placing one on the sofa to see it from a distance. Beth and Sally could not read his face at all. He studied the boards for a good hour. Finally he sat behind the desk. "I am impressed. I would like to go mainly with the Wedgewood interpretation and I like the idea of fabric and leather in the sofas. What did you come up with for the bedrooms?" They cleared the desk and showed the two boards. One had bold colours, almost stark in contrast to the muted beige and barely peach of the other. "Is it possible to take something from each board to come up with a statement?" They tweaked a bit here and took something from there and roughly created an interesting concept. He was delighted. Not in an 'Oh my God' kind of way, but they felt they had struck the right balance. He said he would be in touch and thanked them for their work on his behalf.

Rosemary was also very happy as the girls reported back. They felt it had gone well and with the few suggested tweaks it would not be long before a final presentation could be made. Craig telephoned the next day giving the green light to what turned out to be mainly Sally's creation. They were buzzing. The final presentation was really a formality but it cemented the deal. This would mean so much for the business. All twelve apartments would have the same makeover and this was a huge feather in their cap.

The next step was to get the concept to the drawing board. The company had a complete set of tradesmen on their books. The flooring was left till last after the painting of ceilings and walls. The furniture would be a sizeable contract and Sally suggested the company she had used for her own apartment, based in Chelsea. Beth sourced the material for the drapes and the print over the fireplace was ordered together with the various photographs and occasional tables. The dining room furniture would also come from Chelsea.

Sally knew from what Beth had told her that they would be in at the beginning to see the whole design process through to conclusion. She was secretly pleased that it was mostly her design work that Craig had selected and she called Desmond to thank him again for the introduction to the world of interior design. He asked her if she would join him for dinner but she explained this was now all systems go and she would be working all the hours she could to complete the contract.

Her mobile rang as she was putting her key in the door. "Sally, it's Ross, how are you getting on? I have tried your landline but you are never at home!" She laughed. It was good to hear his voice. "Hey Ross, great to hear from you. I am now a working girl would you believe?" She told him all her news and he was glad she sounded so excited about actually working. "Really happy for you. I wanted to talk to you about a possible investment opportunity. There is some land about to come on the market and it has planning for fifty houses. You could easily afford to buy the land and build on it. It would give a very good return on your money. I just wondered what you thought about it." Sally walked into the lounge and sat on the sofa. "Ross I know nothing about investing anything. That's why I rely on you. Where is the land?"

"It's on the outskirts of Bath. It is a golden opportunity Sally and I am so lucky to have the heads up on this one. A friend of mine owed me a favour. He knows I have clients in a similar position to you but I wanted you to have first refusal." Sally thought that was very kind and generous of him. "Do you know what Ross? I could really do with a break this weekend. Are you free? Could we go together to see the land? Don't know why because it's probably just fields but I do love Bath and it would be so good to see you again." Ross wasn't quite prepared for that. He had always enjoyed being in her company but thought she was so far out of his league. "I would love to see you Sally. Yes, it sounds a great idea. I would like you to see exactly where it is. Saturday or Sunday, whichever day is best for you."

"If we can go into Bath itself I would prefer Saturday. I won't presume to drag you around the shops of course, but I know some good restaurants there. It will be my treat. You are giving up your weekend on my behalf and it will be my pleasure. Is ten too early?"

She ran a bath and had a lovely soak, almost falling asleep, when the telephone shrilled into her hazy state. She grabbed a towel. "Finally I get to speak to the interior designer pluperfect." Desmond's voice was warm, inviting even. "Well right now, Miss Pluperfect is dripping soapy bubbles on to her luxurious rug." His imagination ran wild. "Shall I dry your back?" She roared with laughter. "And how would you manage that?" He laughed back. "Open the door and find out."

She grabbed her robe and tied it loosely around her waist. She opened the door and there he was, champagne in one hand and what looked like a takeaway meal in the other. "I know you wouldn't have time to come to dinner so dinner has come to you." He kissed her cheek and went through to the kitchen, turning on the oven and unloading various dishes. She got the champagne flutes, which miraculously hadn't shattered in the violent whirlpool of the dishwasher, and he popped the cork.

He looked so smart in his chinos, open necked shirt, sleeves rolled up to the elbows. "Well, Mr Johnson, your timing is immaculate. The food smells gorgeous and so do you." He laughed again. God she was something else. They raised their glasses and she told him how everything was progressing. She was so animated, pausing now and then for a sip and as she reached to put the glass on the table her gown fell open to reveal one beautiful breast. Either she hadn't noticed or she just didn't care as she settled back. No, make that of course she was aware and of course she cared. They finished the bottle and he pulled her from the sofa. "Are you hungry?" he asked. "I am starving" and with that she undid the robe and stepped out naked as the day she was born. She took his breath away. He had no idea of just how lovely she was. To see her naked aroused him in a way he had experienced before, but not like this. Not this bold young woman, undoing his shirt, reaching for his belt. He picked her up and carried her to the bedroom.

Gently he laid her on the bed. He sat on the edge and took off his shoes and trousers, while she tugged at his shirt. She sat up and moved to the end of the bed, pushing him back so that she could get astride. No kissing, just straight to it. She was good and he held back so that she could reach her fulfilment and then he let go. She rolled off on to her back. Then he kissed her. It was a long lingering searching kiss. She responded and they lay back.

She went into the lounge and came back with the glasses and got some wine from the fridge. He corked it and they sat up. "What kind of unprofessional was that?"

she asked. "The most professional unprofessional I have ever encountered."

"I am actually quite hungry now," she said and they went to the kitchen. She put on his shirt and he grabbed his shorts. The Chinese meal was just what was needed. They ate, talked, drank more wine, both aware that they had both enjoyed a special moment. "Can I see you again, Miss Pluperfect?" More laughter. "Well I should jolly well hope so. I have never been a one night stand kind of girl."

"I ought to go." Sally looked at him. "Can't you stay?" Her eyes were searching his. "I have an important meeting in the morning, a new developer is interested in some land we are selling. Are you free on Saturday?" She realized she was meeting Ross. Strange that all this had happened when she had been looking forward to seeing him after quite a long time. "I am sorry, Desmond. I have arranged to go with Ross to Bath. He told me about an investment and I asked him if he could take me to see it, I just love Bath." Desmond's disappointment didn't show. "That's okay, Sally. We can do it another time." Something stopped her asking what about Sunday. He dressed and took her face in his hands. He kissed her head, her eyes, her nose and then her lips. Her luscious inviting lips. She held on to him, she really didn't want him to go. "Thank you for a wonderful evening, champagne, wine, Chinese and bed." She smiled as she said it. It had been amazing actually.

She closed the door. It had been a while, she thought to herself. Desmond was an attentive lover and she couldn't wait to do it all again. It was funny how she hadn't said about Sunday. She cleared the containers into the swing bin and got into bed. She could smell him and she fell asleep with her head resting where he had laid his.

31

"You are an early bird," Beth said to Sally as she put her jacket on a hanger. Sally had been there since seven. She had had an idea about one of the bedrooms and wanted to create a new mood board. "I know we can't really change the concept Craig decided on but I thought if we introduced a scarlet edging to the drapes it would complement the soft peach." Beth looked at her idea. It certainly introduced a different angle, making the room appear wider. "That's great, Sally. I will call Craig and ask his opinion, he may want to see it first." Craig had no problem with it, if they thought it would suit then that was fine with him.

They got sandwiches from a nearby deli and worked through. Not too many hiccups so far. They needed to complete just one apartment as the prototype for prospective tenants to view. The furniture could be delivered in ten days and the material for the drapes was already with the machinists. A team of workers had pulled out all the stops and the floors were being laid that evening. It was exciting to see it all coming together and so far there were no hold ups on the future furniture orders. Sally was enjoying being in at the deep end, gradually seeing mood boards become more than just a concept. She finally felt she was doing something creative and useful. Desmond called to thank her for a great time last night and to say he hoped her visit to Bath would go well.

Ross rang the bell at ten on the dot. She was ready, dressed in a silver satin shirt with belted tight- legged denim jeans tucked into Jimmy Choo Bryelle ankle boots. Her Ted Baker soft leather Hobo bag was slung over her shoulder and she carried a cashmere wrap. He smiled hello and said she looked lovely. He didn't look so bad himself, she thought, looking approvingly at his checked shirt and black chinos. Not a hair out of place and she hadn't realized what a deep brown his eyes were as he held the car door open. It was an Audi Sports with comfortable leather seats.

The journey was just over an hour and they spent the time catching up. He was excited to have been offered the opportunity to broker what he hoped would be a very profitable investment. She said should it all go ahead and the houses were built, she knew a very good interior design company and they both laughed.

The agent was at the farmhouse and they had arrived in good time. Ross introduced Sally to Arnold Maynard, a fairly senior gentleman in a Harris Tweed suit, the trousers of which were snug in a pair of Hunter wellingtons. He explained that the farmer had died and the farmhouse and two hundred and forty acres were on the market. There was outline planning permission for the construction of approximately fifty dwellings. It was designated as brownfield land and the vacant farmhouse and outbuildings could be knocked down to accommodate the new build. Sally thanked him for allowing her first refusal. As the agent he could have gone to anyone but Ross had told him she had the money and was in a mortgage-free situation.

The farmhouse was a bit rundown and the barns were really beyond repair but this had once been a vibrant working farm. None of the family wanted to try and revamp and run the farm. They would appreciate a quick sale. Ross assured her he had contacts in the building industry, but that was a bit further down the line. Did she think it was a viable proposition? There didn't seem to be any glaring obstacles in the way, nothing to stop the sale. Arnold said obviously she would need to appoint her own solicitor to do the relevant searches and Ross said he would be able to arrange all of that himself. He would act as her agent in that regard.

She didn't relish the tour of the land in her Jimmy Choos but Arnold had his Range Rover and they clambered in. It seemed a vast area and was surprisingly flat but it wasn't like buying a house where you could ooh and ahh. They got back to the farmyard and shook hands with Arnold. Ross said he would be in touch once Sally had expressed her views on the project, for that is what it would be. He would let him know on Monday.

It took fifteen minutes to get to Bath and park near the canal. She knew an inn situated next to it and hoped they would be able to find a table as they hadn't booked. They were shown to an alcove by a roaring fire, the canal side was a little cool at this time of the year. He ordered a cask ale and she opted for a bottle of Sauvignon Blanc. They really needed to pause for breath. It had been a busy and interesting morning. "Well, cheers Ross, thank you so much for this. I know nothing of what's involved in buying land, let alone building houses. I need your guidance one hundred percent." He couldn't really tell if she was keen on the idea or not. Looking at acres of fields and antiquated farm buildings was not top of her bucket list, and he couldn't expect her to see the potential. "Cheers! I can see that this is viable and could be hugely profitable. The number of houses obviously would be down to the architect, however it is entirely your decision. If you have any doubts, then say no."

The waiter asked if they were ready to order and they asked for five minutes. They chose from the a la carte because they felt they could eat three courses. The fresh air had given them an appetite. The waiter took the order and Ross asked for a red wine although apparently you had white with fish. He refreshed her glass.

"I have every faith in you, Ross. I am ignorant about most things, property developing included. If you consider this is a good investment and you will oversee all the angles, then I would like to go ahead. Obviously we will negotiate your fee but also, have you the time with your commitments at the office?" The waiter brought the olives with balsamic vinegar and oil and large chunks of crusty bread. "I would love to do it. My office commitments are manageable and this is a totally new project for me to get involved in. Obviously I will call on others to sort the basics as I will need to be guided by the experts. We will need to appoint a project manager to oversee the construction but a reputable builder will have such a person on their books." Sally smiled at his enthusiasm. He seemed to be relishing the whole prospect, and it was a huge undertaking.

The sea bass with capers and parsley served with rosemary new potatoes was perfectly cooked and not too heavy. They did wonder if they could manage dessert but taking the time to enjoy another glass of red and white wine made way for fresh strawberries with vanilla panna cotta. He poured the last drop of wine and she said have another red. "I think I am already over the limit. Would you like more wine?"

"No, thank you, but I would love a coffee." They lingered over the coffee and the waiter topped up the cups. "Have we time to just go to Milsom Street? It is my favourite place in Bath." Ross paid the bill. "We can get a taxi and leave the car here."

Milsom Street was a real fashion runway, home to Jolly's the UK's oldest department store, although now it's another equally famously named store. So many Georgian archways through which they glimpsed Bath

Abbey. They walked past the Roman Baths across Abbey Churchyard to Abbey Green to see the old plane tree. Ross was no shopper but he did appreciate the architectural splendour of the city. They realized they were not that far from the car park and were relieved to sit down and relax. "Would you like to go for tea somewhere?" Ross asked. "Right now I am as full as an egg, but thank you anyway."

They decided to set off for home, at a leisurely pace and arrived at six. She turned to him and thanked him for an amazing day. She said she felt confident putting her trust in him to begin the process of purchasing the land. "No, thank you Sally. I am very pleased and honoured that you will let me represent you in the deal. I don't know if it's ethical to ask, but would I be able to see you again, but not in a business capacity, as a friend?" Finally! "I would really like that Ross. I know we are both going to be very busy but I am not working tomorrow. Could we maybe do something then?" Ross got out and opened her car door. "Free as a bird, that would be lovely. You say what you would like to do because I have completely taken over Saturday." She stepped up to the front door. "I will think about where to go and what to do. Shall I pick you up?" He held her wrap while she got out her key. "I will be here at ten. Thank you, looking forward to it already." She watched him drive away as she turned the key. I think I know why I didn't suggest Sunday to Desmond, she thought to herself.

There was a message on the answerphone. Desmond hoped she had enjoyed her day and wondered what her decision would be on buying the land. She really wasn't in the mood to go over it all right now. She sank into the sofa, undid her boots and wriggled her toes into the deep pile rug. Ross was a real gentleman, she thought. He was open and honest. Is it ethical, she mused? I really don't care if it's ethical or not. I would love to get to know you Ross Smythe. You are not like anyone I have met before. Harriet had always said manners maketh man. Ross was the man. He was also very attractive in an unassuming way. She liked the way he dressed, the way he talked. She wondered what he would be like in bed. She hoped she would find out but she didn't want to rush things. Desmond was a different kettle of fish entirely. He must be almost twenty years older and with that comes a confidence you cannot always have when you are young. Plus he has a lot more experience in all things.

She still had a lot to learn about an awful lot of things. She enjoyed sex enormously but now there was the work ethic in the equation. She wondered what Harriet would think of her now. She would obviously be pleased that she had inherited what was rightfully hers. She did wonder if Harriet had ever loved her father. She hoped so but felt that it might have been the love of money before true love. Obviously she had no idea of Harriet's sexual encounters. She had been away at boarding school, then finishing school. The last year of

Harriet's life had been special because they had been there for each other. She was grateful for that.

She went to the fridge and took out a bottle of wine. She wasn't hungry but there was an open packet of smoked salmon and the blinis were still in date. She spread some cream cheese and topped them with the salmon. She poured a glass of ice-cold wine and took it to the lounge. The phone rang. "I just wanted to thank you so much for today. Are you absolutely sure you want to go ahead Sally?" She was pleased to hear from him. "Absolutely I am and thank you too. See you at ten."

She snuggled into the sofa with her wine and nibbles and happy thoughts.

32

She woke early and called Ross about nine to say to forget the car today. They could explore on foot and she would be outside at ten. Her Jimmy Choo ankle boots came into play, comfortable for walking and as the weather could be chilly she had chosen Ted Baker skinny ankle grazers in black, a duck egg blue cashmere sweater topped off with a black boucle jacket by the same label. Ross was right on the button and they had dressed in a similar fashion, although his Burberry diamond quilted jacket offered a bit more protection.

She took his hand that seemed perfectly natural to her. He knew Cheltenham and she suggested they go to the Brewery Quarter that was about fifteen minutes' walk. It was a crisp bright day and they looked what you could call a "golden couple", good looking, young and happy. They had a game of indoor adventure golf that lasted far longer than it should because she took about nine shots to get in the hole compared to his normal three. "You've done this before, Ross" she laughed. It was good fun and they had a coffee at the bistro in the square. "What about bowling, are you better at that than golf?" he asked. "I would love to say yes but I can't remember when I last had a go." She was slightly better and when she threw it down the alley and got a strike she jumped up and hugged him. "Beginner's luck," she said ruefully, then proceeded to get a spare and her score was gradually coming up to his. Too late, the game was over and he scored one hundred to her ninety. "We will not keep score will we?" She looked at him as if to say, don't you dare. "Well, for a small fee" and they laughed as they walked towards the square with restaurants and bars.

She told him she had hoped to make a day of it so perhaps a light lunch and dinner later? They sat outside at The Soup Kitchen, ordered a glass of wine and were spoilt for choice with so many different soups on offer. Sally chose pea and ham with mustard croutes and Mark opted for Dolcelatte and leek with Parmesan crisps. A huge chunk of crusty bread accompanied two delicious choices. They enjoyed another glass of wine. "Can we walk to Pittville Park from here?" she asked Ross. "It's about fifteen minutes. I think after that hearty soup we should manage it, don't you?"

She last visited Pittville Pump Room when she was a schoolgirl and even then she thought it was amazing. It is the grandest survival of the town's spa buildings. She did remember "tasting the waters" and spitting it out. A very unpleasant tasting liquid that supposedly had the power to cure all ills. She thought if you weren't ill before, after tasting you would probably die. The Regency architecture was breathtaking to look at and you could imagine the swirling dancers in the ballroom and hear the music playing in the bandstand. It was a wonderfully nostalgic step back in time.

The lawns swept down to the boating lake and the Boathouse was busy, bursting with a charm all of its own. Ross suggested they take a rowing boat for half an hour. He was adept at handling the oars and she sat back trailing her hand in the water. They lost track of time, discovering an island almost hidden by a weeping willow. Ross scrambled onto the grass and tied the boat to a piece of wood sticking out of the water. He held out his hand and as she stood to take it the boat moved and he held on for dear life to pull her up on to the grass. She was a bit wobbly and clung on to him. He was worried she was really scared but she laughed, only a little shaken. He kept hold of her and she relaxed into him. He led her on to a firmer path. He held her face in his hands and very gently kissed her lips. It was the sweetest kiss she had ever had, she thought. Nothing urgent, nothing demanding, and she kissed him back. She nestled into his shoulder and they stood together for what seemed an age. "Oh, I think our time is up," Ross said as he looked at his watch. "They will think we have absconded with the boat. Now I will go first and help you down into the boat. I will pull it further onto the grass so it won't move." She managed to get in and move to the seat at the back while he undid the rope and pushed off with the oars. "That was one of the best boat rides I have ever had, thank you Mr Oarsman." He grinned from ear to ear. "Do you know what? I agree entirely."

He apologized to the boatman and paid the full amount for an hour with a good tip. The boatman knew they had nowhere to go but all the same he was pleased to see the boat come in. They wandered hand in hand past the aviary with chattering birds of all colours. "Where shall we go for dinner, it's nearly six already?" Ross knew a restaurant in Rotunda Terrace and suggested they get a taxi at the park gate. They had certainly had their exercise for the day.

It was a delightfully modern restaurant, spacious with wooden floors and although it was comparatively early for evening dinner, it was busy. The maître d suggested they wait in the lounge area and a table would be free in about twenty minutes. Ross asked the waiter for a bottle of champagne. He raised his glass and clinked hers. "Just a perfect day, thank you Sally." She smiled. "That's a song you know. I think we have done most of the things, except the zoo, but we had a rowing boat on the lake and saw the aviary." They laughed. "Oh and don't forget bowling and golf." Their table was ready and the waiter carried the champagne. Ross said he would go on to red wine and ordered a Merlot while the waiter took his glass and topped up Sally.

The waiter recommended the crab platter and a matured Ribeye steak. They decided they wouldn't have a starter and Ross ordered the platter and Sally chose Cedar Pink Salmon with blistered tomatoes. "That man cannot take his eyes off you" Ross remarked as Sally smiled back at him. She gently turned her head to meet the staring eyes. They didn't waver. "Well that reminds me of a joke." Ross just loved watching her, being with her and was ready to hear the funny story. "A small girl was at a family gathering and didn't touch her food, just kept staring at her uncle opposite her. He was becoming embarrassed, had he food on his face, had he dropped it on his shirt? He patted his hair and the rest of the family was now very aware. Her uncle asked her, do I look odd? You keep staring at me Anne. Oh no, said the little girl, I am just waiting to see how you drink like a fish." Ross roared with laughter and her eyes danced.

The waiter served the food that was superb. They chatted away and Sally said you would always be able to tell who is married in a restaurant because they didn't really talk much at all. Ross looked around and said, "Well, I don't think the couple behind you can be, he is all over her. Feel like saying get a room." Sally laughed. She needed to sneak a peek. She dropped her serviette and as she bent to pick it up she recognized the side view of Desmond. She turned straight back. "Are you okay, Sally, you look like you have seen a ghost?" She dabbed her mouth with her serviette. "That's Desmond Johnson, he sold my apartment to me." She just didn't want to get involved in this. "Should you introduce me to him then?" he asked. "Can you see who he is with?" He wondered why she wanted to know. "She is attractive, about thirty-five to forty I would say. Got your hair colouring — not your stunning looks though." He grinned.

She didn't think he knew it was her. He was far too interested in his companion. This mustn't spoil our evening, our whole day, she thought. Actually it would be on her if it was spoilt and she had no intention of so doing. She tried to concentrate on what Ross was saying but that was hard when her head just kept asking who on earth who he was with. The dessert menu was tempting. "Chocolate caramel tart with cream for madam and hot marshmallow fudge sundae for you, sir." The waiter cleared the plates after refreshing Sally's glass and ordering another red for Ross. There was no talk of work. She asked Ross about his hobbies. He enjoyed golf, although often found it frustrating and he tried to get a swim in after work, but had been too busy of late. She told him her hobby was really her work; she enjoyed the art of design in so many ways. The desserts were delicious and surprisingly light. Two cafetieres of coffee were the perfect end to the meal.

Ross asked for the bill and Sally covered it with her hand, no this was her treat and she ignored his protest. She placed her card in the machine and the waiter gave her the receipt. She left a twenty-pound note on the tray for which he thanked her. Ross stood and the waiter pulled back Sally's chair, knocking Desmond's chair in the process. Not good. He apologized profusely as Desmond turned and saw Sally. Now what? "Oh, hello Desmond." He stood up, his face displaying absolutely no emotion. "Sally, how lovely to see you." By now Ross was by her side. "Let me introduce you, Ross this is Desmond." The two men shook hands. "This is my wife Janine, meet Sally. I was lucky enough to be the agent when she bought the apartment recently." Janine shook hands with Sally and Ross. "Delighted to meet you, I have been out of the loop recently so am not sure what is going on." Sally thought oh my God, what is going on? Obviously she cannot have a clue or this would not be a pleasant encounter. Ross helped her into her jacket and they said their goodbyes. It had not gone unnoticed to Sally that there was a ring on his finger. She didn't allow her feelings to show anything but surprise at seeing him there. They would surface later. Not right now when she was enjoying her time with Ross.

The taxi dropped them at Sally's apartment. "Time for a nightcap?" Ross took her in his arms. "Honestly I really would love to, but I have to be in the office by seven tomorrow morning and I still have some work to do on the meeting. Can I take a rain check?" He tilted her chin and kissed her, this time a deep lingering wanting kiss. She responded, both of them aware that this kiss was a beginning. "I have had the best of all days, thank you Ross. I know we are both busy, sounds funny to hear me say so, after all I haven't been in the market long!" They both laughed. They kissed again. "I can't wait to see you again, can I call you tomorrow, to make another date?"

"Look forward to it, please make it your number one priority." He took her key and opened the door, walking her to her apartment. Another kiss. He opened the apartment door. He just couldn't leave it there. He followed her inside. He took off his jacket. She didn't say a word. She pulled him on to the sofa, that wonderfully deep soft welcoming place. They kissed again. He was so gentle, yet so wanting. Not forceful, willing her to want him as he wanted her. He touched her breasts and she lifted her arms to take off the sweater. He undid her bra and caressed her with his tongue. She undid her belt and rolled to one side to ease off her trousers. He stood and stepped out of his while she undid his shirt that he pulled up over his head. He eased her panties to one side, his fingers flitting while she grabbed him and caressed him. She pulled her panties off, and he spread her legs. An easy movement that became more intense, as he entered her and the rhythm was perfect reaching a crescendo that left them both wanting yet sated. He rolled on to his knees and kissed her, making her want him again. "That beats going home and working on a meeting." She laughed. "That beats a lot of things." He sat back and she got up and came back in her robe while he was reaching for his clothes. She watched his body, his very able bodied body. She could not have been happier. Right now what she had hoped for had been.

He got his jacket and they kissed again. "You are a very beautiful young woman Sally Harvey Smart.

Thank you for the best day of my life." She held on to him. "I have to thank you Ross Smythe for the best time. The perfect ending to a wonderful day." He stood in the doorway and she kissed him again. "I will call you tomorrow." He just stopped himself from saying those three words. He wanted to because he was falling, but he had to be sure she felt the same. He couldn't take rejection right now, if ever again.

She was almost asleep, drifting on cloud nine when her mobile rang. "Hi, gorgeous man." There was a pause. "Sally, it's Desmond." She sat up in bed. "It was nice to meet your wife, exactly where in the loop was she?" He sounded tense. "She asked if we could get together. That was the first time we have met for ages." Sally didn't know what she felt, why was he phoning her if it would appear they were together. "Well, I am glad it has worked out for you both." Silence. "You certainly seemed to be enjoying yourself." I beg your pardon, she thought. "Enjoyment is a two way street. I certainly don't have to justify my feelings to you. I hope you and your wife stay happy together. Goodnight." She clicked the mobile shut. Now she was angry. He must have been in touch with the wife to meet with her. Ross had no idea who they were and had said they were all over each other. Well, why was she so bothered? Her mobile buzzed again. "Goodnight, sweetheart." Her tummy flipped. "Goodnight, sweetheart." She closed the phone. Now that is a totally different ball game. She lay back and as she closed her eyes she felt happy. She had a purpose, her job doing something she loved, but so much more than that, a wonderfully warm feeling deep inside. Nothing can take that away, she thought, isn't that what love is all about?

33

Stan Roberts had always counted his blessings. They all centred around Dorry, his wife of nearly forty years. They were sweethearts at fifteen, always together after school and at the youth club. Funny how you just kind of know, not take for granted but just accept that you will always be together. He was nineteen and she was eighteen when the wedding invitations were sent out. Their parents were aware of several raised eyebrows and although no one mentioned the word "shotgun" the wedding was in Stan and Dorry's eyes the very best of days.

Youth is oblivious to a lot of things but not to the fact that hard work pays off. Stan had learned how to take a car apart when he was fifteen and had always tinkered with scooters and motor-bikes. Completely self-taught, he got a job in the local garage at weekends and many was the time he would be underneath a car when a pair of legs would appear, foot tapping. Dorry said if she had a pound for every time he was late they could live in a mansion.

She had a Saturday job at the bakers but her forte was mathematics and she did the books for the local greengrocer. He recommended her to the other shops on the street and she was building quite a little business. They had enough saved for a deposit on a flat and when they returned from honeymoon, camping on a nearby farm, they felt very proud to be buying their own home.

Stan was offered a full time job at the garage and Dorry used the second bedroom as an office to do her accounts. Although their lives were busy, they were young, and in love. They kept Sunday free. Stan was not allowed to go to the garage and she didn't go in the back bedroom. "Stan, I am two weeks late. I am always bang on every month." He looked at her, beaming from ear to ear. "Well, guess you had better go to the doc, girl, he'll let you know." They were both ecstatic, but Dorry said they wouldn't say anything till after three months, that was the doctor's advice. She wondered if he knew something she didn't because eight weeks later she was in the toilet and clots came away. She felt so sick. When Stan came home from work he knew from her face something was very wrong. "What's up, you're not right, girl?" She clung on to him. The doctor confirmed she had lost the baby. "Now this doesn't mean you won't have another," he reassured her, "you are both young and fit." She felt she had let Stan down. No matter how much he tried to tell her it wasn't her fault, she just couldn't think otherwise.

They kept their Sundays and gradually she felt stronger and he said thank goodness, he finally had his old Dorry back. A year went by and they were beyond sad when she lost the baby at just five weeks. Stan wondered if they should stop trying, they really wanted to have a baby and Dorry wouldn't hear of it. Stan was in the yard when a black taxicab pulled up. Someone must have some dosh to come by taxi to the garage, he thought. The man asked who was in charge and Stan took him into the office. Pete Cartwright wanted to sell his cab. He had been a cabbie all his life and now he felt he had earned his retirement. The boss told him to leave it with him. They would give it the once over and get back to him.

This was right up Stan's street and he set about doing a very thorough post mortem. That's what he called it whenever he had to do this. You had to look for any kind of problem, no matter how small. Every part was checked and when the tyres passed the required standard, it was complete. He told the boss the cab was in good nick, even the speedometer didn't register a huge amount of miles, but he made a mental note to check with Pete what kind of mileage he normally did. He told him it was mainly West End business. He did nights and was busy with theatre pick ups and drop offs to stations, occasionally he had a Heathrow run but mainly he was local to London.

The boss asked him how much he wanted. She has been good to me, never let me down and I think two grand is a fair price. Stan had no idea how much a used black taxicab was worth but his boss had done his homework. He told him he would go to one thousand seven hundred and fifty pounds cash. They shook hands, both parties were happy with the result.

Stan and Dorry were happy with their lot. They had managed to save quite a bit while they both worked. Dorry had formed a company, Roberts Accounting. She had been to night school to learn how to use accounting software. This combined write-up, trial balance, payroll, financial statement analysis and would allow flexibility to handle all types of industry and entity types. Stan was very impressed. He was aware his boss seemed to be losing interest in the day to day running of the garage. He had virtually taken over the everyday business, booking cars in, hiring two more mechanics and ordering the parts. Failing health and lack of interest caused him to ask Stan if he would take the business over. Dorry was able to step in, looking over the accounts to come to a reasonable asking price.

Stan and Dorry sat up all night. Could they afford it, should they take it on, was it viable? The price asked, Dorry knew, was really far too cheap. The boss said he had relied on Stan who had never let him down and if he could help out by giving them a good deal, it would make him happy. The paperwork was organized and the solicitor told them they had a very good business on their hands for not a lot of outlay.

Roberts Accounting acquired another new client and they went to the pub for Sunday lunch, a rare treat that they both thought they deserved. Stan said the taxi was still in the yard. It came with the deal and he wondered what Dorry would think if he wanted to train to be a cabbie. She wondered how on earth he would find the time. Their friend Arthur was a cabbie and it had taken him nearly three years to do The Knowledge. He had told them he did it on his bike. There are thousands of streets and landmarks within a six-mile radius of Charing Cross and he had to memorise them all. She said she thought you had to be fully committed to it. He was already running the garage. He was ready for that. He told her he could do it at night after work in the summer and at weekends in the winter. Maybe Sundays might have to go by the board for a little while. It had to be a joint decision. She could see he was keen, he had been talking to Arthur, getting his advice and so it was sorted. He would learn the knowledge of London.

34

The nurse roused him from his reverie. It was time for more meds. Dorry had told him she would be back in the afternoon. She was spending some time with her cousin Barbara who was staying at their house. The plan was that they were going to see *War Horse* but the accident put a stop to any thought of that. Barbara had been a great help to Dorry. She comforted her when she would suddenly start to cry, reassuring her Stan was in the best place and he did seem to be making progress.

His injuries had been treated and the physio was doing her best to get him to walk again. The airbag had prevented more serious injury to his chest but the bruising was considerable and it hurt if he breathed in too deeply. He had asked the doctor how his fare was. He told him she was a model, he had seen her on the television and in Dorry's gossipy magazine. He was told she had been taken to a different hospital, no need for him to know that she had died.

He didn't realize just how tired he felt. He was an active man, driving his taxi in London at night, making time in the day for a game of golf or running errands for Dorry. Her business had really taken off and with his income from the garage, he now had a dealership, and they were able to get a mortgage on a house in Kilburn. She had two rooms converted into offices on the first floor. Two bookkeepers were employed to do "the legwork" and Dorry had studied for the Association of Taxation Technicians qualification. She thoroughly enjoyed this side of accountancy being able to advise her clients to avoid paying unnecessary tax.

The baby, or lack of baby, situation took care of itself. The heartbreak of being unable to carry beyond two months took its toll on both of them. Stan couldn't bear to see the huge sadness that had descended. It was all consuming and one Saturday afternoon he suggested a walk in the park. They sat on a bench in the spring sunshine, she leaning into him as he cuddled her in his arms. "We can't do this any more, Dot. We aren't getting any younger and your health and wellbeing are far more important than being parents. No one could have tried more, Dot. I cannot tell you how proud I am of you. You are beautiful in every way." His voice was choking up and tears were falling down her cheek. "Oh Stan, I cannot tell you how dreadful I feel. You are a wonderful uncle to all the kids and I know you will be a great dad." He kissed the top of her head. "Dot, no more. I love the kids, like you do, but we have each other and a very happy home. You are not going through this any more. Arthur has had the snip and I have made an appointment at the surgery. Can you agree it really is for the best?" Strangely, her tears stopped. She looked at him, would he really do this for her? "Sybil told me that she felt it was the greatest gift a husband could give his wife, after four children she was dreading any more. Funny isn't it Stan, what she would dread, I would die for." He held her tight. "Don't even speak that way. We have a future together. You have been so good, standing by me while I did four years of doing The Knowledge and you building up your business, studying as well. Can you be happy with just me?" Now she did cry, sobbed. "Just you my Stan, just you! I love you so much, thank you for all your love."

That had been nearly thirty years ago now, he thought. Maybe it was the sheer relief that there was no more hoping, wanting, anxiously waiting, that things settled into a far happier routine. He loved his work in the West End. His cab had given up the ghost after fifteen years and they had invested in a nearly new replacement that was easier to drive, not so heavy on the steering although most cabs could turn on a sixpence.

Lying in his hospital bed he thought back over his career, for that is what it was. He had progressed from the essential bacon sarnie to muesli, fresh fruit and low fat yoghurt. Dorry was delighted and they always ate a good lunch with hardly any red meat and she packed a wholegrain bread sandwich with tuna or salad with avocado for when he got peckish around two in the morning.

He had installed a dash cam in his cab. One of his mates told him that while he was moving slowly through traffic someone threw themselves on to his bonnet, then claimed they had sustained injuries. If it hadn't been for the dash cam he would have been hard pressed to prove otherwise, not carrying a fare at the time. He also installed CCTV in his cab with a sign informing the passengers of its existence. He always agreed the fare with the passenger before moving off. That way there could be no arguments, particularly if alcohol was in the equation.

He was just finishing his sandwich and sipping coffee from his flask when a man approached his cab. He put his hire sign on, and in the dimmed headlights he could see this was some gent. His suit was immaculate, jet black hair tight to his scalp, smart black boots. He noticed his hands, long fingers with manicured nails. He wondered if he was a fancy boy, not that that would bother him. "Where to Guv?" he asked? "Carlisle Place," was the reply. No surprise there, apartments in that mansion fetched over two million. Seven pounds fifty pence was the agreed fare and he turned the meter on as he got in the back. "I have to deliver a package, it won't take long. Can you wait while I do so? I will make it worth your while." He couldn't determine the accent. It wasn't British, just sounded a bit foreign. "No trouble, mate, I'll wait outside." He certainly didn't mind waiting while the meter clicked up. This was what he called his dead hour, not much going on at all.

After ten minutes he got back in the cab. "Belsize Park, please. Rowland Hill Street. Fifty pounds if you can get me there in twenty minutes." Stan noticed the meter was at fifteen pounds. He still couldn't work out the accent but knew the quiet leafy lanes attracted wealth and some celebrities. This is an earner, he thought, and with hardly any traffic on the road he earned his fifty pounds and a generous tip. He thanked him and drove off. That was a good night wrapped up, he thought. Knock it on the head for now. Be good to get home a bit earlier than advertised.

35

Anderson Beckett, known as The Chameleon because of his ability to change his identity completely, walked three hundred yards down the road and turned into a parking area for the apartments. He walked between the cars to the side entrance of Brondesbury House. His gloved hand pushed the button of the private lift that took him directly to the penthouse suite. He pressed the keypad and inserted a key. The door opened onto a spacious lounge and he made his way to the bathroom. He took down the bathroom cabinet and removed two tiles taking out a steel box. He took the gun apart, removing the silencer, and placed it inside returning it to the compartment, replacing the tiles and putting back the cabinet.

He checked his phone. One hundred thousand pounds had been deposited in his Cayman account. He undressed, carefully removing his arched eyebrows and black moustache. He stood in the shower and the black hair was soon rinsed out revealing a sandy colour that was in stark contrast to his almost black eyes. He poured some acid into the basin that dissolved the eyebrows and moustache. He opened the case on the bed and took out beige foundation, massaging it into his face. He inserted blue contact lenses and lightened his eyebrows with a highlighter.

Wrapped in a towel he went into the lounge to pour a Scotch. He took time to relax. His plane wasn't for another ten hours. His papers were all in order. He had arrived at Heathrow five days earlier entering the country with his American passport under the name of Wallace Lulsgate. The package containing the code and key for the penthouse was in the locker, the key to which had been sent to him before he left.

He used the time to check how the land lay. During the day he had watched the building, the comings and goings and timed travelling to the building from central London. At night he was aware the same taxi was in the rank for thirty minutes from two a.m. This was opportune because the concierge in the entrance hall of the building left his desk at about that time to make his coffee. He was also aware the hit was using opiates, which although not taking him out, made him drowsy, almost vacant. The keypad clicked the door open. A man was sitting, almost slumped on the sofa. He was vaguely aware of a large man, who was holding a gun in his hand. The opiates numbed any pain. He didn't even register surprise. Death in this case was easy to come by, no mess, a clean shot above the right eye.

Anderson Beckett had been born thirty five years ago to a Romanian sex worker, who had been trafficked from a village outside Bucharest to work in Reading.

She was fifteen, one of the Romani people, also known as Roma. What she didn't know was the father was the client who abused her and beat her mercilessly. Had she realized he was a criminal psychopath she maybe would have tried to abort the foetus. She didn't want this baby but her Catholic teaching was instilled from when she was born. Her pimp provided a room for the baby and as it suckled she felt nothing. She was now sixteen. She didn't know what to do because she needed to work to live.

Her friend Ana Maria felt sorry for her. She should have known how not to have a baby. She also confided that one of her regular clients knew of a family who were desperate to have a baby but couldn't. He had asked her if she would carry a baby for them, they would pay a lot of money. Ana Maria had other plans. She didn't want to lose income, and her figure, even for a lot of money. She told Gabriela she could act as a go-between. Her client could tell the rich people that a baby was available. He was named Florin but obviously not for long. Gabriela and Ana Maria got one thousand pounds each, the client pocketing the same.

Anderson Beckett was a "gift from God" to Lilane and Tarquin Beckett. They had all but given up any possibility of getting a baby. Adoption agencies had made it clear that although there was no upper age limit, as long as they were fit and well, they always favoured younger people. At forty and forty-two they knew they stood no chance. Tarquin would never forget Lilane's face as Anderson was placed in her arms. The client had organized a nurse to take Florin from Gabriela who showed no emotion. The combination of a psychopathic father and an almost brainwashed abused mother didn't bode well for Florin.

A nanny was employed and she was in charge of the night feeds while Lilane spent all her waking hours with him. She pushed his pram, brought him far too many cuddly toys and picked him up whenever he cried. Tarquin was keen for him to follow in his footsteps and put his name down for the Backwell Pre-preparatory School that was conveniently situated a few miles from their home in Surrey. Anderson was not used to other children. The mothers seemed to be twenty years younger than Lilane and they didn't invite her to take him to play dates. Having said that, Anderson seemed fine on his own. He could build Lego at two. He progressed to making models, and learned the alphabet and by the time he was admitted to Backwell he could read the Janet and John books.

His teachers were impressed. He was adept at most subjects. He just didn't seem to interact with the other children. They were asked to attend the parents' evening after a year and one of the teachers suggested he would benefit from a home tutor to increase his knowledge because he was so far ahead of the class. He could enter the preparatory age groupings at seven. Lilane was grateful that so far Tarquin hadn't suggested boarding.

It was no distance for her to take and fetch and she was so proud of his achievements.

He was growing and developing and he was a good-looking young man. Tarquin was offered a post in America. It was a huge compliment and although money would never have been a problem, the salary was considerable. He would be a Vice President for a building consortium. Lilane was happy. It would be a new adventure for all three of them. Tarquin explained that Anderson's education was paramount. The dreaded word boarding was mentioned. She was crestfallen. What she couldn't see was that she was smothering Anderson. She would turn up for after school rugby, he was a tough and good player, and she'd wait for him outside the changing rooms. The other boys were in a group that excluded Anderson, even though his prowess in the game put them in the shade. He just didn't seem to want or care about friendships or being part of a group.

He entered Backwell Boarding School for boys aged eleven. Lilane cried all the way back to their house. Tarquin had gone ahead and the company had arranged for several property viewings. He spoke to Lilane suggesting that they rent before they buy, to get to know the district to decide if it would be a permanent residency. The firm sent her several brochures but they settled on an apartment in the iconic Walker Tower, perched high above Chelsea with panoramic views of Manhattan and the Hudson River. She wouldn't be phased by the move. During their marriage they had spent time in Europe and Kuwait. A brief spell in Canada meant they could cross to New York with ease and she had enjoyed visiting the city. She felt it would be a good move. The only fly in the ointment had been leaving Anderson.

They never discussed the fact that Anderson seemed remote, disinterested in becoming involved. She rented a flat near the school for the half term holidays but Anderson travelled to New York for the summer vacation and Christmas. He took it all in his stride. They assumed he liked the apartment and the various activities that were available. One of Tarquin's associates had a son of a similar age and although there didn't seem to be any enthusiasm for a friendship on Anderson's part, he introduced him to the gym and contact sports. Anderson found his niche. He had learned the diverse martial arts discipline of karate at school. He knew the techniques of straight punch and elbow strike, kicking such as round kick and front snap kick. He had the proper balance, speed and power and used the different stances involving positioning the feet, being ready to engage.

He found a studio specializing in Krav Maga. It is a blend of Muay Thai, boxing, judo, grappling and fight training. The idea is to achieve the goal of delivering enough damage to the adversary to quickly finish the fight. Soldiers in the Armed Forces excel at defending against chokes, bear hugs and overpowering headlocks. Working out at the gym and his training at the studio was paying off. He was fast becoming a very fit athlete, albeit in an isolated way.

His GCSE results were reasonable and the teachers suggested he pursue his language skills at A level. He had mastered French, Spanish and Russian. He could easily accommodate Arabic at that level. One teacher approached Lilane on what he described as a more personal footing. It had been recognized that Anderson had a problem in communicating with his peers. They suggested he meet with a counsellor. It would be discreet and in his own time after class. She agreed it was becoming more noticeable, she had hoped with time he would become more sociable, but was pleased for any help. Anderson begrudgingly began to open up to the counsellor. After several sessions he realized Anderson didn't know or truly understand the concept of happiness, love or how to be loved. The afterschool activities enjoyed by him were not only a way of hurting people but also improving his agility, making him stronger. He was feeding a rage and stirring the darkness within. The counsellor didn't give up on him, he gave up on the counsellor. He felt no benefit whatsoever from talking about what he didn't feel.

Following on from his graduation and with no interest in university he travelled to his parents in New York. He had no idea what he wanted to do next. Tarquin and Lilane were pleased that he had achieved so much. They were aware of his prowess in his physical attainments. The Master at the Krav Maga studio had asked them to let him know when he returned to the US. He felt he had a career in utilizing his martial arts accomplishments. They had never known any form of enthusiasm be displayed by their son, but on hearing that the Master was interested in seeing him, a smirk, couldn't call it a smile, was at the corner of his mouth.

The Master had watched his progress, he was an exemplary student and his commitment to fitness was remarkable, to the exclusion of all else. His friend owned an escort business. He moved in the very highest social circles and his escorts had a first class reputation. He suggested Anderson might like to meet him. He considered there could be a good job opportunity where he could apply his skills.

Tarquin took Anderson to his tailor. He would look good in a garbage bag the tailor thought and set about creating a suit that emphasized the build and strength of this young man. He supplied the shirts, ties, belts, shoes everything that would create the very best impression. One week later Anderson went for his final fitting. Tarquin was impressed. His son turned heads as soon as they left and called the cab. Now he was ready to meet one of the highest rollers in New York.

Jackson Willard met Anderson Beckett at his apartment in 1010 Fifth Avenue in the Carnegie Hill neighbourhood. First impressions counted in his book and he was not disappointed. The Master had selected one of the finest specimens of a young man that he had encountered.

He offered tea but Anderson politely declined. He outlined the job he had in mind. His clientele were the cream of New York society. He supplied the escorts for any occasion and it would be Anderson who would ensure they came to no harm. He would need to be discretion itself, a timely tap here, a word there, just so everyone kept in line. He said he would start him at one hundred dollars an hour, if that was acceptable. A trial run of one month to make sure everyone was singing from the same hymn sheet was agreed and he started on the following Monday evening.

His education in one of the best public schools in England ensured that he achieved academically, as well as displaying good manners confidently in any situation. This was not lost on Jackson. The first occasion he had to use his fist was when an overzealous photographer got too near to the escort. He stepped forward and almost lifted the man off the ground and half carried him away from her. His fist connected with the man's jaw and he was out cold. This was out of sight of the rest of the paparazzi. He had to do this on several occasions. An admirer wanting to touch was almost maimed as he swiftly head butted him out of the equation.

Anderson told his parents he really couldn't keep living with them. He needed space and they agreed the hours he kept were not in keeping with their lifestyle. They rented a small apartment for him in the same building as Jackson. A lot of clients had acquired their wealth from illegal trading. There were several drug cartels in the immediate area around the Walker Tower. Anderson didn't ask any questions but he guessed Jackson was not strictly legit. His wealth was not inherited. He had got to where he was by fair means or foul. It was not a problem for Anderson and when he was asked to do a hit he considered it a natural progression, one that he relished.

Turf wars frequently erupt between the different cartels. Brian Donoghue was alerted to the fact that his sales were dropping. Someone was taking his customers. The Joaquin Lichtman cartel operated out of Mexico. It had established a base in Queens and Donoghue was aware that the eldest son was overseeing the business from there. He was the hit. With him gone the family may consider their business operations in New York were not viable.

Donoghue met Anderson in Jackson's apartment. He showed him the photo and gave him the address. Twenty five thousand dollars would get the job done. Anderson visited the address three times, watching the movements of the man that owned the apartment on the twentieth floor. His business was done mainly at night. He ordered food in during the day, always at noon. A blond-haired smart young man in a tailored Zoot suit took the lift to the twentieth floor in 35th Street in Queens. He pushed the bell at five minutes to midday. "Delivery". A maid opened the door. She dropped like a stone and he stepped over her into the lounge. No sound came from the open mouth of the eldest Lichtman son. Anderson closed the door and took the stairs to the thirtieth floor. He pushed the lift button and was out of the building at four minutes past midday.

No rush of adrenalin, just a job perfectly executed. His career was determined by that one day. He became known to Jackson's associates. His reputation grew as he made the hits. He changed his address. It never occurred to him to get in touch with his parents. He was an adult, independent and got his clients through an advertisement in the *New York Times* under recruitment/help wanted. A name and contact number which opened the door to so many diverse and interesting requests. He wasn't cheap and his clients had large wallets.

It was through this portal that he travelled to England. He was very thorough. He poured another Scotch. He was neither hungry, nor tired. He was still on full alert. He had to get to Heathrow with his face matching that of George Hartley, businessman, on his way to New York. The cleaners, or sweepers as they were known, would have disposed of the body. How or when was of no consequence. Another group of them would visit the penthouse as he left, removing any evidence of him ever being there.

He hailed a cab. He had changed into more casual clothes, suitable for a long flight. He was through security that had been busy. It was far more painstakingly thorough since the advent of terrorism on the streets of London a few years ago. It was crowded.

Someone was pushing and shoving to get by. He had the lounge in sight, a more direct shove would have toppled a less fit man. He didn't feel the needle go into his thigh. He just felt a sudden pain in his chest. He stumbled, a fiercest sharp pain. He fell to the floor. A woman screamed but he didn't hear her. A man watching from the upper floor took out his phone. "It's done, no loose ends, clean as a whistle."

Jackson Willard replaced the receiver. He had been planning his retirement. He enjoyed good health and at sixty he was ready to take his foot off the gas. He appreciated Beckett's skill and attitude to his work, but he had never warmed to him. Actually no one had "warmed" to someone so cold. This was business. It was a necessary precaution and he wanted a clean break.

He had been made aware of some discontent by one of his escorts. She considered she could go on her own, she had made enough connections in the right places. Obviously she thought she was better than she was. Opening the door to Anderson Beckett she turned to grab her bag. She turned back to a gun pressed tightly into her chest. A squeeze of the trigger ensured she wouldn't be making any more ridiculous assumptions. Once discontent raised its head above the parapet there could be more. Enough already, he had served his time. He had many friends in many different walks of life and he told them he was moving on.

He had bought a house on the waterfront in Durham, New Hampshire. A boat came with the property and the

Oyster River, known for its shellfish, lapped at the mooring. There was access to the local woods where he would be able to hunt and trap. His friends threw him a party and he appreciated their sentiments, but he wouldn't miss them. They were really more acquaintances along the way. He settled into the first class seat, the plane taxied to the runway and he felt a surge of excitement. Another new start, but this one was not fraught with obstacles. This was going to be one long extended holiday and he would make the very best of all that was on offer.

36

The physio had managed to get Stan walking with one crutch and he was so looking forward to going home. He had to prove he could walk up and down a flight of stairs in the hospital, which although caused pain, the urgency to get home overcame that. Arthur and Sybil collected Dorry to take her to the hospital. She caught her breath as she hugged him. He had aged, almost appeared shrunken, but she knew she could feed him up and get him strong.

Arthur said that one of their mates, old Ronnie Blythe, had taken a fare to Heathrow the other day and blow me down, he dropped dead of a heart attack in departures. Arthur's humour could always be relied on. Departed in departures, poor sod. He laughed. Lucky it wasn't in the taxi though, that really holds you up, let alone, how would he pay? Stan had read in the paper about that. An apparently fit youngish man had suffered a fatal heart attack in the airport. Ronnie recognized the face as that of his fare. Stan would never have recognized the man that he had taken to Belsize Park, that is what a good disguise is for.

His stay in hospital had given him time to think. His brother Roger had sorted out a good pension scheme when he got the dealership for the garage. He didn't have private health insurance. They had always hoped that if it was necessary they could afford a private consultation, assuming that it would be later in life. They had been mortgage free for five years and their combined earnings ensured a very good standard of living.

Dorry had insisted Arthur and Sophie stay for supper, they were good company and it was good to see Stan laughing again. She cleared the table and put the kettle on. Arthur and Sophie wouldn't stop for a cuppa so she took a tray into the lounge. Stan was fast asleep. She gave him a gentle nudge and he started awake. "Sorry Dot, I must be more tired than I thought I was." She hugged him. "Now you can show me how good you are at stairs." He slept deeply, no machines buzzing or alarms going off. She made him breakfast in bed, but as she took the tray in he was coming out of the shower. "How did you manage that?" He smiled. "Arthur told me he had put a handle in for me. I can hang on and wash and rinse." They sat on the edge of the bed. "Not really hungry, Dot, but would love a cuppa." He opted for some jogging bottoms and a sweater, easier than a belt and zip.

The morning paper had arrived and the telephone rang. It was Roger, wanting to know how his brother was settling in. Dorry said for him to come and see for himself, in fact to bring Polly and have coffee with them. They were so relieved to see Stan, considering what he had been through he looked far better than they thought he would. "What are your plans, Stan? Do you think you will go back to being a cabbie?"

Stan stared into his coffee. "I am not sure Rog. Haven't talked it over with Dot yet. My leg will need a bit more physio and I am not sure sitting in a cab is the best thing right now." Dorry offered more biscuits. "Well you take your time. I can tell you your pension will give you a very good return for your money." He was so pleased he had almost had to insist he take it out.

When they had gone, he said "I've been thinking" and they both laughed because whenever either of them said those words, something was about to be revealed. "How would you feel if I gave up the taxi, Dot?" She sat beside him. "I would be very glad, Stan, but it's been your way of life for a long time." He nodded. "I know Dot but I have to say it's lost its appeal. I don't know if I would feel confident, do you know what I mean?" She held his hand. "You have the garage Stan. Walter has been so good taking it over. He could run it with his eyes shut. What do you feel about a complete break?" He wasn't quite sure. "Do you mean completely retire, sell the taxi and the garage?" She looked at him. "You have provided a wonderful home, we have no money worries and I am easing off my book work. In fact one of the girls said she would love to have first refusal on the business."

She poured another cup. "Goodness, Dot, that's a lot to take in. What do you really think, about selling everything I mean?" She stood up. "I reckon we have earned ourselves a break Stan. I have no idea what anything is worth, I am sure Roger would help us out there. I feel ready for a change. Thinking I nearly lost you, I couldn't go through that again." Her voice faltered. "Come here, old girl, you would never lose me. Tough as old boots me." The tears rolled down as she clung to him, as she had done so many times before. They both sat there, thoughts going into overdrive. "I think we have both really made up our minds Dot. I really haven't the heart to go back to taxiing. Don't get me wrong, I have loved it but something like this makes you take a fresh look. Also you don't need to be working. I know while I was on the road it was something you enjoyed and you have succeeded in creating a really good business. What say we call it a day? No taxi, no garage, no Roberts Accounting, just no more working." She grabbed his arm and held on.

"Well, you've only been home one day and you have changed everything, and so much for the better. I was excited when we got the garage, then when you drove the taxi. Building up our company was good for me. Now we can make plans for our future, just for us." He hugged her tightly. "Do you know what Dot, all of a sudden I could eat a horse."

37

You get used to the daily routine. Stuart goes off to work. Mavis wonders where she will shop. Except things were far from going well. No matter how hard he tried, how many hours he worked, he could never make her understand that they were in trouble. He was grateful for the job, but there were only so many hours in a day when a company is open for a sales pitch. Sometimes he could get an appointment at eight a.m. That was usually with a secretary or a diligent office worker who wanted to impress. He was good at cold calling. It never fazed him when he was shown the door, mainly because that was becoming more and more rare.

He was aware of pain. He couldn't move, nor open his eyes. He could hear a vague sound. Someone was talking. Where was he? He remembered he had been on his way to an appointment, what was he doing here?

The doctor stood at the end of the bed. He thought this poor woman has no idea of how bad things really are. He moved to the side of the bed and gently touched her arm. "Mrs Dunwoody?" she started, she was talking to Stuart. Surely he could see that, not interrupt. "Yes, who are you?" He took her arm. "Let's step away from the bed for a moment." He guided her to a chair behind a bank of machines that were whirring, almost in rhythm. "I am Mr Lehman, an orthopaedic surgeon. I have been assessing your husband." She looked at him. "He is going to be all right isn't he?" He pulled up a chair, his voice was calming which seemed to her that there was nothing to worry about. "Stuart has lost a lot of blood and his right leg has been severely crushed. My colleagues and I have done our very best but the leg cannot be saved. We will have to amputate below the knee."

She physically slumped in the chair. He fetched some water. She tried to sip but her mouth wouldn't work. "You can't do that. He drives for a living. He needs both legs to walk to his appointments. There must be another way." Richard Lehman had seen it all before and he knew how dangerous shock could be. "Believe me, Mrs Dunwoody, if there was any other way. The lower leg is so badly injured, coupled with the loss of blood, we must operate to save your husband's life." Oh dear God, how can this be, thoughts were pounding in her head. "Is there anyone I can call? A lady came in with you didn't she? Can I call her?" Mavis remembered Katherine Carlisle, such a kind lady from Stu's office. She told him her name and he sent someone to make the call. "Mrs Dunwoody, speed is now of the essence. Stuart is as ready as he will ever be. We have given him blood transfusions and he will be prepared for surgery. I plan to operate this evening using a general anaesthetic. The length of the operation can vary but this will give Stuart the best opportunity to get well. He will be in hospital for up to two weeks." A nurse came to tell him that Katherine Carlisle was still in the hospital and would come straight away.

They took Mavis to a side room. They needed to prep for the operation and it was important she didn't see the damaged limb. Katherine rushed into the room and hugged Mavis. They had briefly told her what was about to happen and she had relayed it to the office. Stuart was a popular employee, he had been with the company since he was sixteen and it was impossible to contemplate that he would lose his leg at thirty-years-old.

She asked Mavis if there was anyone who could stay with her. She told them they really only had each other. She had a friend where she worked in the Post Office but she was a young mother with responsibilities that lay elsewhere. Suddenly Mavis felt so tired. Too tired to cry. She couldn't take it in, this sort of thing happened to soldiers in the war, not to her Stu. Katherine left her to find a nurse. She explained the situation, was there any point in Mavis staying at the hospital? She was told it would be far better for her to go home and call the hospital in the morning. Stuart would be out of it for a long time. Quite often patients in the Recovery Suite were there for many hours.

She repeated this to Mavis who was not taking anything in at all. She offered to drive Mavis home, then she would go to her house and collect a few things so that she could stay with her. This was such a kind gesture and the tears finally came. Nonsense, it is the least she could do. She called the company and told her boss of her plans. He was grateful to her for her selflessness. Knowing Katherine as he did he would expect nothing less. She got a takeaway from the supermarket, and together with a bottle of wine made her way back to Mavis's house. She was once told that it's very easy to say "busy" when someone needs you, but it's very painful to hear "busy" when you need someone. It had been her mantra to live by. She would never be that busy.

Katherine was married once. She often thought it was a blessing they had never had children. They were often the most damaged in an unhappy marriage. It wasn't unhappy at first. It was a bit of a whirlwind courtship. She was amazed that such a gorgeous man could want to spend the rest of his life with her. She was too hard on herself. She was an attractive young woman, hard working in the advertising department of a marketing company. He was the new boy on the block and marketing can be very competitive. He asked if she could show him the ropes, every company had different ways of working and he wanted to fit right in.

He was charm personified. Everyone, or those of the opposite sex, thought he was just drop dead gorgeous. No one questioned why he was single. They guessed he just liked to play the field. One of the typists literally threw herself at him, almost crashing into him at the photocopier. This didn't bode well because the material he was copying was in chronological order and her clumsiness caused it to go all over the floor. Her aim was for him to notice her, but all she achieved was a curt, please don't worry, as he gathered it from the floor. Katherine had witnessed the whole episode and was laughing as she went into his office. He wasn't at all impressed. She started to collate the paperwork, and finally he could see the funny side, or if he didn't he made out that he did. She put it all in order and he thanked her.

Troy Hubbard's forte was design. The company had landed a contract to market e-books. He had to create a design strategy that was neither intrusive nor boring. He held meetings to brainstorm content ideas to establish goals and marketing objectives. He brought his website experience into play and threw ideas and challenges to his colleagues. One such challenge was to design how to hold back time. A clock with the hands in handcuffs was the winner. Simple, the best designs often were. Katherine was impressed by a lot of his designs. They had been approved and were now in the advertising stages. Katherine and Troy were involved in the process and although the deadline was a bit ambitious, they worked late in order to make it.

The presentation to the client was well received. They would go with it. Given the green light, the pressure was off and Troy suggested they go out and celebrate. There was a local pub near the office but he didn't want to go there. They had established they were about half an hour from each other's apartments and he would collect her at seven thirty, giving her a chance to get home and change. The restaurant was new to Katherine, but he was welcomed like an old friend. He made it very clear he found her attractive and enjoyed her company. Their earlier conversations: Are you married? Involved with any significant other? cleared the path. They were free agents. As relationships go it was quite full on. Both had previous relationships. There was no awkwardness, sex was good and they shared a great sense of humour, something which Katherine brought out in him. He wasn't serious, just a bit different in the way he saw things.

Her friend Ruby thought it was a bit too soon to talk of marriage. Why don't you just live together? She'd tried that before, no commitment, although if they were honest they hadn't really tried at all. She said yes, she would marry him. Ruby and Will witnessed the marriage at the Register Office in the Town Hall. They thought it a bit odd that they were the only guests at the restaurant afterwards. Troy's family had emigrated to Australia when he was sixteen and he hadn't gone with them. He wanted to go to art college, his mate Darren was going and his mum said he could lodge with them. His parents gave him a generous allowance and he paid his way. Katherine was not close to her parents. They wanted so much more for her, she could have gone to uni and become a doctor but no, London and the world of fashion beckoned and she thought she would learn graphic design at college.

She fell head over heels in love with her tutor. He was married and she didn't care. He taught her how to be amazing in bed, not so much at graphic design. Suffice to say she hadn't anyone really close in her life and once his wife had realized what was going on, she moved on.

If they had thought it through they would have realized they didn't know that much about each other. A sense of humour is important, but so is fidelity. Troy was offered a job in a rival design company, head hunted you could call it. He was tasked to run the department of an innovative group of people with the common incentive to take their creations to the limit.

He often worked late, but so did Katherine. They were making their way and she broached the subject of a having a baby. This was not received well by Troy. Why on earth would they want to have a baby? It just wouldn't fit in, be realistic.

Katherine supposed that right now it probably wasn't the best time. Perhaps suggest it in a few months. She was approaching thirty. She felt she was ready and would cope. They were financially sound, his way of life would not dramatically alter in the way hers would.

She began to realize that maybe they didn't really know each other that well at all. Ruby's words echoed in her head. She had married in haste. She just couldn't afford to repent at leisure. His late nights became the norm and when she heard his key in the latch at four a.m. she knew she had to confront him. He was very drunk. She should be so happy for him, the team had won an innovative contract, judged on their past achievements. It was no good trying to talk sense to him. She waited until the next morning. He was going in late, all the team were, they had it all planned. He just didn't expect Katherine to be so cold. She was still going on about a baby. She really didn't get it, did she? He told her he was sorry but he was far too young to be weighed down by parental responsibilities.

Will knew a solicitor, his firm used the company, and a marriage born out of lust, rather more than love, was ended on the grounds "the irretrievable breakdown of the marriage". Katherine was lost. She never thought a marriage could end in this way. It really was a forgone conclusion to Ruby and Will. They were good to her, helping her to move her stuff out. Troy was able to buy her out of the flat. Will saw to the business side of buying a new one. The deposit was affordable as was the rent.

She couldn't stay in her job. She opted for a complete break from what she knew and turned her expertise to office management. She knew the ropes, she had people skills and her boss congratulated her when she saw an opportunity to rent, rather than buy, a new brand of software. It wasn't a large company, but it was growing, thanks to the reps like Stuart, totally dedicated to seeing the show get on the road.

Mavis was curled up in front of the gas fire. She wasn't asleep, just dozing and immediately got up when Katherine rang the doorbell. She put the oven on and found a corkscrew. "Whatever am I going to do?" She turned helplessly to Katherine. "Well, first of all we will eat." They were both quite hungry and Mavis cleared the plates while Katherine topped up the wine.

She looked at the paperwork the hospital had given Mavis. There were so many different aspects. The operation itself was straightforward. Richard Lehman was top in his field. He had an air of confidence that put you at ease. If anyone knew what he was doing, it was he. Some individuals receive a temporary prosthesis immediately following amputation. This was the way Mr Lehman worked. The incision would heal over a period of two to six weeks. There was so much to take in and Katherine suggested it would be best to leave it all till the morning. Her boss had told her to take as long as necessary, although she knew it couldn't be too long. Somehow Mavis had to understand that she needed to be there for Stuart, not the other way round.

Mavis called the hospital in the morning. The operation went well and Stuart was in recovery. They expected him to be there for the rest of the morning. It would be fine for her to call around two p.m. Katherine was glad she was there but it was hard to read Mavis. She was on autopilot, getting some cereal and toast, making tea, but not communicating. It appeared as if she was in denial. Katherine suggested they sit in the lounge and look at the paperwork. They would be able to get a better idea of what had happened, and what the next two weeks would be like.

The word amputate finally came through. Mavis crumpled and Katherine held her, reassuring her that it was the only possible way to keep Stuart alive. The tears stopped and together they read what could happen, what will happen and the timescale. "I don't know what he will do when he realizes he has lost a leg. Who will tell him? What will they say? I certainly cannot be the one to say." Katherine told her it would be Mr Lehman who would explain and monitor the situation. She said he would make sure Stuart understood there was no other option, the only way to save his life. Katherine didn't really know Stuart, it was all on the surface but she perceived a very well mannered, earnest young man. She hoped with all her heart he would be able to accept what had happened.

What she didn't mention was the mental side of the operation. The physical surgery she assumed had gone well, the scar would heal in about two weeks. The scar inside his head could go either way. She read some amputees suffer phantom pain that seems to be coming from the missing limb.

She thought the best thing right now was to keep Mavis occupied. Had they been able to prepare for the amputation a physio would have visited the house to see what adjustments would need to be made. A bed would have to be put downstairs and possibly a ramp for a wheelchair. Fortunately the doors were quite wide and the chair would be able to get through. She told Mavis she would return to the office to sort out getting sick pay and any other benefits to help their situation. Unfortunately Mavis was oblivious of the financial side of things.

When Katherine had gone Mavis decided to take a look at her wardrobes. In the cold light of day it struck home. They were full of clothes she had just never worn. A separate shoe cupboard opened on to racks of brand new shoes. She sat on the bed and howled. What had she done? She had spent all of this money. No, she had wasted all of this money. Her friend in the Post Office arrived and she took her upstairs. Jennifer was a young mum, three under four, and a worker. Her mum lived round the corner and could come at the drop of a hat to look after them while she worked in the shop. She inherited her "make do and mend" attitude from her mother and was frugal in every way. She just couldn't believe the amount of clothes and shoes. "Oh my God Mavis, what on earth are you thinking? I've never seen you in any of these clothes. Where do you wear them, where do you go?" She wasn't angry at her, just at the sheer waste of money in selfish indulgence. "I know, Jen, Stuart had cut up my cards twice but then I thought things were better so I got another store card." Jennifer had to hold herself in check. She thought of poor Stuart working himself half to death and now so near to death. She must be mindful, not just charge in.

"You're never going to wear these are you Mavis?" Mavis rifled through the hangers. "No, Jen. I think this is a big wake up call. I didn't really have a purpose in life other than getting to the shops. Three days in the Post Office stopped me going every day but I got such a rush." Jennifer tried very hard to be gentle. "My mate Kanza has a brilliant business in selling new clothes on a website called 'Ragstrader'. The good thing is you don't have to go out and buy your stock. It's all here. I think she picked the site because she doesn't have to pay much commission."

Mavis sat on the edge of the bed. "Can I call her, Jen? I would need to know how to go about it." Jen wrote down her number. "I know she always says the photos of the clothes you are selling are the key. You have to sell it to the buyer. Material, size, quality but the most important thing is the pricing. I am sure she will be able to help and I can always come round when Pete's home to help you." Mavis hugged her. "Jen, you are a lifesaver. I have to call the hospital at two. I am hoping I can go in to see him. Katherine says his work has been brilliant and she said she would drive me. Perhaps later tonight I could call Kanza?" Jennifer was relieved to see a bit of life come back into Mavis. She had had a dreadful shock and this would give her something else to think about, take her mind off things so to speak. "That will be a good idea. I know she works but reckon she would be home by eight."

Katherine returned with sandwiches from the deli. She couldn't believe the change in Mavis. From a crumpled lost and vacant soul this energetic woman greeted her with open arms. She took Katherine upstairs, and like Jennifer, she was aghast. She didn't say a word while Mavis told her of her plans. It all made sense. She also thought of poor Stuart, working all the hours to feed her habit. Bit like drugs, she thought, and actually the rush Mavis felt when she shopped was like a drug. She told her she thought it sounded a really good idea.

The hospital told Mavis that Stuart was back in a side room. It would do him good to see her. Mr Lehman had expertly taken him through what had happened. He was still not fully aware but able to grasp what had happened. He was at the very first stage. Receiving and trying to absorb the fact would take a while. In fact he had no idea of what he would have to go through but he thanked Mr Lehman for saving his life. The surgeon looked at him. He had been the bearer of bad news to so many of his patients and the reactions varied hugely. However, he felt that Stuart was one of the more positive recipients. He had age on his side and he sensed a certain positive upbeat. A positive attitude is quite often more beneficial than a lot of drugs and he left his bedside far happier than when he had arrived.

Mavis kissed Stuart on the top of his head. He had a tube in his arm to administer fluids and a drain was removing excess blood from the op. He was so pleased to see her and thanked Katherine for her support. He said he couldn't feel pain but the nurse had told him to keep taking pain medication because he would soon be doing exercises. There was no mention of the amputation. He said he felt sleepy. Mavis didn't do her usual non-stop verbals but actually listened to him. She held his hand and told him he was so brave and she would help in any way she could. He squeezed her hand and his eyes were closing. She said she would be back tomorrow and as the nurse arrived she thanked her so much for looking after her Stu.

Katherine had instigated sick pay that would start on the fourth day. He was covered under the company insurance for a road traffic accident. The company's insurance department had been given the details and it was felt he could be entitled to compensation. An adviser was appointed to act on his behalf and was already making enquiries. She didn't mention this to Mavis, just said that she was not to worry, she would not suffer financially. The company would make up any shortfall between sick pay and his normal salary.

Mavis felt so much better after she had seen Stuart. He seemed to be all right, naturally tired but aware the surgical team were going to help him get through. Katherine got fish and chips and they discussed how to go about selling the wardrobes full of clothes. Kanza had called Mavis when Jennifer told her about Stuart and how Mavis needed advice on selling on line. She told her to sell seasonally, sweaters in winter, sandals in summer for example. When photographing to find a spot with natural light and use good coat hangers. Include pictures of the sizing and brand labels. A digital camera could show up detail better. It was a good idea to include the size, dimensions and fabric details. When Kanza told her about posting her items she felt she was really on the way. She should buy envelopes that fit within the "large letter size" tops and thin dresses can squash into these. A 200g skirt costs one pound fifty pence to send first class recorded if it's a large letter size. If the same package is even one centimetre over it will cost three pounds fifty-five pence to send as a small parcel.

She had made notes and Katherine was fascinated by the whole prospect. Apparently you can advertise your clothes on more than one site. The fees on e-Bay are quite high. You pay ten percent of the final value, including postage. However, while it's not official, the site routinely runs sell for one pound max promotions every other weekend. The final value fee for items listed during these promotions is capped at one pound. Kanza had told Mavis to always use a tracked postal service and keep all her receipts in a file.

Mavis had blossomed overnight. She had a chance to make a difference and her excitement rubbed off on Katherine. She told her she had a digital camera she hardly ever used and would be delighted to donate it to the cause. Where to start? It was May, so spring and summer clothes would be the best sellers. Mavis called the hospital and Stuart was comfortable. They had rolled towels either side of the stump so that he wouldn't be able to turn and harm it in any way. Mavis caught her breath at the word stump. It sounded so callous to her, but in reality that is what it was and she must get used to hearing it.

Katherine felt so much better about going to work the next morning. Mavis said she would get a chicken to roast with vegetables that night and would do that first thing so she could start sorting out the clothes. The hospital told her Stuart had had a reasonable night and she asked them to give him her love, she would be there at two. She stuffed the chicken and prepped the vegetables.

She decided to use the third bedroom to display the clothes to be photographed, half of which she couldn't remember buying, all of which she had never worn. A new set of hangers set the clothes off and in a natural light she started to take the photos. She wasn't even halfway through when she had to leave for the hospital, setting the oven to turn on automatically.

Stuart told her that a physio had been to see him and explained how she would start to get him moving. He had a programme of upper body exercises which he was determined to do. In fact he was determined that this setback would not stop him doing anything. The nurses loved him. He always greeted them with a smile and asked if he could see the stump. It was heavily bandaged but they encouraged him to gently touch it, an acknowledgement of what had happened to him. He said he was so sorry to Mavis, he was not the man she had married. She rebuked him straightaway. She said thank God, he was the man she'd married, and no one she knew could be so upbeat and positive. He relaxed and she told him that Katherine had sorted the sick pay situation and the company was meeting any shortfall.

He told her that there was a bit of a hiccup money wise. She hadn't realized the depth of the problem and felt sick to her stomach that it was all her doing. He asked her if she was all right, was she coping. Typical, there he was with half a leg and he was anxious about her. She told him about her project. He was amazed at the change in her. She had an air of confidence he had not seen before and told her so. She positively beamed. There would be no more shopping, unless it was to sell on. At the moment, selling her own wardrobe would keep her busy for a month but Kanza had told her there were outlets where you could buy cheap and sell on high. When the nurses came to change the dressing that night he told them that his wife was going to be the queen of eBay, but in a selling capacity.

Mr Lehman was in charge of his medical care, supported by a team of doctors. He introduced Stuart to the rehabilitation consultant who specialized in rehabilitation and amputee care. The physiotherapist taught him exercises to prevent blood clots initially and showed him how to transfer from the bed to the wheelchair. There was a raised platform for his stump and he soon got the hang of manoeuvring around the ward. She also showed him how to use his prosthetic leg. Mr Lehman's policy was to fit one immediately after amputation if he felt the recipient would benefit. He had been doing vigorous exercises to strengthen the muscles in the remaining limb, improving general energy levels to help cope with the demands of the artificial limb. He enjoyed his first bath, the nurses assisting him in cleaning his stump, making sure the stump didn't stay submerged for too long. He moisturized before bedtime and when he wasn't using the prosthesis.

Mr Lehman was aware of negative thoughts and emotions in his patients and hand on heart could detect none of these in Stuart. He was an exemplary patient. He would often wheel himself to the bedside of a new amputee, offering reassurance, saying, "Look at me. I'm doing okay." The nurses said this often did more good than a whole round of physiotherapy. After two weeks in hospital the wound was healing well and he had successfully used a walking aid with the physiotherapist. The swelling had considerably reduced and the prosthetist had made a cast of the stump to make a prosthesis specifically designed for him.

It was a very emotional time all round when Mavis arrived with Katherine to take him home. He had booked his rehabilitation sessions in the gym and was looking forward to using parallel bars to support his weight with his arms. The next stage would be to use a frame or elbow crutches, and then walking sticks if appropriate.

A ramp was in place and as Stuart negotiated the slope in his wheelchair Mavis felt such a rush of pride for him, the tears just splashed down her face. Friends from his work, rallied by Katherine, had moved the bed downstairs. Fortunately there was a shower room that meant he didn't need to go upstairs for anything.

Katherine had gone home the weekend before to give Mavis space, but had come for a couple of hours in the evening to help with the online selling of the clothes. She also took the parcels to the Post Office and Mavis told her she had made nearly one thousand pounds. Admittedly the clothes were the high end of the market, but unlike some sold online, they were brand new and the feedback was full of praise and appreciation.

Mavis waited until after supper to tell Stuart of her success. It was his turn to cry, he couldn't believe how hard she had worked to raise the money. She told him this was just the beginning. In future if she went shopping, it was to spend money to make money.

She marvelled at Stuart's determination to walk again. The physiotherapist was delighted with his progress and his new prosthesis enabled him to move on to elbow crutches. He was told it could take up to a year before he could properly walk again but eight months after his operation he was back at work, in the office, enjoying a different role in a job he knew well.

Mavis went from strength to strength, building her business. She had rented a unit on the nearby industrial estate and employed two ladies who loved fashion as much as she did.

It completely stopped her in her tracks when the doctor told her she was pregnant. She had gone to see her because she was feeling so tired, just didn't seem to have the energy to go upstairs and she needed to be fully fit to keep on top of things at the unit. She told her she was deficient in iron, not surprising when she was three months down the line. She was prescribed tablets and when Stuart was dropped home from work her face was a picture. "Mavis, are you all right, you look a bit different somehow?" She hugged him like there was no tomorrow. "Well, I am going to look a bit more different in a few months." He had absolutely no idea what she was going on about. "You are going to be a dad, Stu."

He felt around for the chair and sat down. "Really, are you sure? Do you mind?" She knelt down in front of him. "I always hoped, Stu. I had kind of resigned myself that it wasn't going to happen. I am three months and I could not be more happy or proud that I will be the mother of your child." Now they were both crying. He felt a wave of emotion roll over him. All that they had been through in the last year, the milestones they had reached and conquered. None of that compared to the deep feeling of pleasure, of endearing love and respect he held in his heart for her.

Neither of them could really take it in. They were in a good place. The debt had all but been paid off. Stuart was happy not to be driving. That was the only difference in his way of life right now. Mavis with her new business had grown in confidence and had adjusted to a very busy routine. Their future had never seemed so bright. "All things bright and beautiful, all creatures great and small." They were waiting to welcome a new little person into their very secure world.

38

Pauline Collins had been an administrative officer for nearly a year now. She enjoyed her work, she could really do it blindfolded. Perhaps that was why she was restless. She wasn't very sociable, or maybe she chose not to be. She wondered if she was afraid of rejection. She had noticed, and been noticed by, Christopher Wright. His smile always made her smile and he made a point of chatting to her. She did like him. She didn't feel awkward or shy with him. Just seemed to lack the confidence to take it further, hoping that he might.

She was nothing like Charmane in accounts who was everybody's friend and confidant. What she didn't know about wasn't worth knowing. She knew Alan and Frances spent too long in the stationery cupboard to be looking for envelopes and consequently everyone else knew too. She had seen Tom Perry from the warehouse holding hands with a man in the local supermarket. He hadn't seen her and she made it her business to mention, in confidence to Barnaby, what she thought he should know. This really freaked him out because he had sensed a signal, a kind of nod, from Tom that he was secretly so pleased about. It taught him you don't mess on your own doorstep that probably saved him from being the next snippet of gossip.

Pauline often thought back to how the spirits had saved her. Her car had broken down on the other side of the motorway, on the day of the worst road traffic accident in years. The breakdown man arrived and the car started, just like that. When she told him she was on her way to Hounslow, via the motorway, he said someone must have been watching out for her. Without the delay she would have been smack bang in the middle of it.

When she closed her eyes at night she saw images, almost behind her eyes, of people who had passed. She didn't know them. They just appeared and always seemed so happy. She hadn't lost anyone close. In fact she dreaded the day that it would happen. Her aunt Evelyn, her mum's sister, had died very unexpectedly and the whole family were distraught. She was only forty-nine and the post mortem results showed a massive trauma to the heart. She was a very fit woman. She had never married but had been in a relationship for four years with Nicholas. No one liked Nicholas. Pauline had met him once and try as she may she couldn't get him to respond to any topic she tried to talk about. Auntie Alice said he just wasn't a people person. He just wanted to be with Evelyn. Her sister, Pauline's mum, asked if she was truly happy. Who is ever truly happy was the reply and everyone thought you could take that two ways.

Madge Collins called her daughter to say the funeral was at the local crematorium in three weeks. She told her she would be there and asked how on earth Nicholas was getting on because he seemed only to exist for Auntie Evelyn. Madge said she and her dad had called round to see him and when they walked in the whole house was a shrine to Evelyn. There were pictures of her everywhere and candles burning in the fireplace. When Madge used the upstairs bathroom she peeked into the bedroom and her nightdress was laid out on the bed with her hairbrush and toiletries by the bath. The wardrobe was full of her clothes and there was a shoe rack with her shoes, colour coordinated.

Madge wasn't surprised about the clothes. Her friend Edna couldn't touch her husband's clothes until a year after he had died. She did think it was odd that it appeared he was just waiting for her to come home. The dining room table was laid for two, two cups were draining on the board by the sink and there were two cereal bowls on the table.

They tried their best to console him, talk to him, but he seemed on autopilot. He hadn't gone back to work. Some colleagues had called in but they were obviously greeted in the same vague way, and they hadn't come again. "What will you do Nicholas, you will have to return to work sometime, won't you?" He shrugged. "No point, Madge. She won't be here when I come back so it's best I stay home, just in case." This really didn't bode well. If he had crumbled and cried, reached out, hugged them, they maybe could have helped. "I can't understand why she died, she was happy with me, why did she leave me? I had her best interests at heart, everything I did I did for her. I know she didn't always like what I did." His voice trailed off. Madge raised her eyebrows and looked at her husband with a look that said what does that mean?

The funeral was a bleak affair, as funerals often are. Evelyn had few friends. Two colleagues from her office and a man aged about forty, Pauline thought, introduced themselves to Nicholas. Pauline looked about her to see if there was anyone she may recognize and gasped as she saw a woman at the back of the chapel. She was the spitting image of Evelyn. Before the coffin was brought in Pauline went up to the woman, introduced herself and asked her to sit with her towards the front. The woman completely froze. "I cannot let Nicholas see me, that's why I am sitting here."

Pauline didn't want to intrude although she was intrigued and as she moved to go back to her seat the doors opened and the music began. She had to stay where she was. Nicholas was walking behind the coffin, completely alone. The woman, Germaine, stood stock-still and then began to tremble. Pauline held on to her arm, trying to steady her as she sobbed. Oh my goodness, who is this woman? Why is she so bothered about Nicholas? Was she some long lost relative of Evelyn, of her own family? Nicholas led the mourners out through the door at the top of the chapel. Pauline still held

Germaine's arm, feeling her gradually relax so that she ceased to tremble.

"I had to come, Pauline. I loved Evelyn, you see. She was desperately trying to leave Nicholas. We were going to be together but she thought Nicholas might have known about us. She thought she saw him get on the train a carriage down when she was coming to meet me. I didn't see him. I was waiting on the platform and rushed to meet her. If it was him on the train he would have seen us." This was really not what Pauline had expected to hear. "Oh I am so sorry for your loss Germaine. How absolutely dreadful for you." Germaine turned to face Pauline. "You can see how I couldn't possibly face him." Pauline nodded. She wondered if the heart attack had been triggered by stress. She didn't know her aunt's medical history but if she was living in this way, trying so hard to leave him yet unable to do so, it could cause huge anxiety. "Germaine, can I meet you somewhere? I can't stay now, I have to go to the wake, but let me put my number in your phone. Can you give me yours? I can only imagine how you are feeling, but I may be able to help you, just by talking things through." Germaine passed her the phone and they exchanged numbers. "I have to go now, but I will be in touch Germaine. Do you feel able to make your way? I have my own car. My mother is in the funeral car. I will check if they have left then the coast will be clear. I will come back and let you know."

The cars were leaving. The next family of mourners was assembling in the foyer and she was able to let Germaine know there was no danger of her seeing Nicholas. Her mind was a whirl; Auntie Evelyn in love with Germaine. How sad they couldn't be together. What kind of hold did Nicholas have over her that she just couldn't up sticks and be with the woman she loved? Quite a turn up really.

The wake was a bit like the funeral, mundane, almost sparse, and when most people would welcome a glass of something stronger, there was an urn that produced something resembling coffee. Sandwiches with curled up edges stayed exactly where they were on the plate and people seemed quite keen to be able to decently leave. She hugged her mum. Madge seemed quite composed really. She was always good at finding the right thing to say to people, putting them at their ease when inside she must have been so sad. "Can I come back to yours tonight, mum? I popped a bag in the car and we haven't had any time to talk here have we? Anyway I want to give you a real hug." Madge's face said it all and after a few words with Nicholas they all made their way out.

39

Pauline hugged her mum. She was putting a casserole in the oven and her dad had opened a bottle of wine. He hugged her, poured her a glass and one for her mum. "Well, Madge, you did well today. Never easy things are they but Evelyn would have been pleased to see us there, especially you Pauly. I would have said a few words at the wake, to toast her life, but coffee doesn't quite cut it. So, please raise your glasses — to Evelyn, may you rest in peace." They clinked glasses and went into the front room.

"Where did you get to Pauly? One minute you were there then gone." Pauline explained that she had seen a woman, an actual dead ringer for Evelyn, sitting at the back. She told them she asked her to join them at the front but she didn't want to be seen by Nicholas. When she told them the reason Madge nearly choked on her wine. "Well, I never did. It just goes to show what goes on behind closed doors. We didn't have a clue about any of this, did we Reg?" She looked at her husband in disbelief. "Well, we knew she didn't seem that happy and I always thought Nicholas was a strange one. I wonder if he knew about it. We also wondered what he meant when he said Evelyn didn't always like what he did."

His voice seemed to be questioning, as if trying to figure it out. "Well, I have her number and I am going to contact her next week. I hope she will meet me. I know I haven't contacted the spirits for a long time, but with someone as close as Auntie Evelyn I think maybe I could connect. Also I have no idea what thoughts Germaine may have on the subject."

Madge mashed the potatoes and Pauline realized just how much she missed her mum's cooking, the casserole really hit the spot. Reg opened more wine and they chatted about Pauline's job and wondered again how Nicholas would cope. "Trouble is he doesn't help himself, does he? He surely has to go back to work. I don't see how he can manage without earning unless he has a stash of cash somewhere. If he did, why didn't he share if with Evelyn?" There were lots of questions and no answers to be found. They could speculate all they liked but no one really knew the truth of it.

It was a Friday and Pauline suggested they make a day of it on Saturday. Just a day to potter and be together and a trip to the garden centre followed by lunch in the pub were thoroughly enjoyed by them all. Pauline left after Sunday lunch and promised it wouldn't be so long next time before she saw them again.

Germaine said she would love to see Pauline and they arranged to meet outside a restaurant in Hounslow that they both knew. They greeted each other like old friends. The restaurant was bright and airy and the menu a bit more upmarket than pub grub, as Pauline put it. They ordered drinks and Pauline asked her how she was coping. She told her it hadn't really sunk in yet. She got up and went to work and came home again. She tried to factor in grocery shopping but a takeaway seemed so much easier. "Evelyn would be cross with me. She always cooked and said I should do the same." Pauline was glad she was able to talk about her. It helped to remember, we did that and we went there, rather than ignoring the fact that she had lived at all.

Pauline ordered gammon and pineapple with chunky chips and Germaine chose the beer-battered cod and chips. They had another glass of wine. So much to learn about someone you have just met and they discovered they both worked in admin, enjoyed swimming and walking. Evelyn and Germaine were planning a holiday in Rome. It was to be their first trip abroad as a couple. Germaine looked so sad, this wasn't going to happen now. Pauline asked why couldn't Auntie Evelyn just leave Nicholas?

"It is never that simple, Pauline. He was subject to huge mood swings. He found it difficult to relate to people and made Evelyn his whole life. He smothered her really. She in turn didn't have any friends. We met quite by chance in the library. She was hunting for a book on Rome and I was rummaging in the travel section. I picked up *The travellers guide to Italy* as she found *Explore Rome* and we both laughed because they were side by side. We clicked straight away. Italy is such a diverse country, the culture, the cities, the history and she had a huge fascination for Rome. We took our books to the counter and she asked if I had time for a coffee. I had no idea she was married. She had no idea I was not. We just put the world to rights and couldn't stop talking. She looked at her watch and gasped. She said she had to run, Nicholas would be tearing his hair out. I grabbed her hand and asked if we could meet the next Saturday, outside the library at ten. Goodness knows why I had to be so precise. I just had to see her again. I had so much to ask her."

Pauline asked for a lemon sorbet and Germaine had a chocolate brownie with double cream. Germaine explained that the Saturday meetings became a regular feature in their lives. She learned that Evelyn was in a very unsettling situation. Her husband was a control freak. She also said she was aware of feelings for Germaine. She had never felt this way before about anyone. She was only with Nicholas, she now realized, because she didn't want to be alone.

They first made love in Germaine's flat. It was an extraordinary coming together of two women, in love, making love, cementing the bond they both knew they had felt right from the start. When they were together nothing was impossible. It was only their time apart that made Evelyn so hesitant. Nicholas was to say the least unpredictable. She told him she had met a friend from years ago and they were enjoying catching up. He didn't seem to mind but he wanted to know where she was going. She lied. They were meeting at the park, would he like to come? Not his scene at all, Evelyn was thankful for that. Their liaison was becoming more urgent and it was important they met whenever they could.

He knew. He had followed her and although they walked side by side their hands didn't touch. They went into the flat and he got the train home. When she told him she wanted to leave him he said that would never happen. They would always be together and if she tried to go he would kill himself.

Poor Auntie Evelyn. Pauline wished she had told her mum or anyone that she was in this dreadful situation. They had decided to book their dream holiday. Evelyn got a new passport claiming the old one was lost. Nicholas had it in the safe. Evelyn had decided that for once she was going to put her own happiness first. If Nicholas killed himself, so be it. How dreadful was that to think that? She did however think he wouldn't have the courage, for that was what she believed it took. She wasn't responsible for his actions, he was.

They settled the bill and Germaine suggested they find a coffee shop. Pauline was waiting for the right moment to broach the subject. "Do you believe in life after death?" she asked. Germaine looked her straight in the eye. "Do you?" Pauline told her about her psychic powers explaining that a bad experience a while ago had stopped her from contacting the spirits any more. "Oh, my God. I always hoped I would be able to contact Evelyn again, but I felt it was too soon and she may not be ready to come to me." Germaine gripped Pauline's arm.

Pauline held her hand. "She is here, Germaine. She is happy where she is but so sorry she had to go. She wants you to know you were the best thing to ever happen to her. She wants you to move on, she is proud of you but no more tears." There and then the tears flowed. "Is she hurting, is she safe?" Pauline squeezed her hand. "She is very safe and healed. She says you will meet someone who will make you happy too. She wants this for you so much. She said you must go to Rome. It was your dream as much as hers." Germaine dried her eyes. "I loved her so much, I don't think I could go to Rome without her."

"She is smiling, she loves you even more now. It would make her happy if you went, she seems so sure it will be the trip of a lifetime."

Germaine sat back and the waiter refilled the cups. "I am so glad you made contact with her. I always hoped for a sign, something to let me know that she is at peace. Now I have her code to live by. Everything is booked for the holiday," Pauline said. Evelyn was standing with her arms around her. "She will be very pleased that you are going to enjoy Rome. She is saying, three coins in a fountain." At this, more tears. "That was our song and we were going to visit the fountain and do just that, throw three coins in the fountain." Pauline hugged her.

"You go for it, Germaine. Evelyn thinks you will find your happiness there and the spirits are not often wrong."

It was late now and they needed to make the last tube home. Pauline was relieved that she had been able to reach out to Evelyn. It was also good to know that she was happy. No mention of Nicholas but why would there be? Her life was with Germaine, her one true love.

"We must keep in touch." They laughed, both saying it at the same time. "Let me know about Rome. We can meet when you come back and I will hear all about it." They kissed goodbye and hugged each other. "Thank you so much Pauline, you have no idea how much you have given to me. The reassurance that we loved each other has made me so happy. I hope you can find someone that will mean as much to you as Evelyn did to me."

Sitting in an almost empty carriage Pauline saw Evelyn sit beside her. She turned to face her. "By the way, you will find Mr Right, Pauly. Your Mr Wright spells his name differently." With that she was gone, leaving a sense of peace, just before realization dawned.

40

Melanie and Laurence Stammers joined the cruise ship at Barcelona. They had never taken such a glamorous holiday. Melanie said the lead up to it seemed almost as exciting as the cruise itself. She had spent two weeks laying out her outfits with accessories, jewellery, bags and shoes. Her wardrobe was extensive. She had accompanied Laurence to so many black tie dinners it was a pleasure to select the clothes knowing it was to please Laurence, not as a status symbol to be checked out by the other wives. She was glad he appreciated dressing for dinner as much as she did. It was all part of the enjoyment.

Laurence was just happy they were able to afford such luxury, and they easily could. His salary in the Civil Service was over £150,000 a year. Their lifestyle could be described as comfortable, but the degree of comfort afforded by the salary was considerable.

The bags were taken to the cabin and they went up the zigzag walkway to enter the ship. It was quite breathtaking. An enormous round vestibule with bars and luxurious sofas greeted them and a pianist was playing one of the biggest pianos they had ever seen.

Huge chandeliers hung from a ceiling four floors up and there were three banks of lifts. Laurence returned from the bar with two glasses of champagne and they found a table in another lounge. The waiter appeared to offer complimentary snacks beautifully arranged on slate casters. They were trying to take it all in. "Mrs Stammers, I would like to propose a toast. To the most beautiful woman I have ever met. Thank you for marrying me, for supporting me and loving me." Melanie felt her eyes prickle. "To the most caring, kind and amazing husband. Here's to the holiday of a lifetime." They clinked glasses and it was announced that the suites were ready for occupation. Melanie sat watching various people standing and making their way to the lifts. Laurence said there was no rush. They could enjoy their champagne before they went.

They took the lift to the sixth floor and Laurence guided Melanie around the corner to another lift. He inserted a key and they arrived at the Queen's Suite on deck nine. Melanie was confused. As the door slid open a man in evening dress greeted them with an enormous smile. "Welcome to the Queen's suite, Mr and Mrs Stammers. I am your butler Basilio, but please call me Baz. I will be looking after you during your stay with us."

Melanie just stared at him. Laurence thanked him and they followed him into a very large room with sofas and a deep pile carpet. Beautiful drapes at the windows created a secure and luxurious effect and centre stage was a huge floral arrangement with champagne on ice and cut glass flutes. "Laurence, how are we here, is this ours?" He smiled and hugged her. "For the duration of madam's stay." Baz gave them the card that was beside the flowers. It read — 'to my dearest Mum and Dad, have the cruise of a lifetime, make memories because you deserve this so much. All our love, Christine, Mark and Hayley.'

Melanie burst into tears. "How did they know we were here? That is so kind of them. Honestly Laurence, how on earth did you do it?" He smiled, so happy she was happy. He tapped his nose. "Friends in high places." He laughed at her face, her eyebrows raised as if to say really? "I booked it as soon as I could. They go so fast and if a thing is worth doing, it's worth doing well."

Baz corked the champagne and asked them to sit down and enjoy while he told them what his duties were. He checked with Laurence if the bar had been stocked as he had ordered and he was there to troubleshoot any complaints or problems that may crop up. He told them they would get priority treatment in securing reservations for dining, entertainment and shore excursions. If they wished to dine in-cabin he would liaise with the ship's galley and would be serving meals course by course. He would be serving canapés before dinner and would be taking care of laundry.

He told them he had unpacked their suitcases and if anything needed to be rearranged he would do it at their convenience. They followed him to a huge bedroom with a double en-suite, one with a shower and the other with a bath. There was a dining room through the other door and a huge balcony ran the length of the suite.

Melanie had stayed in quite a few hotel suites but this topped the lot. She recovered her composure to offer her thanks to Baz who positively beamed at her enthusiastic gratitude. He said he would leave them to settle in and showed them the bell to summon him any time, day or night.

41

Gratitude is a two-way street. Melanie could not have come through her desperately sad, lost, dark time without Laurence. His support of her, once he realized just how ill she had become, was unswerving. His relief seeing her respond to treatment was paramount. She had finally come through the grieving process for their son. By being there for Laurence and Christine she had neglected her need to grieve. Refusing to acknowledge her sorrow plunged her into deep depression. The doctor called it a chemical imbalance in the brain.

Laurence would be forever grateful to Melanie for her strength. She had always been there, encouraging him, appreciating everything he did in his advancement to the top in his career. She rose to every social occasion, escorting him to dinners and conferences. When she lost her confidence, her ability to do even a simple task, he realized just how much she had given of herself to him.

This was so long overdue, time to be together, time to be self-indulgent. They were appreciative of each other and after another glass of champagne they undressed, got into bed and made love. They lay in each other's arms. A huge pressure they had not chosen to acknowledge was lifted. Melanie soaked in the bath. Laurence used the shower. She was looking for the kettle to make coffee. "I think that is what Baz is for," laughed Laurence, as he pushed the bell.

They watched the sail away from their balcony, waving to the people on shore as if they were the king and queen, regular cruisers of the seas. They opted to dine in-cabin, as Baz put it, and the food was superb, skilfully served and probably far too much, but they were on holiday after all.

The next morning Baz knocked on the door as arranged with tea and coffee. He pulled back the drapes and gave them the itinerary and the daily news bulletin. They were on their way to Monte Carlo and would dock late afternoon. He showed them the various excursions and left them to make their choice. He would serve breakfast in-cabin but they told him they would go to the dining room.

Their fellow cruisers were from the suites. It was exclusive to them. They politely said hello to a couple on the next table but chose one for the two of them. Laurence said rather than go on an organized excursion why not take a taxi and ask the driver to take them to the various famous sites. He was a keen F1 enthusiast and wanted to drive through the famous tunnel. Melanie wanted to see the casino. So many old films she had seen featured the ornate gaming rooms with poker tables, roulette wheels and craps tables.

Baz organized a taxi to come to the dock gates. They had told him they would like a light lunch on the tour and he reserved a table at the Horizon Deck. The taxi driver was delightful, full of information. Of course he could take them around the streets of Monaco, the F1 Grand Prix circuit. He told them the drivers got up to speeds of one hundred and eighty to two hundred miles per hour. True respect, said Laurence, he felt a bit queasy just doing sixty miles per hour through the narrow streets and the famous tunnel.

The Palais du Prince sits high above Monaco and dates from the thirteenth century when it was a Genoese fortress. The driver told them because the flag was raised in the main tower the Prince was in residence so they would be unable to visit. He told them about the ornate Throne Room and the Palatine Chapel and drove them around the grounds. Lunch had been booked for twelve thirty and they enjoyed a glass of champagne while soaking in the view of Monaco's Opera House, the Prince's Palace and the Casino, all framed in the deep blue of the Mediterranean. At their driver's recommendation they ordered the richly flavoured long burger that did not disappoint.

They were not dressed to go through to the gaming rooms of the Casino, but could enter the marble atrium with onyx columns glancing up at the ornate decadent chandeliers. Melanie could imagine the rich and famous, dressed to the nines, chancing their luck. *Casino Royale*, the famous James Bond movie had been filmed there.

She loved to see glamour, to be aware of the wealthy people who were oblivious to the amount of money they had. Her mother used to say money makes the world go round. It creates employment.

They had to be back for six p.m., the ship was sailing at seven thirty. The driver took them to the gangway. He had called ahead to Baz who was waiting to greet them. They both thanked him for such a wonderfully interesting tour and he was delighted with the rather over generous tip.

They soon settled into the luxurious experience of being pampered, waited on and waking each morning to different scenery. They opted to dress for dinner and eat in the Grillroom each night. Baz called ahead to the popular restaurants for lunch that they sampled in Florence, Rome, Naples and Messina. Being a huge James Bond fan Melanie loved Montenegro where more scenes of *Casino Royale* were filmed in the Hotel Splendid, and she relived it all. Dubrovnik was so pretty and as they had a two-day stay in Venice they spent the first sightseeing and the second shopping. Melanie loved the Venetian masks and bought several with different designs. "But I will always know it's you," Laurence laughed as she held one to her face.

They went to the ball on the last night and stood on their balcony watching the sea far below and the stars shining as the moon reflected on the dark water. They were both deep in thought, Laurence about the future, Melanie revisiting the various places in her mind. "This holiday of a lifetime has made me put things in perspective." Laurence broke the silence. "We have been spoiled and indulged and it's been wonderful. What are you thinking about?" She turned to face him. "I can take early retirement at fifty. I am fifty-two and can you imagine, after three months' notice, I will be a free man." Melanie wasn't expecting anything like this. "Financially we will be totally secure. I will get a generous lump sum, who knows, a deposit on a villa abroad?"

"But I thought you loved your job. Whatever will you do?"

"I do appreciate I have been lucky to get where I am, but the work will only get more stressful. I will need to take on more responsibility. Not always welcome at my age, but expected just the same." Melanie hugged him. "I only want you to be happy. It would be amazing if you did retire. There is so much we could do, so much to see. *The Spy Who Loved Me* was filmed in Italy and the Bahamas." At this he burst into laughter. "James Bond has a lot to answer for." They stood holding each other. Obviously he had been turning it all over in his mind but it was a bombshell to her.

"Are you sure about this? It is a complete change of lifestyle. Are you sure we will manage on your pension?" He took her face in his hands. "We will be more than secure, we will be in a position to help out Christine as well as enjoy so many more cruises. No doubt you will be able to visit nearly all the places your beloved James did." Now it was her turn to laugh. Tears cascaded down her cheeks. "Please don't be sad. I won't do this if you are not sure about it." She brushed her tears away. "These are tears of joy. Of course I am sure. It's just I never thought we could have a future like this. I thought you would be working for at least another ten years. It is because you worked so hard we can even consider this. I am right by your side." She kissed him and he kissed her back.

They went back into the lounge and Laurence rang the bell. A beaming Baz knocked and entered the room. He was carrying a tray with champagne and two flutes. "We will need one more flute Baz." He returned and corked the champagne. "Please fill the three glasses. We would like to thank you so much for showing us the very essence of luxury. The toast is Baz, thank you for the trip of a lifetime." Baz was delighted. "Thank you both for being the best guests in a lifetime." They clinked glasses and Baz thanked them again as he left.

Laurence refreshed their glasses. Melanie stood. "I have a toast. To the future retiree, Laurence Stammers. May God bless him and all who sail with him." Melanie put her glass down and they sat side by side. "We are just so lucky. Who would have thought it? We have enjoyed two weeks of sheer pleasure and we are returning to a brand new future. Bring it on." There was nothing more to be said. They were embarking on a special journey and were excited at what it would bring. They say into every life a little rain must fall. They had weathered the worst of storms. The rainbow stretched to infinity and beyond.

42

Sarah Cook answered the telephone to her son Adrian. She was always so pleased to hear from him. He checked in most days in his busy schedule. He had also kept in contact with his dad, Clive. Since the divorce Clive had descended into a gloomy existence. He could find no pleasure in anything any more. He never gave a thought to Kiri. She was his past. She had tried at the beginning to keep in touch, but it was awkward. She sensed his reluctance to engage in any conversation and gradually had to accept that the man she loved more than life itself did not love her back.

He now worked out of the office in London. He had no need to travel to New York. He was grateful to have been offered his current post, totally Europe based. No old contacts to have to face when his life was crumbling. They wouldn't see his loss. They had actually thought he was not one hundred percent in the last few months. The car crash that nearly killed his wife seemed to have half killed him.

His daughter Sapphire asked him to stay with them, until he could sort out a place of his own. He was glad to accept. Anything that appeared normal helped. He even adapted to his granddaughter Molly's non-stop talking about total rubbish. At three she was full of life and expected him to play hide and seek if he wasn't blowing bubbles or building towers for her to gleefully knock down. One of twins, she was the livewire to Liam's less dramatic approach to life. He had spent several weeks in Great Ormond Street Hospital for children when he was two because at birth he weighed twenty-five percent less than Molly. The hospital regularly checked on him and with careful monitoring he was gradually gaining weight. Sapphire was with him at the hospital when her mother had the accident. Her husband John's mum, Isobel, had come up trumps looking after Molly while she was with Liam. She wanted to go to her mum but she was also needed at the hospital with Liam. John said they would keep her up to date and Clive was with her and Adrian could get there within the hour.

Sapphire was worried about her dad. She told her mum he was kind of broken. She couldn't go on about it too much. After all he had cheated on her, not the other way round. It wasn't anything to do with her mum. It was all self-inflicted but he was her dad after all and if she could do anything to make things easier for him she would.

After a few months he seemed to be coming out of his despair. He always responded to Molly, who went into his bedroom every morning to make sure he was awake. "Are you awake, Granddad?" He tried desperately to keep his eyes closed but each morning she whispered that she knew he was awake really and bounced on his head. Liam was happy just sitting on his lap looking at books.

There was a new account he had acquired for the company that operated in London and France. The London agent set up a meeting with him and Clive in Paris. The trip had done good things for his confidence. He had a smattering of French but they all spoke English so there was no language barrier. He was a good salesman, now fully committed to proving he hadn't lost his spark. It had been temporarily dimmed, but was now sharper and brighter.

Sapphire could see this change in him and she felt relieved. She supposed that in a way he had been grieving. Grieving for his wife and marriage. Their paths never crossed. Sarah had completely changed her way of life.

Immediately after the accident she began her slow recovery. Physiotherapy and occupational therapists did their job and she gained strength in her body. It was her soul that needed equal care. Her confidence had waned. Little by little her sparkle returned. She smiled a lot more. She didn't think too deeply. She took things at face value, didn't look for any hidden agendas. She delighted in the twins and was pleased to see Liam gaining weight and playing more.

She had always been attractive with a good dress sense. Her friend Tessa worked at the airport meeting and greeting VIPs and she loved it. You never knew whom you might be escorting from one day to the next. She suggested Sarah might enjoy it. There was no pressure. You had to be articulate, attractive (although that wasn't on the job description of course) and a people person. Sarah had been feeling bored. There were only so many Pilates classes you could do. Shopping wasn't her forte. Her wardrobe from when she worked for John Bartlett was full of designer labels.

Tessa drove her to the airport. Junction Four on the M4 loomed. She realized she must be a lot stronger now because to go past the site where she nearly died didn't really bother her: A little flip in her tummy that was all. She was introduced to Maurice Fieldman, the director of the company. He liked what he saw. Really, being attractive was a very important part of the job. He was impressed by her c.v. and the way she conducted the interview. It rather felt like that to him. She was leading with the questions and he was following. He offered her the job. The starting salary was generous. Her hours could be flexible. Obviously it was a twenty-four seven operation but she could choose. Some people wanted the late flights, early mornings. She said she would let him know. She needed to talk it over with her son.

Adrian was delighted to see his old mum back, animated and hugely excited about the job opportunity. "You don't need my input Mum, look at you, you are bouncing." Tessa preferred the late afternoon early evening flights and Sarah went for the morning shift, eight to four. Her job was to meet her clients at the steps of the plane and escort them through customs. Once their luggage had cleared it was taken to the hire car or to the gate of the next onward flight. She took them to the VIP lounge, signed them in and arrived promptly to take them to the next gate. Quite often she rode in the buggy with them.

She was a good conversationalist and could engage in many topics. Film stars, television personalities, famous people from the world of sport and fashion editors, she greeted them with the same professional courtesy. She particularly loved the young unaccompanied children. They were so confident, obviously used to the trappings of wealth but not precocious, as some of her clients seemed to be. Precious was what Tessa called that particular type of client and she was glad that Sarah enjoyed the job as much as she thought she would.

She listened to Adrian who sounded very excited. "Mum, I am going to get married." "Oh my goodness, finally." This woman had to be someone very special. All his other romances never stayed the course. He had brought her to meet Sarah several months ago. She was introduced as Nicole, Nicky for short. They had met at a party and had stayed together ever since. Sarah always went by first impressions and she thought Nicky was delightful in every way. They were so at ease with each other. She thought they made a handsome couple. He could be volatile, very charming and always polite.

Nicky introduced a great sense of humour to the equation.

Sarah smiled. She remembered the first flush of love, the heady rush you get, the feeling of pure joy. "Darling, that is wonderful news, I am so happy for you." He said they would love to meet up with her. She looked at her shifts and she was clear Friday through to Monday. They settled on Saturday. He suggested they pick her up and they make a day of it.

Sarah selected a cream trouser suit with a pale peach cashmere jumper, Gucci handbag and a pair of Jimmy Choo ankle boots in pale peach. She still used her signature Red Door perfume and was ready at the door when they both knocked. "Please come in Nicky. Would you like coffee, tea?" Nicky kissed her, both sides of her cheek and hugged her. Adrian was smitten to say the least. She was stunning.

Her fair hair was pulled back into a pleat and the pale blue sweater complemented her eyes with huge lashes. She wore a pair of black leather trousers that enhanced her stunning figure. "No thanks, we haven't long had breakfast, but you go ahead." Sarah said she was fine and they sat in the lounge, side by side, holding hands. "First of all I must congratulate you on your news. Are you engaged?" Nicky jumped up and showed a stunning aquamarine stone surrounded by diamonds on her wedding finger. "That is very special, Nicky." Adrian said she would be very proud of him because he asked her dad for permission to marry his daughter, manners and all that. "Obviously he said yes," Adrian laughed. "Well if you call, you make your bed, you lie on it, meant yes, I guess he did." It was Sarah's turn to laugh out loud.

There were so many questions she wanted to ask but she decided things would come out gradually rather than a barrage of who, where, etc. Adrian had booked a table for lunch in Covent Garden. He suggested they leave the car at Hounslow and go by Tube to Covent Garden station. It was only a short walk to the historic market and its sprawling traffic-free piazza. There were so many upscale fashion and beauty boutiques with restaurants and bars lining the streets. He took them to a large area of tables and chairs under umbrellas, gave his name and they were directed to a table for three.

They could comfortably sit and talk face to face and when the champagne arrived Adrian stood. "I would like to propose a toast to my beautiful fiancé, thank you for agreeing to marry me. I don't want to be presumptuous but I believe our future is beyond bright." He sat down and they kissed and clinked glasses. "Do you have any brothers and sisters?" Sarah asked. "I have a younger brother Charlie, named after my dad and a sister Nigella who is married." They scanned the menu. Sarah ordered fish and salad and they chose a seafood platter to share. "Have you told Sapphire and John yet?" The waiter brought a sample plate with little canapés. "Not yet. We wanted to tell them in person so they will be our next visit."

They chatted away. Nicky was brought up in north London, living with her mum and dad. Sadly her mother had passed away far too young and she had stayed at home to help out. She said her dad was a strong man and although it had hit him hard, he was determined the family would stay together. He changed his job to be nearer home and was a photographer in his spare time. "He has done quite well, you may have heard of him, Charlie Gilbert."

Sarah hadn't heard of him, but she knew the name. "I wonder, years ago, before Clive obviously, I went out with a Charlie Gilbert. He was really tall and he was always playing tricks on me. Would be too much of a coincidence really wouldn't it?" The waiter cleared the canapés and the food arrived. "Where did you grow up then mum?" Sarah sipped her champagne. "Finsbury Park, north London. Charlie and I went to school together. I was Sarah Robinson then." The food was superb. Her plaice, stuffed with prawns and served with a lemon sauce was complemented by a herb salad. "Oh my goodness, wouldn't it be crazy if he was the same Charlie?"

Nicky was really excited. "I can't phone him now, he is doing a wedding today. Actually he will do ours and that will be wonderful. I will call him tonight and find out."

Adrian said they could recommend an Expresso Martini as they were too full for dessert. Sarah hadn't had one before but it was delicious and what with the champagne, she felt quite light headed. They sat enjoying the sun, watching people strolling by, carrying smart carrier bags with their recent purchases.

Adrian ordered another two expressos but Sarah just wanted a black coffee. "So when is the big day? Have you found a venue? There must be so much to organize." Nicky took Sarah's hand over the table. "I would love it if you can help with the planning, Sarah. You will become my mum and without you I wouldn't have Adrian. I would be so pleased if you can be in right at the start." Adrian kissed her. "She's all right, isn't she mum?" Sarah was very touched. "All right doesn't do her justice Adrian." And she kissed Nicky. "I would be honoured to help in any way I can. That is just so sweet of you, thank you." Adrian said they had sourced a venue, a hotel in a country park. They had been lucky, there had been a cancellation and it was to be Friday the twelfth of August. "This year?" asked Sarah. "I know, four months away, and that's four months too long!"

They left the restaurant and walked to the Opera Quarter, the Yards and the Seven Dials. It was such a vibrant, buzzing atmosphere it took hold of you and carried you along. It was a very happy day, not least because of the wedding plans. Just to see her son so happy with such a beautiful young woman thrilled Sarah's heart.

Later that evening Nicky called. Her dad remembered Sarah Robinson. He said she was very pretty with very long legs. Sarah roared with laughter.

"Well, it will certainly be good to meet up after all this time. I'll leave it in your capable hands Nicky. Thank you both so much for today. I have had a wonderful time." Nicky blew a kiss down the phone. Well, well thought Sarah, stranger things have happened. She remembered a good kisser, but they didn't do any heavy stuff. They were more mates than boyfriend and girlfriend. She found herself looking forward to meeting him again. A lot of water under the bridge, life does that.

43

Sarah told Tessa about the engagement and she was so pleased for her friend. Monday evening Sapphire phoned to say how thrilled she was for her big brother. "I really like her mum and the ring is a whopper. Dad likes her too and she asked me to be matron of honour with her sister Nigella." Sarah could see things so far seemed to be falling into place. Of course she would meet Clive again. It wasn't a problem. It's just strange that someone who once was your whole life is no longer in it. She said to Sapphire that they should all meet up. Sapphire couldn't believe Nicky's dad and her mum went to school together. "Did you love him then mum?" She was laughing. At sixteen you can fall head over heels but this wasn't the case. They were good mates and it would be fun to meet up after so long.

Nicky arranged with Sapphire, Nigella and Sarah to meet the following weekend for the all-important dress shopping. She asked her matrons of honour what sort of style, colour they had in mind. She was going for ivory and as it was a summer wedding any colour would go. There were so many different styles. They suggested concentrating on Nicky's dress first so they would have a rough idea of possibly replicating the style.

Sarah remembered Sapphire's wedding, as clear as day. Clive was so emotional as he walked her down the aisle, such a proud father of a beautiful bride. Now it was happening all over again, for their son. The pressure was nothing like before, as in mother of the bride and checking that John's mum's outfit didn't clash with her own. She felt far more relaxed and this was due in no small part to Nicky's calm approach. However, when she emerged in the fourth choice, they all burst into tears. She was so graceful, exquisitely beautiful. "Don't start me off." She laughed. After trying the ball gown effect, the mermaid and the sheath style, the trumpet wedding dress did everything the others did not. The silhouette was less fitted through the hips and gradually got wider at the lower thigh. The strapless bodice created the dramatic look and the overall impression enhanced her natural curves. The ivory silk had a sheen that seemed to reflect her glowing smile. Simplicity personified.

The wedding consultant tweaked it in a couple of places and the final fitting would be in two weeks. They found a bistro and had a glass of wine and a sandwich to prepare them for the next round, the matrons of honour. Another huge selection was available for them to choose. They were both about the same height and both felt the sheath style would not take away anything from the bride. Nude and blush were the colours and both girls felt very comfortable and looked amazing standing side by side.

"Just one thing," Nigella said. They looked at her. She wasn't going to cry was she? "I may be pregnant." Nicky rushed up and hugged her and everyone was crying now. "Oh Nigella, I am so thrilled for you, that is such happy news." Nigella sat down. "We're not supposed to say anything until twelve weeks. I think I am eight. Do you still want a fat matron waddling down the aisle?" Nicky roared with laughter. "It will be the icing on the cake." The consultant checked that the dress could be let out and there was room. "You will be possibly five to six months by August, all being well. We can easily accommodate you in this style."

She took the measurements of both girls and their final fitting — although not in Nigella's case — would be the same day as Nicky's. They had a coffee on the top floor of the department store and all in all had enjoyed a very successful shop.

Sarah hadn't really thought about her own outfit, but felt she should buy new. She asked Sapphire, Nicky and Nigella if they were up for yet another shop and they jumped at the chance. Harvey Nichols on the corner of Knightsbridge and Sloane Street in London was the venue and Sarah had reserved a table in the terrace on the fifth floor for lunch. She had always admired the designer Stella McCartney and felt she would be able to select something from her exciting range. Bearing in mind the ivory and nude blush shades the bride and bridesmaids would be wearing, she chose several dresses in pale shades of pink and pastel blue.

The girls were enchanted by her elegance, she had such confidence and it was hard to choose. Sarah was hoping they would agree on her preferred choice: a ruffled silk and lurex jacquard dress in the palest pink. She didn't need to have any doubts. They jumped up when she entered the room, the most beautiful mother of the groom. She wasn't sure whether she should wear a hat or fascinator. The girls were not sure but the assistant, who could have been a model, selected a "hatinator" a cross between a hat and a fascinator. She placed it on her head on the right hand side, towards the front and it looked stunning. A slightly deeper shade of pink and when teamed with a pair of nude shoes with a dainty heel, the picture was complete.

Lunch was deliciously light and flavoursome and champagne was the only possible accompaniment. Sarah was thrilled with her shopping and it was a good opportunity to learn more about Nicky and Nigella. Sapphire also enjoyed their company, chipping in with various anecdotes of her own and the non-stop chatter and laughter ended a perfect afternoon.

44

Charlie Gilbert was an entrepreneur. When he was fourteen he bought five chickens. He built a henhouse and used the leftover vegetables to cook up for the mash. He then sold the eggs to his mother — but he did give her a discount. He left school at sixteen and began working in the sales office of a local stonemason's yard in North London. His father was more than relieved that he had found work that kept him busy six days a week.

Prior to leaving school he and his friend worked on motorbikes, buying them from a dealer in Harringay for not a lot, repairing them and selling them on. He used the garage to store the machines and worked on them in the drive. Oil spillage was the least of his worries. The neighbour complained about the noise of the revving engines and his father rented him a lock up around the corner to take the whole messy noisy affair out of his domain. He and his friend Lionel, known as Li, were doing very nicely, thank you. Li drove the bike to the buyer while Charlie followed in his second hand Ford Capri. He had applied for a driving licence and his father had paid for specialist insurance for the first year known as PIP. He realized his father had put up with quite a lot to get him on the road, literally and metaphorically.

The stone yard moved to near Heathrow Airport and that added three hours driving to his day. He would leave at six thirty to avoid the traffic and return after eight p.m. He was a popular young man and by talking to the masons he learned all about the stone they cut and where it came from. He earned good money and after paying rent to his mother he was able to save, mainly because his work gave him little time for anything else.

It was a shock to be told that the company was going to be taken over by a large building concern. His job was not in the equation. His knowledge of the types of stone, the suppliers and buyers stood him in good stead. The company's supply of stone was part of the package so he focused on finding a yard nearer to his home while he worked his month's notice.

Yet again his father stepped in as guarantor for the rent, which, although it wasn't a lot, freed up his savings to buy in stock. He kept his contacts in the building trade, offering to supply them at ten percent less than any rival. His father told him it was a tight margin, could he still make a profit? He actually could and took on two stonemasons and a yard foreman to make his business grow.

He went on the road, upgrading his car to create the right impression to source new customers. He secured a contract from various councils when they needed to clear cemeteries (which you could when the graves were more than one hundred years old) and the stone stock grew considerably. He formed another company to build fireplaces in natural stone. Quite often the customer would also want a garden wall in the same stone that presented another opportunity to make money.

He was so happy to be able to pay his father back and made him a director of his new limited company. He was going from strength to strength, supplying garden centres with rockery stone, patio slabs and gravel and asphalt for driveways.

By the time he was twenty-four he had a flourishing business. He had built an office that housed a secretary (who was also the receptionist, telephonist and cleaner). Mrs Caplain was the bookkeeper. She was very popular with the masons as she always had a supply of cake.

It was when a prestigious client wanted to visit the yard to see the "whole operation" Charlie realized he would need to smarten things up. He had always referred to the yard as 'head office' giving the impression it was top of the range. Consequently he extended the office to include a modest reception area and employed a very attractive young lady to run it. A kitchen was built on at the back and tiles and carpeting were a good replacement for the wooden floors. He had told the client he was refurbishing the yard and invited him six weeks later to see how things worked. The client was very impressed, particularly with Jacqueline, the receptionist. He told Charlie he was lucky to have such an employee, efficient as well as totally stunning.

Charlie had not really noticed just how lovely she was. His mother and father came to see the new layout and his mother said how on earth had he managed to find such a glamorous lady to work in a rather off the beaten track place?

Jacqueline was completely unaware of the fact that whenever she got out of her car, swinging her long legs out of the door, straightening up and reaching for her bag, every eye was watching her walk to the office door. Charlie had not really had much time to think about anything but work concentrating on the general running of a very successful business. He had the odd date but couldn't really spare the time to be a full time boyfriend.

He was sharing a flat with a mate and when he left he decided he would go to live at his parents' house until he could find somewhere else. He got the third degree when he returned for supper, albeit it at nine. "Charlie, what a stunner Jacqueline is. Is she married, she looks about twenty, just a bit younger than you?" his mother asked. He was hungry and said between mouthfuls he really didn't know, his secretary dealt with the hiring of staff. "Well, you must be totally blind Charlie Gilbert. Not only is she efficient, she lights up the room. There is more to life than just work you know."

He was in the office most mornings for seven and when her car arrived at the depot he looked at her for the first time without thinking of the next order to be sent out. He was very aware of how everyone was looking at her and even more surprised she seemed not to notice. "Hello Charlie, how are you?" He smiled. "I am very well thank you Jacqueline, how are you?" She put her jacket on a hanger on the coat stand and settled in behind her desk. "I am fine thank you. I think we are on top of the backlog after the printer broke, so that's a relief." He really hadn't looked at her before. Her brown hair was cut to frame her face. Her smile was all encompassing and it came from her hazel eyes as well as her mouth. He hoped he wasn't staring. He wondered how on earth he hadn't noticed her before. He was always in work mode, never had much time to be sociable.

He went into the office and searched in the filing cabinet for the personnel files. She was twenty, single, and living in a flat in Edmonton, about half an hour's drive away.

He walked back to the reception area and a florist was delivering the biggest bouquet he had ever seen. Jacqueline was saying they couldn't possibly be for her. "Are you Jacqueline, Miss?" The man seemed a little cross, he thought such a lovely young lady must be used to this kind of attention. "Yes, yes that is my name, but I don't know who would send me flowers." The man just looked at her. "Really? There is a card Miss, I suggest you read it and you will know." She opened the envelope. The card read — Flowers are not able to hold a candle to you, kindest regards, Jason Greenwood.

"I don't know a Jason Greenwood." Charlie felt a little tightening in his chest. "He is one of our best clients, Jacqueline. He saw you when he visited the office. He was obviously very impressed — and quite right too." He felt a little superfluous standing there. Mrs Caplain was totally amazed by the magnificent bouquet. "Luckily they are in water so they will last till you get them home." The scent was already permeating the whole area. "Oh no, I couldn't possibly take them home. I will bring in a vase tomorrow. They really brighten up the whole area. Do you have a phone number for Mr Greenwood, Charlie?" He scrolled down his phone and wrote down the number. "Thank you, I will call him from here if I may?" Charlie said of course, and made a hurried exit to his office.

He reckoned Jason was about thirty and he knew he wasn't married, not that that made a difference these days. Jacqueline was a free agent and if he chose to send her flowers that was fair enough. He was miffed though. It was as if he was moving in on something he himself felt he should be doing.

He went into the yard and checked over the next order that was the stone to build a fireplace, checking on all the materials. He busied himself outside, checking with the mason who was going to build it, making sure he was confident about what he had to do. Of course he was, he had been doing it for a long time.

That night at supper, and he was early for a change, he told his parents about the bouquet and his mother smiled. Finally, he was taking an interest and he didn't seem that pleased about it. He went to the pub that evening and met up with a few mates to celebrate a birthday. They were all about the same age, one had just passed his articles in an accountancy firm, one was a sales rep and one was a van driver. They knew how well Charlie had done for himself but that was all down to hard work while they enjoyed a busy social life and playing the field. Colin was quite a ladies' man. "Hey Charlie, why haven't you got a girl? I reckon you could have your pick if you stopped thinking about work all the time." Charlie smiled at him. "Well actually, there is someone at work but I don't think she even notices me." He went to the bar and ordered another round. "How do you know that mate? She could be fancying the pants off you." Charlie put the tray of drinks on the table. "One of our best clients sent her flowers today, I think he fancies his chances with her." He sat down. "Oh really. How do you know she fancies him?" Charlie stared at his beer. "Well, it was the biggest bouquet I have ever seen. She said she would bring in a vase tomorrow because she thought they brightened up the reception area." Colin looked at him. "So she isn't even going to take them home then? Can't think that much of the bloke, can she?" Charlie hadn't looked at it that way. "The way I see it, she can't go up to you, the boss, and make a pass now can she? You can though. Ask her if she would like to go out for a drink Friday night." They were all on the case now. "If you don't ask you don't get mate, take it from me. She can always say no, but if she says yes, well, you have scored."

Charlie lay awake that night. He turned things over in his head, not only stuff about Jacqueline, but his future in general. He had enough money to put a sizeable deposit down on a house. His father had always said you would not go wrong investing in property. Things gradually began to become less foggy. He was beginning to make a plan and he was beginning to get a positive feeling that things may just be starting to happen.

Jacqueline was arranging the flowers when he walked into reception. He didn't really want to know what Jason had said when she phoned to thank him. It wasn't his place to ask, although he was dying to find out. "Aren't they beautiful, Charlie?" He nodded. He wanted to say you are too. "Mr Greenwood was pleased I liked them and wondered if I would be able to join him for supper at the weekend." Charlie's heart sank. "That is nice of him, Jacqueline." She turned to face Charlie. "It is, but I politely told him I was busy. To be fair I vaguely remember him and not in that kind of way." Charlie went from despair to hope. "Oh, I see. Can I ask are you with someone?" She roared with laughter. He was taken aback. Had he been rude, intrusive? "No Charlie, I am free as a bird. Little white lies aren't that bad, are they Charlie?" If you don't ask, you don't get. "I was wondering if you might like to go out for a drink after work on Friday night. I could pick you up around seven if that would be all right?" He didn't expect the enormous smile that lit up her face. "I would love to

Charlie, seven would be fine. I can give you my address, I don't live far away." He nearly said I know where you live, but nodded and took the slip of paper from her.

His mother noticed a far happier Charlie than she had seen in a long time. He had spoken to his father about buying a house. It would have to be fairly near the yard and he had contacted a couple of estate agents in the area. It was all a bit sudden. A huge change of heart and when he said he had asked Jacqueline out his mother jumped up and hugged him. "Well Charlie, in one day you have asked a beautiful young lady out and decided to buy a house. Whatever next?"

Jacqueline always looked smart and attractive but when she opened the door in a figure-hugging red dress, his heart flipped. He opened the car door and her legs seemed to go on forever showcased by really high heels. She immediately put him at ease, chattering away as they entered the pub and again the heads turned and she just looked straight ahead. She asked for a white wine and he ordered a pint and they sat in a corner, totally absorbed by one another. "Have you eaten?" Charlie asked. "No, I thought it would be a bit of a rush." He asked for the menu and they both chose fish and chips with mushy peas. He ordered another wine for her and he learnt how she had gone to secretarial college gaining a diploma in shorthand and typing. She had left her previous job because the boss wanted the salesmen to use Dictaphones. It was more economical than going back into the office to dictate to her. Also he was considering retiring so it didn't bode well. He told her how he had always wanted to work for himself. Also that he was going to buy a house, to get on the property ladder.

On the way home he said he had details of a couple of houses to view on the Saturday. Would she like to go with him? She said she was flattered to be asked and would really enjoy it. He walked her to the door and she put her key in the lock. "You are welcome to come in for coffee, Charlie." To this day he still remembers how he hesitated and said it was a bit late, he had a few things to do but could he pick her up at nine thirty? All the way home he was kicking himself. He didn't have anything to do, he was just not used to dating.

The details of the first property they looked at were, to say the least, using poetic licence. The rooms were obviously photographed using a telescopic lens and the 'conservatory' was slightly better than a lean to. You would have to be an athlete to manage to get into the bed in the main bedroom and the 'box room' was just that, suitable for a box. Charlie was disappointed but she told him how she experienced exactly the same when she was looking for her flat. "You have to kiss a lot of frogs," she told him, then thought, did I really say that?

The agent called him while they were on their way to the second property telling him that a detached house in his price range had just been put back on the market after the sale had fallen through. Charlie told him that they would look at the scheduled property first and would it be possible to have a viewing around three. "I know a lovely restaurant in the forest for lunch, would that be okay with you?" She smiled. "I am in your hands Charlie, sounds wonderful." I wish you were in my arms, thought Charlie.

The bungalow was compact with a beautifully laid out garden. The agent explained that the elderly widow really could no longer manage the garden and the property itself was too big for her now. He liked it. When they were back in the car he asked her what she thought. "I thought it was very nice, maybe a bit out of the way, but it's your home, not mine." He appreciated her thoughts, but was thinking actually, it could be ours.

The restaurant was fairly busy and they sat at a table looking out onto the rear garden with roses in full bloom. It was a steak house but the menu was extensive. They shared a plate of nachos topped with Cheddar cheese sauce, tomato salsa and cream, smashed avocado and jalapenos. Jacqueline enjoyed a white wine and Charlie tried the local ale. She chose the sea bass and he a rib eye steak.

Charlie said that she was quite young to be able to rent her own flat that was quite an achievement. Her face clouded, as if a huge shadow was over her. "My mother and father were killed in a motorway accident. I was their only child and I inherited quite a bit of money. I didn't want to commit to buying anything until I could clear my head." Charlie was mortified. The last thing he wanted was to upset her. "Please forgive me. I had no idea." He covered her hand with his. "How could you know? It was two years ago, yet it still feels raw. However, life goes on and you have to pull yourself up and get on with it." The food arrived, piping hot and cooked to perfection. "Please don't worry Charlie, I would have told you sooner or later anyway. In a way it was a blessing they went together, they were devoted you see." This didn't make him feel any better. "They will be more than proud of you. You are totally amazing. Beautiful and talented and getting on with life. I am so happy you came to work for me." She smiled. "I am too, very happy." The waiter brought them the dessert menu. "Oh my goodness, my absolute favourite, raspberry crème brûlée," exclaimed Jacqueline. He laughed. "If that is what madam would like, madam will have." They both laughed and he decided on the same.

The ice was broken. He felt so much more at ease with her, she seemed to glow, he thought. The detached house in red brick had a sweeping drive and a huge green beech tree in the front garden. Charlie checked the price on his phone. With a wing and a prayer he could afford it. Jacqueline's eyes opened wide as the agent took them through the hall. A sweeping staircase led to a landing. There were three good-sized bedrooms and a bathroom and shower room. A short flight of stairs led to a huge en-suite bedroom.

In the hall one way led to a kitchen with utility room. The dining room was adjacent. From the other side of the hall you entered a huge lounge with a fireplace central to the two main windows with two sets of sofas. The agent explained that the previous buyers couldn't raise the capital but he considered it to be reasonably priced. "The kitchen is the room that is important to the lady," he smiled at Jacqueline. "It is very important, what do you think?" She dug him in the ribs. "It seems perfectly equipped, even two ovens doesn't appear too much." Charlie laughed. The agent said he would leave them to have another look around. They felt less hurried without the agent and really noticed quite a few more nooks and crannies.

Charlie told the agent he would like to make an offer. He could see Jacqueline was blown away, but even if it was just for him he felt immediately at home. The agent said he would contact his client and let him know by the end of the day. The name of the house was Sanscesse. She googled it. "It means constantly, forever Charlie." This just gets better and better, he thought.

"I am parched, maybe there is a coffee house around here. Did you like the house?" he asked. "I thought it was amazing. The rooms are large and I don't think there is anything I would change. Oh that came out all wrong. What I mean is it all seems just fine as it is." He laughed. There was a café with bow windows just along the high street that was a five-minute drive from the house. The waitress brought a cafetiere and gave them the cake menu. "Goodness, I couldn't eat another thing, thank you." They squeezed two cups each and settled back. "I am taking up too much of your time aren't I? It is your Saturday off work after all." She looked him straight in the eye. "I am having the best time. I do hope the agent comes back to you soon." He checked his phone. "So do I. In fact it would be lovely if you can wait with me to hear what he has to say." She smiled and brushed his hand with hers. "I have absolutely no plans. I would love to know how it turns out." They didn't have long to wait. The agent called and said his offer had been accepted. The sellers were anxious to get things moving as soon as possible. Would it be possible he could get to the agent's office this afternoon?

"I will wait in the car, Charlie. This is your personal business." He leapt out and opened her door. "There is nothing private or personal. You were in at the start of it all and I hope you will be in at the end." That didn't quite come out the way he thought it would. "I love the way you thought two ovens didn't seem too much." He took her hand and he thought this could be the first day of the rest of my life.

He gave the agent all the necessary information. He would use the solicitor he had before when he bought the yard. He asked if a deposit was required and the agent said that would be needed when contracts were exchanged. The agent said that for a small fee, they would be able to use the searches carried out for the buyer who couldn't complete so that would speed things up. The agent shook their hands and said he would start the ball rolling and would keep in touch.

It was all a bit of a whirl. He hoped he wasn't jumping the gun but he felt he really wanted Jacqueline to be a part of this new venture. "Shall we go and have another look?" He took her hand as they walked around the garden and peered in the windows. "It seems to be a very happy house to me." She was laughing as she said it and he just looked at her. He pushed her hair away from her eyes, took her face in his hands and kissed her. She kissed him back. "Where do we go from here?" he asked. She kissed him again. "I think this calls for champagne." They found a pub just down the road. It was a lovely welcoming old-fashioned type of place and they went through to the garden. He asked the waiter to bring champagne. They clinked glasses. "The toast is Sanscesse, a forever house." They both started talking at the same time. She was so happy for him. It certainly was a lovely place. He poured her another glass. "I had better stop right now or I won't be able to drive." She smiled. "Then let's take the bottle to my flat. We can finish it there and there is wine in the fridge."

They didn't finish the champagne, at least not until much later. She opened the front door and he was kissing the back of her neck. She turned and their lips met and she opened the bedroom door. It was so normal and so necessary. He unzipped her dress and she faced him, her breasts brushing his face as she undid her bra. He was naked and laid her gently on the bed. He tugged at her panties and kissed her mouth, her neck. She was trying to reach him, to caress him but he slid down to where she ached to be touched. He kissed her, stroked her with his strong fingers, feeling her inside as she began to moan. She drew her legs up and as he entered her she felt a deep want, an almost raw need. He moved slowly, then more urgently, wanting to please her before himself and as she gasped and gripped he let himself give his all. He moved to lie beside her. Tears were falling down her face. "Darling, did I hurt you?" he asked anxiously. "Oh no, I just feel so wonderfully happy." He learned very early on in their relationship that whenever she was truly happy, she cried.

45

He left Sunday evening. They hadn't really got up. She made some toast when they woke and found some chops in the freezer for supper. It all just flowed. No awkwardness, as if this was always how it was, how it would be.

She had admired the way he ran his business. He was a handsome man, not in any way showy but he just oozed confidence and he was very fair. She knew deep down it was more than just respect for what he did. She really wanted to be a part of his life. It seemed as if that could possibly happen. She could dare to dream. How could you know how things would turn out? She knew he felt the same, whispering words of love and as he went out of the door, he came straight back, kissed her and said he loved her. She held on to him, tears came again. Happy tears, he knew that now. "I love you too."

His parents were thrilled. So much had happened in such a very short time. He took them to see the house. They were delighted by the property and equally proud that their son was able to afford it, and manage the mortgage. They were even more impressed when he took Jacqueline for dinner. Privately they had thought he would never get around to romance, far too busy with work, but were so glad they were wrong.

The house completed in two months. Charlie was very emotional one morning when Jacqueline arrived at the office. "Charlie, what's wrong, you seem upset?" He took her in his arms. "Maybe I am catching your happy tears. Mum and Dad have paid the deposit on the house. They had arranged to meet the solicitor without me knowing. I called to say I would make an appointment to sort it and they told me it has been done." She hugged him so tight and kissed him right there in the office. "What a wonderful gift Charlie, I am so happy for you."

She helped him move his stuff in and the sellers had agreed a price for the furniture. He ordered a takeaway and produced a bottle of champagne. She sat on the sofa and he went down on one knee. "Jacqueline, you have made me so happy. I want to be with you always. Will you do me the honour of being my wife?" He produced a small box that contained a diamond ring, a huge diamond actually. Tears, laughter, she couldn't speak. "It is I who am honoured Charlie. Yes, yes, oh my goodness, yes." The deliveryman thought he had the wrong house but finally Charlie got to the door, apologizing saying he couldn't find his wallet. "That's okay, mate, thought I would be eating it myself. Enjoy."

She moved her belongings in the next day. The rent was paid to the end of the month but that wasn't at all important. When his parents opened the door to see two beaming young people, Charlie holding out her left hand, they were delighted to say the least. "Dad, you look as though your horse has just won the National." Lots of hugging and kissing ensued. His dad found the wine and they toasted the happiest of futures. They didn't want a big wedding. Although Charlie had said to her that her parents would be so glad for her, he sensed she would miss them too much.

It was just a quiet affair in the village church. She asked her best friend to be her bridesmaid and Colin was the best man. His mates couldn't believe the transformation in such a short time, but when Charlie's dad walked her down the aisle, there really wasn't a dry eye in the house.

46

Their marriage was made in heaven. Charlie decided to invest in property, still running the stone business, and buying up rundown houses. He used his stone company to do the renovation work and was often away overseeing the build. Nigella came into their lives a little unexpectedly. They wanted children but hadn't planned for them just yet. Jacqueline was a wonderful mum and Nicky came along eighteen months later. Charlie was the son they had hoped for and family life and work ran smoothly, in no small way due to Jacqueline's juggling school runs and office work. Mrs Reynolds came to clean and generally help out around the house and they always had a holiday every year. It was a special time to spend together.

Jacqueline began to feel tired. Charlie's mum said she was doing far too much but Charlie told mum she loved it. All the same he noticed she was losing weight and made a doctor's appointment. Blood tests showed nothing abnormal but things were not right. She went for a scan that showed no abnormalities. It was a test for insulin that showed the pancreas was not producing what it should. This led to another scan and a fearful diagnosis. Pancreatic cancer is so hard to detect. The stomach hides it. Incurable, even in this day and age, nothing could be done.

Forty-one is far too young to die. Charlie's father said it should be him, not this vibrant wonderful beautiful young woman. Charlie wanted to die. He didn't have anything if he didn't have her. His mother said he must think of the children. They needed him now more than ever. They were heartbroken but children are far more resilient than you give them credit for. He got strength from them, not the other way round. He did his grieving in his bed, their bed. He heard a dreadful howl come from deep inside him, and he thrashed and wailed as if he could exorcise his grief. God will hear you, his mother said, but that was the same God that took her and he was very unsure about Him.

He organized a project officer to oversee the building programme. It could run itself really. He had just loved being so involved. He needed to be at home every day. He concentrated more on the stone company and his best mason Joe asked him to his wedding, six months after Jacqueline had died. His mother said he must accept. This is not all about you and she would be there for the children. Joe asked him if he was any good at taking photos, their wedding planner had been let down at the last minute. He had enjoyed taking family photos, but this was more of a big deal. He said he would have a go. Joe felt it could be a distraction for him, not having to circulate and make small talk. Actually he was rather good. He had made a dark room in the garden shed. It was his man cave he told Jacqueline, and was quietly smitten with what he had produced. He had a knack of taking photos that were not all posed, the pageboys fidgeting and the flower girl swinging her posy as if it was a tennis racquet.

When they came back from honeymoon they couldn't believe the quality of his work, the different angles he had captured. Joe told him he had missed his vocation, although not to detract from the stone business.

It took Charlie out of himself. He hated weekends, the time they would all have a Sunday roast and he would take Charlie to football. Joe had shown his work to Angela's bridesmaid who was getting married and she wanted him to photograph their big day. "You need to charge for it Charlie," Joe told him. He said he wouldn't know where to start but weighed up his costs and his petrol and added a bit on and his rates were more than reasonable.

Weddings used to always be at the weekend but more and more couples were finding it far cheaper midweek and purely by word of mouth he found his diary filling up. He preferred midweek because Charlie was now in the school cricket team and he wanted to support him on Saturday afternoons. Football was fine because not many people had winter weddings.

A year after Joe's wedding he found he was really enjoying this new lifestyle. It was something that

Jacqueline hadn't been a part of, something that didn't drag up those tug at the heart memories and he relaxed into it.

Ten years later he was looking forward to photographing his daughter's wedding. A few years earlier he had hired a manager to run the yard. He was a young man who reminded him of him. He had always looked for the 'hunger' in the applicant's attitude. Laid back didn't work. You had to be hungry for the contracts. He was delighted in the young man's success, happy in the knowledge that the yard was in safe hands, enabling him to expand his photography work.

He rented a studio in the town. His man cave wasn't quite up to the progress he had made. He also took portraits, either in the studio or on location, but he remained fairly close to home to be there for the children.

He was very aware that Nicky could, may be should, have left home when she was eighteen. She stayed because she wanted to. She wanted to support her dad and be there for Charlie. This had stood her in good stead. She was not needy, always putting others before herself and this was one of the attributes that had attracted Adrian to her.

Charlie had liked Adrian from the outset. Well dressed, well spoken, confident and obviously over the moon in love with Nicky. He would be able to support her without her having to work but she enjoyed her job in the travel agency. She needed her independence and he respected that. Charlie told Nicky that her mum would have loved Adrian, and they both hugged and shared happy tears.

47

Two months before the wedding Nicky organized a lunch at the wedding venue. All the family was invited to get together before the big day. Clive, Sapphire, John Liam and Molly were the first to arrive. Nicky and Adrian took Sarah. Charlie, Nigella and Piers accompanied Charlie, now seventeen. He was a very tall young man and quite at ease in his navy suit. Charlie senior wasn't sure about the trainers he had chosen but what did he know?

Clive kissed Sarah on the cheek and she reciprocated. It was fine. There was no atmosphere, water under the bridge. Nicky grabbed Charlie and introduced him to Sarah. "I would have recognized you anywhere Sarah Robinson. You look stunning, but then you always were the best looker in the class." Sarah laughed. "Well, Charlie, you certainly still have the gift of the gab." When she was introduced to young Charlie she gasped. "You are most definitely your father's son. You take me back to my school days, looking the image of how Charlie looked then." Drinks were served in the conservatory and everyone agreed it was a magnificent place. "We were so lucky to get this, weren't we

Adrian? I cannot believe it's only two months and we will be here to tie the knot."

"How on earth do we begin to catch up after so many years?" Sarah asked Charlie. "I think the here and now is what matters Sarah. Right here and right now I am so happy to see you again. It sounds daft but you haven't really changed that much." Sarah looked at him, tilting her head. "Does that mean I have always looked this old?" He looked aghast. "Only kidding Charlie Gilbert. Remember how you always used to play tricks on me. Making me jump when you put a spider on my desk and a worm in my gym bag?" Charlie looked at her. "Who me? Never would I do such a thing" and everyone laughed as they went into the dining room.

Lunch was delicious, a promise of things to come on the wedding day. "Got your speech sorted Adrian?" Clive asked. "Actually I have, Dad. I am lucky in a way because I have had to do presentations so hopefully it will be okay." Clive laughed. "Think you will be a bit more personally involved in this one." Everyone was very relaxed and coffee and liqueurs were available in the lounge. Sarah sank into a huge sofa and Charlie moved a small table for her to rest her cup. "Anything with?" he asked. She shook her head. "The wine has gone straight to my head, thank you Charlie. I will go flat on the floor if I have anything else." He sat next to her. "How are you really, Sarah? Nicky told me about the dreadful accident and how well you have progressed, but some scars stay deep." She became serious. "I think the scars you bear are far deeper than mine. Adrian told me how you lost Jacqueline. Nothing can compare to that desperate grief." He looked at her. "You have answered my question with another." She turned to face him. "Honestly, I am fine. I have been more than lucky. I have a new job and I am happy in it." He put his hand on hers. "I too have been lucky. I feel very blessed to have been a part of Jacqueline's life. To have had her, for however short a time, she is always in my heart." He lifted her hand and kissed it.

Clive saw her reaction. She seemed happy and relaxed and turned to reach for her coffee. Of course it was going to be tough, to see her again and accept what he had lost. Charlie went to find his son who was sitting with Nigella and Piers. Clive went up to Sarah. "May I sit?" she smoothed the cushion. "Of course Clive, how are you?" He found it hard to look into her eyes. "I am doing all right. I am opening an office in France and that keeps me really busy." He looked away. She touched his arm. "Clive, I am so happy for you. We have both gone our separate ways yet we will always be friends, please assure me of that." He turned to face her now. "For as long as I live I will rue the day I let you down." She took his hand. "No Clive, that is all in the past. We have both moved on and will have our memories. Just look at our children, didn't we do well?" He smiled. She always had the knack of making things feel better. He leant over and kissed her cheek. "Thank you Sarah, of course we will always be friends."

They got ready to leave and Charlie went up to Sarah. "I would love to have a real catch up. Learn about your new job, where you live now and I could show you my studio." Sarah took his hand. "That sounds a wonderful idea. When did you have in mind?" He still held onto her hand. "Can I call you on that one? My diary is in the studio." She still held his hand. "I will check my shifts. Work is quite flexible and I am sure I can juggle the days if I need to." He walked her to her car. "Do you live far from here?" He opened her door. "About half an hour away. It has been so good to see you after all these years Charlie. I look forward to hearing from you." He closed the door. "Oh, better have your number." They both laughed and she handed him her card. He produced his and as she drove down the drive she felt a feeling she hadn't felt in a long time.

Nicky looked at her dad. "It was lovely to see how well you and Sarah seemed to get on. It was almost as if there was a spark from a long time ago." Charlie hadn't realized it was so obvious. "It was a long time ago and yes, I felt very at ease in her company. We do have so much to talk about, I have asked her if we can meet again." Nicky nudged Adrian who knew how her mind worked. "That's great, dad. Everyone enjoyed the lunch and thought the venue was brilliant. Will you be able to walk me down the aisle, and take photos?" Charlie laughed. "I will be fine. I enjoy all the pre-wedding photos and will be at your house to photograph you and the bridesmaids getting ready. That is a fun time and Joe at the yard has offered to photograph the guests before the ceremony. He will film when we arrive at the hotel and us walking down the aisle. Then I will work among the guests before the meal and then Joe will film the speeches." Nicky was most impressed. "Gosh dad, you have it all completely sussed." He smiled. "It is what I do Nic" as he kissed her.

48

Charlie called that evening and Wednesday evening suited them both. He had asked Nicky where she lived and there was a good restaurant about ten minutes away. He said he would pick her up at seven.

Sarah chose her outfit carefully. She had told Tessa that Charlie had asked her to meet again — did she think that was a date? Tessa looked at her quizzically. "Well, of course it is. I am so pleased for you. It will be so good to know you are actually getting back into the social side of things. Life isn't all work and no play."

She didn't expect her heart to flip when she opened the door to Charlie. He was quite striking. Being tall he carried off whatever he wore perfectly. Smart casual, beautifully pressed trousers, pink shirt and navy jacket. Her grey linen suit with a vibrant pink blouse didn't clash, and she loved her nude high heels. A clutch bag completed the outfit. She was always more confident when she had something to hold.

They both felt immediately at ease. She thought she would be nervous but seeing him swept all thoughts and jitters far away. The restaurant was in the high street and a table in the corner had been reserved. Charlie pulled out her chair and the waiter eased the napkin over her lap. They both just looked at each other. "You look stunning, glad we both chose pink." Charlie's eyes twinkled as he looked at her. "Thank you, Charlie, you don't look half bad yourself." The waiter took their drinks order and the menu was extensive. "Their forte is seafood, do you like that?" Sarah glanced at the various dishes. "Actually I do." There was a platter for two to share. "Shall I order the platter?" She nodded. "That is a good idea. Thank you." Charlie refilled her glass, and poured more red for himself. "So what does meet and greet actually involve?" She put down her glass. "Exactly what it says on the tin. The clients are all first class passengers and quite often famous. My job is to wait at the bottom of the steps. They always disembark first. The company has its own buggies and the porters load the luggage and I sit with the driver to take them to the VIP lounge or to their onward flight. I engage them in conversation. The Americans love the English accent and are very good tippers."

The platter arrived accompanied by lemon wedges, sprigs of dill, parsley and basil and a selection of sauces. The presentation was superb and Sarah waited for Charlie to serve himself, she didn't want to spoil the look of it. "How can I serve you, you point and I will spoon it to your plate." She chose a little of everything and he passed her the sauceboats. "Oh my goodness, it is so tasty. It's hard to say which is the most delicious. What a wonderful choice Charlie, thank you so much."

Charlie agreed and they both enjoyed the different selection of flavours.

"So what is the most famous person who has sat in the back of your buggy?" Sarah dipped her fingers in the bowl of lemon water and dabbed her napkin around her mouth. "Actually she didn't use the buggy. I don't think I am allowed to say who uses our services but suffice to say it took two buggies to transport her luggage and another two for her dogs and their carers. She is always in the news with her outbursts on the film set but insisted on walking with me to the lounge. I can honestly say her skin was flawless and she was very beautiful. She asked me all about myself and did I enjoy my work. I guess she is a true professional."

Charlie sat back. "Goodness, you move in very important circles." He laughed. They couldn't eat another mouthful and the waiter cleared the table. The dessert menu was innovative and the cheese board looked amazing. "I really cannot eat anything else but when I was with Adrian and Nicky they introduced me to an Expresso Martini." Charlie checked the wine list. "Perfect, I will join you, I have never had one before." The waiter arrived and they sipped and chatted and sipped some more. Charlie told her how he kind of "fell" into photography and although his stone company and building work were the backbone to his work, he found photography to be therapeutic. He looked at his watch. The waiter asked if they would like any more to drink and they both declined.

He settled the bill and the waiter pulled back Sarah's chair. He helped her into her suit jacket and took her hand as he led her to the door. The touch of his hand sent a shiver right through her. He opened her car door and as she sat down he remembered her legs from all those years ago. "Well, what a wonderful evening, thank you so much Charlie." He sat behind the wheel. "We never actually went out-out, did we? Nothing heavy." He looked at her. "Never mind your first class celebs, you are beautiful through and through." She turned to face him. She went to say something but words didn't come. He kissed her full on the mouth. Just like that, as if it was what they had always done. She sat back in the seat. His eyes were twinkling. "I had hoped to show you the studio but it's getting rather late. That will be our next date." She admired his confidence. "A date it is."

She didn't ask him in. Actually she wasn't sure how things went. She had been a long time off the dating scene. She put her key in the lock and he whirled her around. The kiss seemed to last and last. She responded in a way that surprised her, feelings were running deep. "Can I call you when I have checked my schedule?" She nodded, whispered thank you and went indoors.

The phone rang half an hour later. "Are you free Friday evening? I have a wedding on Saturday but that is a five o'clock service so I don't have to be there until three at the bride's house." She knew her schedule inside out. "Perfect and thank you again for tonight." He seemed to hesitate on the other end of the phone. "I loved it Sarah. Sleep tight."

Tessa came in early to see how the date had gone. She really didn't have to ask. She hadn't seen Sarah like this, ever. She was always elegant, confident and professional. Add ethereal to the equation and that told her all she needed to know. She hugged her. "I am so happy for you Sarah. I can see you must have had the best time. Can I be bold? Did you ask him in?" Sarah sat down. "No, I did not. To be honest I really wanted to but I wasn't sure if it would make me seem cheap." Tessa gave her one of her unreadable looks. "You, appear cheap. You are having a laugh." She sat down next to her. "You are both adults. You are not kids experimenting. If you have those feelings for him you should really let him know." Sarah looked at her hands. "Tess, I do have those feelings. It's almost a need. I haven't been with a man for so long, what if he doesn't want me in that way?" Tessa took her hand. "If he doesn't want you in that way he must be a monk." At that they both burst out laughing. Sarah was glad she had confronted that obstacle, even if only with Tessa. "He has asked me out Friday night. I am going to see his studio." Hooray, thought Tessa. "Perfect. Just make sure you select your very best underwear." A frown crossed her face. "I may have to go shopping, it's been a while."

For all his outward confidence, this was a first for Charlie. The first time he had felt feelings he thought he could never feel again. He didn't feel guilty or disloyal. He felt a bit lost. He realized how he longed to be with Sarah. He felt the first stirrings when he met her at the venue. It was funny how they hadn't got together at school. In a way he thought that it was far better now, both having experienced true love, although Nic had told him for Sarah in the end it was true lies.

49

The only garments lacking in Sarah's wardrobe were good quality lingerie. She hadn't felt the need, good old Marks and Sparks worked well. She visited the bespoke range, Janet Reger Atelier on line and was fascinated by the elegance and quality of bras and briefs, silk, satin and lace. She ordered several sets of colour coordinated bras and briefs, choosing a white lace Brazilian brief with matching white lace bra for the date. A pale blue pleat deep midi dress by Karen Millen with a Michael Kors clutch bag and strappy sandals completed the outfit.

Dressing to be undressed felt incredibly sexy and her confidence soared as she sprayed her Red Door perfume. Charlie handed her a beautiful bouquet when she opened the door. She asked him in while she put them in water. "They are beautiful, thank you so much." He kissed her. "My God Sarah, you look amazing. I booked a table in the same restaurant because the studio is just down the road from there."

The food was of the same high standard and the conversation flowed. She asked him if he had ever had a disaster, had a bride not turned up? He told her he hadn't experienced that as yet but one of the worst times for him was when the bride was over an hour late due to road works and had to make a large detour once free from the jam. The venue was a cider farm and fruit drinks were served to the guests and the time for nerves, will she/won't she turn up came and went. Unfortunately wasps have no sense of occasion and made a point of buzzing the guests' drinks. They somehow got under his collar, up his sleeve and inside his shirt. He kept calm and worked hard concentrating on the images of the day, all the time wanting to rip his shirt off and scream get away you pesky wasps. Sarah was horrified. "Oh no, that is just dreadful" while also thinking, I would like to rip off his shirt. Charlie laughed. "Fortunately that was a one-off and I am happy to say the photos do not reflect the pain of the photographer!"

The studio was surprisingly large. The lighting equipment was along one wall and an assortment of backdrops along another. Three large umbrellas at different angles were around the room and the walls were all stark white. The dark room was through a door at the back with reels suspended from the ceiling. He could develop colour and black and white and the majority of couples wanted a digital format, stored on a CD. The cameras were most impressive Sarah thought. He explained one was fitted with a wide lens to shoot the loose shots of the scene and the other (he always carried two) was fitted with a long lens for when he wanted to get closer to the action but couldn't move his feet. There were two mounted on stands for portraits.

"Wow, Charlie, you certainly are a professional and from the portraits around the studio you have a way of relaxing your clients." He thanked her. "Shall we go for a drink, there is a bar down the road?" "I would like to show you my house, now that I have seen your studio." She was quite surprised she felt so at ease saying that. If you could photograph anticipation it would appear as a nervous expectancy of hope, emerging in a warm smile.

He took the key and opened the door. The lounge was on the right off the hall. She went ahead and asked what he would like to drink. He chose a red wine and put the glasses on the table while she went to the kitchen for the cold white wine. He poured and they settled on the sofa. "Good health and I toast the day I found you again." They were totally relaxed, at ease. He put his glass down and pulled her to him. "I want to make love to you Sarah." She kissed him and took his hand. "I am so happy you said that." The bedroom was spacious with an en-suite. There was no fumbling. He unzipped her dress and she stepped out, slipping her sandals off as she turned to face him. "My God you are exquisite" he said as he loosened the straps of her bra. She started to undo the buttons on his shirt but he stopped her and pulled it over his head. She unzipped his trousers and they both sat on the bed while he took them down. He just held her and lifted her to put her head on the pillow.

She pulled at his pants and he undid her bra. Her breasts were full and he sucked her hard nipples as she stroked his hardness. She gasped as he pulled her panties down and spread her legs. His tongue traced her breasts and stomach and she moaned as his tongue teased her, making her arch her back, wanting him to be inside her. He stroked her and gently eased himself entering her with a gentle forcefulness. They were in total rhythm. She wanted this so much and when she found she could wait no more she reached that place she had not been to for the longest time. He felt her and then let go, a huge need fulfilled.

He lay back on the pillow, kissing her as he encircled her with his arms. "Well, Sarah, I cannot believe my luck." They both laughed, so happy, so glad that they had made love. Sarah sat up and reached for her dressing gown. "Oh no, don't cover your beautiful body, I just have to keep looking at you." Naked, she went downstairs and came up with the wine. She knelt on the floor beside him, offering his wine. He sat up and put it on the table. He reached down to lift her on to the bed and they kissed and stroked and she sucked him, and they made love slowly, him deep inside her as they rocked in unison.

They finished the wine. "Can you stay Charlie?" He looked deep into her eyes. "If you are sure?" She pulled him on to the pillow. "I don't think I have ever been more sure of anything in my life."

They made love in the morning and he pulled on his trousers while she put on her dressing gown to make coffee. He said he made mean scrambled eggs and she griddled some bacon and they made short work of a delicious breakfast. She went upstairs to shower and he opened the door and ran the sponge down her back and turned her around. He soaped between her legs and rubbed himself against her. She stepped out of the shower and lay on the thick pile rug, reaching for him, holding him, opening her legs and closing them over his back as he entered her. They came together, both enjoying the rush of pleasure, both so aware of each other. They finally got dressed. She put on matching silk underwear in a delicate pink that he immediately wanted to take off. "Charlie Gilbert, you are insatiable. Don't forget you have the wedding to go to." Reluctantly he let her go and went downstairs to pour more coffee.

They sat at the table. "Did I actually go to bed with the most beautiful woman in the world?" She kissed him. "You did, because you made me the happiest woman in the world."

He had to go to the studio to collect his equipment and get to the bride's house for the first photos. He told her it wasn't going to be a long day. There was no evening do, which could often mean he wouldn't be home before two in the morning. "Would it be forward of me to suggest you could come here afterwards?" He kissed her goodbye. "Forward? If that's forward God only knows what went on last night. I will call you when

I can and I will be forward and bring a few clothes from home."

She was in a whirl. Everything she had hoped for had surpassed her wildest dreams. He was amazing in bed, in every way and she hugged herself tight. She wanted to shout it to the world. She had found a man who seemed as happy to be with her as she was with him. She couldn't sit still. She drove to the supermarket to stock her cupboards with something a little more extravagant and top up the fridge. She called Tess who had a day off and asked if she could come round for a glass of wine. She needed to tell someone how she felt, how it had all gone. Tess was beyond delighted. Her oohs and ahhs and really? That much. They both giggled and when Charlie called around seven to say he hoped to be there by nine. Tess called a taxi and made a discreet exit.

He showed no sign of tiredness. He didn't want it to end, this euphoric feeling, this feeling of belonging, finally, to someone he cared so much about. He didn't use the L word. Neither did she. Deep down they both knew they had discovered something very special and didn't want to jinx it.

They knew they had to tell the family. He had left a note for Charlie saying that he was staying at a friend's house and would be back Monday morning. He could make his own way to college with his mates so told him not to worry. He would see him when he got back. "It's a big step to take don't you think?" Sarah looked puzzled. "What step is that?" he grinned. "Well you and me sort of living together." She kissed him. "Is there somewhere else you would rather be?" At that he led her upstairs and made it very clear he only wanted to be with her.

Charlie looked at his dad. "You and Sarah?" It was a statement rather than a question. "Dad, you don't need to ask me what I think. I can see how happy you are. You have always been there for all of us and I can tell you Mum would want you to find happiness again. It has been a long haul and I am really glad for you." He hugged him and Charlie felt his eyes prick as a tear slid down his face. "Thank you, son, I know it's all a bit quick but it just feels so right." Charlie just smiled. Fancy him thinking it was all a bit quick when he and his mates, if they met a girl, just got together. He reckoned it was an age thing. Mind you his dad wasn't that old, not like really old.

They told Adrian and Nicole the next evening. Over the moon didn't cut it. They were ecstatic. Nicole threw her arms around them both and Adrian opened a bottle of champagne. "I did wonder because I thought I saw a spark." Adrian laughed. "You and your sparks Nic. Seriously we couldn't be more thrilled. You both deserve this. You have always put everyone else first. Your time now and you are so suited." Nigella and Piers reacted in the same way. Piers wasn't one for showing emotion but he hugged Charlie so hard happy tears nearly came again.

Sarah hoped Sapphire would react in the way the others had done. She had reservations because she had worried so about Clive in the divorce. John opened the door. The twins were in bed and Sapphire was in the lounge. They had made it clear when they told the family that they wanted to be the ones to tell each of them together. Sarah looked at Sapphire and she smiled. "I think you may have something to tell us mum." Sarah looked puzzled. "I haven't seen you this happy in forever. I guess it's something to do with you Charlie." She went up to her mum and hugged her. "Are you okay with this, Sapphire?" Charlie asked as John shook his hand. "You have no idea just how happy I am." She kissed him and that told them all they wanted to know.

50

Sarah moved in with Charlie. That was the natural progression. It gave young Charlie security and their lives carried on in much the same way as before. Charlie had broken up from college and hung out with his mates most days, skateboarding or in the park. Sarah continued to meet and greet and Charlie had three more weddings before the main event. The dresses had been collected and Sarah had them at her house. Nigella blossomed in pregnancy, she looked beautiful and the dress discreetly covered her bump, not that she didn't want it to show, of course.

The men in the wedding party were in evening dress and Piers had been tasked with collecting them the night before. Adrian was staying with John the night before and Nicole, Nigella and Sapphire were with Sarah at her house.

That night they enjoyed a takeaway and consumed quite a few glasses of champagne, deciding to stop a little earlier than usual because they wanted to be fresh for the next day. They didn't stop talking, so much to say. So much to look forward to, the future had never seemed so bright. Nigella was emotional, explaining it was her hormones, but when she stood to propose the toast to her baby sister, hormones or not, everyone was in bits.

Their hair appointments were first thing in the morning and Nicole's hairdressing friend was at the house by eight. Charlie arrived in his suit, cameras at the ready and Sarah's heart did a three sixty, he was so handsome. They were arranging Nicole's dress when he knocked on her door. He went to her, beaming at his beautiful daughter. She burst into tears as did he. Happy tears. "You are beyond the loveliest bride in the world. Your mother will be so proud." He put his arms around her, careful not to tread on anything or smudge her make up. He hugged Nigella, and Sapphire. Sarah brought him a glass of champagne and they kissed each other. "God, I missed you." She smiled. "Me too."

This was Charlie's favourite part of the wedding day. Everyone was relaxed, there was always champagne to relax the situation and he captured some wonderful moments.

Sarah had called Adrian to wish him good luck, how was he? Just can't wait was his reply. She had also spoken to Clive, wishing him a good day. He had heard about her and Charlie and wasn't surprised. Sometimes you can just tell when there is chemistry.

When Sarah came into the room the girls just screamed. "Oh my God, you look so amazing" Nigella gushed. Charlie turned to see and he was speechless. "How can you look even more beautiful, you gorgeous girl." Sapphire hugged her mother and helped her with the hatinator, tilting it at just the right angle. Sarah was going with the bridesmaids in the first car leaving Charlie and Nicole sat with their champagne.

"I just want you to know how proud I am of you Nic. Adrian is one of the good guys, you are a perfect match. I can say it now because if I choke up, it's only us." Nicole squeezed his hand. "I am equally proud of my very handsome dad. We are all so glad you have found Sarah. You just go so well together. Thank you for all you have always done for me dad. I don't want to cry, even though the mascara is supposed to be waterproof!"

Sarah entered the hotel leaving the bridesmaids to wait for the bride. Charlie came flying up to hug her. "You look really nice Sarah." She hugged him back. "Well, Charlie, I do believe you could be a model you look so handsome — as does your dad by the way."

She found Clive and kissed his cheek. He couldn't believe how beautiful she looked and said so. Molly was clinging on to him for dear life, a little overwhelmed by the throng of happy smiling faces. Liam was with Isobel who was chatting away. You would have thought it would have been the other way round. Adrian came up to her and hugged her. "Mum, you look stunning, I love the hat thing. How is Nic? Is she okay? She will turn up won't she?" Sarah kissed his cheek. "She is the loveliest bride and is ready to make you a wonderful wife Adrian."

The bridal party in their evening suits cut quite a dash, moving around the room as Joe snapped away.

The Master of Ceremonies banged a gavel and the guests were ushered into the huge hall where the wedding would take place. Nothing was left to chance. The chairs were decorated in nude, ivory and blush. There were three huge floral arrangements as a backdrop for the ceremony. There were red roses for passion, white roses for purity and pink to signify joy and admiration and they scented the room.

All of Me by John Legend signalled the guests to be upstanding. Sarah stood next to Clive, both admiring their son and his best man. Adrian said he would wait till she was beside him before he looked at her, but he turned and the look on his face said it all. He was beaming from ear to ear. Charlie and Nic walked slowly down the centre of the room. Her veil covered her face. The bridesmaids followed and as they reached the groom Nigella stepped forward to take Nicole's bouquet and lift her veil.

The music stopped and the wedding ceremony began. Charlie handed Nic's hand to the marriage officiant and sat down. That was the first time Sarah cried. They had both written their own vows, so sincere and deeply meant. They turned to face each other, slipping the rings on their fingers. That was the second time, dabbing at her eyes. "I now pronounce you man and wife. You may kiss the bride" and the huge applause seemed to relax the situation, no need to cry.

They walked hand in hand, man and wife, through to the lounge and the guests followed. Joe was on good form, videoing the ceremony and now taking the official photos. Charlie felt he could have left it all to Joe, but he got his cameras and took various photos where people were not posing. Charlie saw his son and stopped dead. "You look very smart son." Charlie beamed. "I remind you of you dad!"

He went up to Sarah, took her hand and led her into the garden. "Did you feel the love they have for each other?" She kissed his cheek. "I felt it through the whole of my being." Joe appeared and they laughed as he snapped away, their first official photo of being a couple.

The guests were called to the dining room and stood to clap the bride and groom as they entered to take their places. Tradition ensured that Sarah would sit next to Charlie and Nigella sat next to Clive. Charlie couldn't resist playing footsie with Sarah who was grateful there was a tablecloth to the floor in front of them.

It had been decided that the speeches would intersperse throughout the meal and Charlie stood as father of the bride to thank everyone for coming. He praised and thanked his beautiful daughter and also his family for their support. He said he knew Jacqueline would be so happy as he welcomed Adrian to the family. He ended his speech toasting the newlyweds, the bride and groom and sat down to thunderous applause.

The first course was served and Adrian stood. He couldn't resist starting with "my wife and I" that was greeted with raucous laughter and much table thumping. There were lots of thank yous and Nicole and he presented the best man and bridesmaids with gifts. Sarah was given a beautiful bouquet and Charlie and Clive both received engraved tankards. Loud cheers followed and the main course arrived which was impeccably served and piping hot.

The best man stood to huge applause. He also thanked everyone for coming and true to tradition, cracked a couple of jokes. "All those amongst you who know Nicole well will know that she is a wonderful and caring person. She deserves a good husband. Thank God Adrian married her before she found one." Laughter and applause ensued. "Just some last messages here to read out: one from Adrian's football team to Nicole. Apologies we couldn't all be here today. Good luck with Adrian. We found him to be useless in most positions, but wishing you all the best for tonight." He raised his glass to the bridesmaids and sat down to more clapping.

Dessert was the last course and absolutely deliciously decadent. Coffee and liqueurs signalled the end of the banquet and guests drifted into the lounge. Nicole and Adrian worked the room. Joe had videoed the speeches and Charlie thanked him profusely. Joe told him he was so happy to see Charlie with Sarah. "It just looks so right, mate."

The first dance with the bride and groom signalled the start of the party. Adrian asked Nigella to dance and Nicole asked Charlie. All the guests joined in and Molly was in Clive's arms laughing as he whirled her around. Liam had crashed out and was lying across two chairs.

Weddings are so special. They join two people together in love and hope, happy and sad but mainly glad. It is so heart-warming and positive, a great decision cemented in love. Charlie was dancing with Sarah. Well actually they were more just moving together, holding each other. Charlie tilted her face. "Happy?" She kissed his lips. "Oh yes. It has been a wonderful day, very happy." They went into the garden. The music had changed to disco and the floor was packed with movers and shakers.

They found a bench near the lake. "Sometimes, when you meet someone, you just know. Gut feelings, first impressions, they all count. I love you Sarah." She caught her breath. He said it. He meant it. He was looking at her, willing her to say something, anything. "I love you Charlie. I had never dared to hope that I might find love again. It is all just perfect." The kiss was long and hard. "Do you think we will be missed if we just disappear, right now?"

No one missed them at all. The disco was in full swing, the guests were dancing and enjoying themselves and you could feel a sense of great joy. A wedding does that. It reminds you of the good things in life and brings a new energy.

For Charlie and Sarah it was their new beginning. Their love was assured. No looking back, just forward to a very bright and positive future. They slept in each other's arms and would awake to a new adventure, the two of them together. It did bode so well.